MW01241099

SEEDS OF WAR

Book 1: Invasion
Book 2: Scorched Earth
Book 3: Bitter Harvest

Dr. Lawrence M. Schoen &
Colonel Jonathan P. Brazee, USMC (Ret)

Semper Fi Press

Acknowledgements:
We want to thank all those who took the time to offer advice as we wrote this book. A special thanks goes to beta readers James Caplan and Kelly Roche for their valuable input.

Edited by by James Caplan, Micky Cocker, and Kelly O'Donnell.

DEDICATION

To the SMOFs and fans who created

the San Juan, Puerto Rico NASFiC
and the Helsinki, Finland WorldCon.

Your tireless efforts produced many wonderful outcomes, including
two authors from different worlds coming together in the unlikely
partnership that resulted in this book.

Thank you.

THE SEEDS OF WAR TRILOGY

Book 1

INVASION

Schoen & Brazee

Part I: Dreams and Response

"General, Second Battalion's lines are crumbling. What are your orders?"

Colby looked up from his console as he tried to comprehend what the red-faced colonel was asking.

Second Battalion's lines were crumbling? Which second battalion, and how the hell could that happen?

The fact that one of his units was engaged was a complete surprise to him. The division was only deployed as a show of force, not to kick off a war.

"General, what now?" the colonel insisted.

Colby didn't even recognize the colonel, but he cut the connection with his boss, the force commander, with whom he'd been discussing the political situation, and turned back to his console. A moment ago, the display had been clear, but now, red alarm stars were pulsing over the entire front. A swarm of red arrows were pushing through the blue unit symbols of his Marines. As he watched, Second Battalion, Fifth Marines disintegrated, down to 20 percent.

"General!" the colonel insisted once again.

Colby shook his head. He didn't have an operations order for this. His G3 would have 50 such plans in the files for any contingency, but Colby wasn't prepared for this. He looked around the Command Post, but his Three wasn't there. Twenty faces looked to him for orders.

Hell, I'm Lieutenant General Colby Merritt Edson, Republic Marines, and this is what I'm trained for.

"What's the status on the arty?" he asked, transitioning into command mode.

"Two heavy and one light battery are in place, the mobile and one light are displacing," a major replied.

Colby powered up the terrain model in the middle of the CP, instructed his AI to overlay the battle onto it, and said, "Give me sheath volleys, here, here, and here. It's too late for Two-Five, but maybe we can stem the tide and give us a moment to dig in."

A heavy battery, with its 24 tubes of 225mm shells, could create a virtual wall of steel, covering 1200 meters of front.

"What's the status on the Navy? What do we have in orbit? Can we get support?"

"That's a negative, General," a lieutenant commander said. "The ship's inner system drive is down."

"Tell the captain that he'd better get that drive up and running. We need those guns now!" he shouted.

Damned piece-of-shit Navy! Never there when we need them.

That wasn't a fair accusation, he knew. He had Academy classmates in the Navy, and they were plagued by the same lack of replacement and spare parts as the Corps was, and half of the parts they did receive were faulty.

No use bitching about it now. If no naval guns, then it's got to be air.

"Air Officer," he shouted, "what do we have on station?"

"Nothing on station, sir," a lieutenant colonel said.

Colby had to take two deep breaths or he was going to go off on the woman. "And why the hell not?"

"Your orders, General. You said not to waste flight hours. You said you didn't want to break the aircraft."

Colby didn't remember giving any such orders, although that had become standard practice. Air capability had become a balancing act between pilot hours and airframe hours. The pilots needed them to remain proficient, and the planes needed limited hours so the crews could keep them airworthy.

"What can we get in the air, then?"

"Two Specters and a Wraith, sir."

"Out of eighteen craft in the squadron? Hell, I'm going to have to fire me a squadron commander. Get those three in the air, now, priority of fire to. . ." he paused, taking a look at the developing battle on the terrain model. "Priority of fire for the Specters to Fifth Marines, the Wraith in general support."

"Who exactly is attacking us?" he asked. "Two?"

Colonel Juan French, his G2, said, "The Defenders of Truth, General."

"What? The DOT?"

That didn't make any sense at all. The DOT was all talk and bluster. They'd never shown the will nor the capability to launch a military offensive.

"Roger that, sir. It's them."

"If they want to play with the big boys, we'll crush them," he muttered.

He took a moment to digest the battle. Amateurs or not, they had pushed right through the division's lines. Even if the Marines had not expected an offensive, there was no way they should have been able to prosecute their assault so well.

"Who's got Seventh Marines," he asked, confused as to why he didn't know such a simple fact.

"Colonel Harris Bellemy-Mohamed," the red-faced colonel said.

Harris? My classmate? How did that slip my mind? he wondered before pushing the thought aside.

He opened up the comms on a Person-to-Person line and passed, "Colonel, this is General Edson. The DOT is sweeping through Fifth Marines. I need you to pull back, then create a hasty line of defense along the ridge running from zero-three-three-eight to zero-three-four-five. I'll give you air and arty support, but you need to move it now. You've got forty mikes to get into position."

"Uh, Colby, I'm not so sure we can do that. We're having problems with our ammo. I think you gave us a bad shipment."

"I what?" he asked astounded.

"You're the Commanding General of the Marine Corps Logistic Command, so yeah, I put in on your shoulders."

"What the. . . ? Logistic Command?" he asked, going apoplectic. "I'm your fucking division commander, and I'm ordering you to move, now!"

5

"Get us good ammo, and maybe we will. I'm not going to fight without it, Colby." The colonel's smug tone underscored addressing him as "Colby" and not "General."

Colby stood up in his chair, barely keeping the volcano inside of him from erupting. Classmate or not, this. . . this refusal to follow orders was completely unsat.

"I'm going to court martial his ass as soon as this is over. He'll rot in the brig!"

No wonder he never got his star, the piece of shit. How did he even make O6?

He forced the colonel out of his mind. He had an entire division under his command, and he didn't need the Seventh Marines to crush the DOT. Maybe if he slid Ninth Marines to the north. . .

"General, one of the Specters just went down," the air officer told him.

"The DOT have Gen Six Anti-air? Since when?"

"It wasn't shot down. One of the ion thrusters fell off," she told him in the same calm and collected voice as if telling him his hover back at home needed a new rearview cam.

"It. . . it fell off?" he said, wondering to what level of hell he'd been sent.

"That's what the pilot said."

An explosion shook the CP, dust rising from the ground to obscure the terrain model. Captain Jersey Rialto, his long-time aide, rushed in and took him by the arm.

"We've got to get you out of here," the captain shouted, pulling him towards the hatch. "I've got a Hydra ready for you."

"Wait, Jersey," he shouted, resisting the burly captain's pull.

The dust was settling enough so he could see the terrain model. Seventh Marines was falling apart before his eyes, blue lights winking out as the running count of Marine KIAs kept rising. Ninth was in contact, and as he watched, the Wraith was shot out of the sky. Unbelievably in less than five minutes, a Marine division had been rendered combat ineffective. It was categorically impossible, but there it was right in front of his eyes.

"Sir, the Hydra won't wait forever," Captain Rialto said.

"Tell the pilot to take off," he told his aide. "I'm staying."

Captain Rialto hesitated, and for a moment Colby thought his aide would bodily pick him up and load him on the shuttle, but then the young man nodded and stepped aside.

A series of snaps filled the CP, making everyone duck, including Colby. He looked up, and a line of holes stitched the walls of the CP. They'd taken fire. He turned back to the terrain model, and where a moment ago there were no DOT forces within five klicks of the CP, now they were surrounded. The rifle company assigned to CP security was in a fight for their lives, and they were losing that fight.

Generals didn't fight battles, they planned them. That was the SOP, at least. But Colby was a warrior at heart, and there really wasn't any option left to him.

"You, prepare a report back to Force, let them know what's happened. Everyone else, suit up! We're going to fight!"

There was a loud "Ooh-rah!" as Marines and sailors rushed to the line of battlesuits in their cradles. Captain Rialto beat Colby to his suit and had started powering it up for him. Colby jumped up and grabbed the support bar, twisting his body like a pro as he slipped into the suit.

"Ready?" the captain asked.

"Hit it."

A moment later, the suit surged to life, straightening and coming back erect. Lights flashed as systems came online. Colby inhaled deeply. He'd had a long career, both as an enlisted Marine and officer, and he'd spent much of that time in his combat armor. There was a smell, a cross between a locker room and a garage, that both got his blood pumping and made him feel at home.

Colby had no idea how the DOT was defeating Marines, and he didn't have much of a hope that any of them would survive, but if he was going to go out, he couldn't think of a better way to do it, fighting with his fellow Marines.

As his suit gave a final confirmation, Colby reverted to company commander mode, quickly outlining a basic plan which the colonels, sergeants major, and other senior officers and enlisted acknowledged, Colonel French became a platoon commander. Sergeant Major Lammi, who'd been his sergeant major when he was a recruit all those years ago, became his first sergeant, as the entire CP staff thundered to the sound of gunfire.

"Get some!" he shouted, filled with elation.

He charged forward, seeking targets as the Marines around him opened fire. Two DOT fighters hesitated as they saw him bear down on them. Their bright red T-shirts emblazoned with the insipid logo of a hand holding a star made them easy targets. The younger one, a slender, pock-marked youth who couldn't have been twenty, raised his old rifle.

Youth or not, he was the enemy, and Colby raised his own 18mm chattergun to cut him down. The young man fired, his round pinging harmlessly off Colby's chest carapace.

You shouldn't have come, son, he thought, as the sights of his chattergun locked on the boy's center of mass.

Colby triggered the gun, but instead of a whine of 20 rounds being fired, there was a clunk. He tried to fire again, but nothing happened. In front of him, the look of terror on the young man's face disappeared to be replaced by one of surprise first, then satisfaction. His buddy had already fled, but he started walking forward.

Colby didn't understand why his gun hadn't fired, but the boy was playing with fire. Not only was Colby experienced in combat and fighting, but he was in a battlesuit, armor that massed 540kg empty. He'd crush the boy with one blow of the fist.

He stepped forward to meet the boy, but the suit remained motionless. It would not respond to his movements. Colby checked the readouts, and 18 of the 23 were red. His suit had crashed hard, and it wasn't going to be moving again without a complete overhaul.

Colby didn't understand how a suit could fail like that, but he couldn't just sit there, spam in a can. He hit the emergency molt. . . and hit it again when nothing happened. The bottom light, which he'd never noticed before, was clearly marked "Molt," and it flashed red.

The faceplate of his armor was clear, and even without his combat display being projected on it, he could see the battle unfolding, at least what was in view. Over the young man's shoulder, he saw Captain Rialto rushing toward him. Colby allowed himself a small exhalation of relief before his aide exploded in a huge ball of fire.

"No!" he shouted, unable to believe that Jersey was gone.

To his right, he caught sight of Colonel French, on his back, with three DOT fighters prying at him with what looked like crowbars. French's arms waved feebly until one of the fighters managed to push his crowbar right through the colonel's torso despite the armor.

This cannot be happening. It's impossible!

And then the young man was standing in front of him, his pimply face up against Colby's faceplate as he tried to peer inside. He held up a hand beside his face as if trying to cut down the glare. After a moment, he shrugged, and with a wicked smile, reached into his cargo pocket and brought out a small GT-3 grenade.

'Oh, shit," Colby said, his heart jumping to his throat.

The GT-3 grenade burned rather than exploded, and at 2300 degrees Celsius, Colby's combat armor wouldn't even slow it down.

The young man held the grenade up in front of his faceplate, making sure Colby could see it. He pointed to it with his free hand and opened it suddenly, then dropped the open hand slowly, mimicking a detonation and it burning down through his armor.

He's enjoying this, the piece of shit. Just get it over with.

The man placed the grenade on Colby's shoulder, steadied it, then took half a step back. Colby tried to move, hoping to knock it off, but his suit remained stubbornly frozen. His tormentor cautiously reached over and set the detonator before hopping back five meters. Colby could just see the grenade sitting there, but he chose to focus on the young man instead, vowing to put on a brave face.

A small sun erupted on his shoulder, blinding him, and a moment later, an unbearable blast of heat engulfed him.

"NO. . .

. . ." he shouted, kicking out his leg. Duke yelped in protest as she fell to the floor.

It took a moment for Colby to come to his senses, his heart pounding as if to burst through his chest.

"Sorry, Duke," he muttered as he sat up in the dark.

Colby's dreams haunted him. They all had a similar theme. Sometimes he was a sergeant, sometimes a captain, sometimes a general, but he was always in a position of authority, and the situation was always dire. He never actually knew what was going on, in the same way he'd often dreamt as a kid that he had a test for a subject he hadn't studied. In these dreams, his Marines looked to him for answers, answers he didn't have. Whatever he could devise never worked, not necessarily because of his plan, but because equipment always failed.

"Sergeant Major Lammi, glad you could make an appearance," he muttered.

He often dreamt of people he'd known as a Marine or as a child, but this was the first time his boot camp sergeant major had been in one of his dreams. Heck, he hadn't thought of the man for decades.

The clock on his nightstand flashed a subdued blue 0423. He considered trying to go back to sleep but knew better. Once his nightmare woke him up, sleep tended to escape him. With a sigh, he rolled his feet out of bed as Duke crept back up and lay beside him. She gave two whumps of her tail and was fast asleep again.

"That's right girl, it's easy for you."

The long-haired, ruddy gold dog had been a bedraggled mess when he arrived and took possession of the farm. Four baths and a bar of soap later, she emerged as a rather pretty dog in the golden retriever vein.

He got out of bed, took care of his toiletries, then sat at the battered desk he'd scrounged from a neighboring farm when he'd first arrived. He pulled up his account. As usual, the inbox was pretty empty. There was a message from a former Marine who'd been lance corporal in the battalion he'd commanded some 17 years prior. The lance corporal was inviting him to his wedding. Colby didn't remember the man, but if the former Marine thought enough to invite him, he deserved a response. The wedding was on Ceylon 2, so he couldn't really go, but he wrote a congratulatory message with what he hoped were enough semper fi platitudes to fill the bill.

He pulled up the latest crop prices, but that somehow got sidetracked to a story on ancient Phoenician agriculture, and that led to the god Ba'al, which led to Norse gods which led to. . . suffice it to say that two hours later, he was still at his console and hadn't yet learned the day's price for pyro berries.

He needed to cut the deep dive into trivia, so he got up to make a cup of coffee. As soon as he opened the cupboard, Duke came bounding out of the bed, begging eyes fixed on him. He couldn't resist a pretty female, so he poured her a bowl of kibble, which she wolfed down, tail wagging. She looked back up at him hopefully, but when he didn't pour her more, she wandered over to the couch and plopped herself down on it.

Time to get to work, he told himself as he took his coffee back to the desk. He pulled up the prices, which had jumped higher from the day before. Next, he checked the maintenance schedule, created after his ag AI had performed its morning analysis. As usual, there was nothing that had to be fixed. His farm pretty much took care of itself, and the equipment was reliable.

Not like in the military, he thought, going back to his dream, which stubbornly refused to fade away.

Not that the military was as bad as in his dream—not *quite* as bad, that is. But still, with his last command, maintenance and parts acquisition had been his prime focus.

Lost in the past, he stared at his readouts for a full minute before his mind returned to the task at hand. He shook his head once, then focused on the data dump. After nine months, the complex algorithms were only beginning to make sense to him. Not enough, though, for him to make a rational decision. With a sigh, he hit the "Accept," and the day's irrigation plan his AI had recommended went into effect.

He didn't have to review the AI's recommendation, but at least by doing so, he could pretend that he was vital to the process. It still grated on him that he was little more than a caretaker on his own farm. He'd commanded a Marine division in combat, after all, and now he couldn't even make a decision on how much water went to each field. Most of the other farmers on Vasquez, heck, probably throughout human space, let the ag AIs do the work, but Colby prided himself on being a man of action. As usual, he was tempted to override the AI, to adjust what it recommended, but he realized that would only result in a lower yield, and that would be detrimental to the war effort. He may have resigned his commission in disgrace, but he still understood his duty. If this was how he now served the Republic, then he would salute and march on.

He knew he couldn't complain about his situation. He might no longer be on active duty, but life on the farm wasn't so bad. The work wasn't difficult, and as he looked out the window to his fields, there was a sense of accomplishment. His farm provided much needed supplies to both the teeming masses of the megablocks as well as to the armed forces. A man could take pride in that, should take pride. And yet. . . he felt a hole in his life. Transitioning from being the commanding general of the

Marine Corps Logistics Command to being alone on his farm had been an adjustment, one he hadn't yet completed.

He turned around, his eyes drawn to his "I Love Me" wall, where holos, flat pics, and plaques hung, all he had left to commemorate his time in the Corps. They covered the entire back wall of his small one-room farmhouse. I Love Me walls were supposed to be celebrations of a military man's career, but Colby's reminded him of his failure, it reminded him of what could have been. He'd been tempted to take everything down, to pack the items in boxes and store them in his vault, but he'd kept the wall up. Taking his holos and plaques down would be giving in to Vice Minister Greenstein, of ceding the field of battle to a man even pond scum would look down upon. Colby had never fled any field of battle, and he wasn't about to start now. Instead, he kept the mementos of his life hung on the wall as he lived alone on a backwards planet in the far reaches of human space.

He wasn't completely alone on the farm, however. "Let's go take a look at the morning harvest, Duke," he said to the old dog that he'd inherited when he'd taken over the place.

Duke wagged her tail twice, but didn't get up from where she was lying on the couch. As a career Marine, Colby had never owned a pet, and it had taken him awhile to realize that the dog he'd named "Duke" was a she, not a he. He never bothered to change her name.

"Come on, Duke. I mean it."

Marines used to jump at his slightest whim, but this old dog was a different story. There was an ancient saying about letting sleeping dogs lie, but he was a general, dammit, and besides, she was not technically asleep. He walked over to the couch and gently pushed on her butt until she gave in to the inevitable and slid off. Once down, she looked up at him with hopeful eyes.

"No. You had breakfast already."

At "breakfast," her tail started wagging in earnest.

Ah, hell, he thought, feeling like a patsy as he went to the cupboard and took out two Happy Pooch doggie treats to give to her. He waited while she gulped them down without so much as a single chew, then with her on his heels, walked out of the door and onto his porch.

He took a deep breath, filling his lungs. Vasquez might be a backwater planet on the edge of human space, but the air was clean and brisk, something that all the scrubbers back on the more densely populated worlds of the Republic couldn't duplicate. The terraformers had done an amazing job on the planet, eradicating all traces of the native vegetation—everything from ancient forests of spike trees to inhospitable plains of poisonous thorn grass—to make it into a human paradise. Crops grew as if on steroids and without the pests and diseases that plagued other worlds.

There was still a trace of morning dew on the grass, and he made a show of kneeling to touch it. "Another twenty minutes, Duke, and the harvesters can start."

The AI had determined that the lowest 20 hectares of pyro berries were ready for harvest. The genetically modified berries were calorie-dense food at 18 kwH/kg. A year ago, Colby didn't know a watt-hour per kilogram from a hole-in-the-ground. Now, he knew that 18 kwH/kg was damned good. By midmorning, he'd have 400 tons of the berries harvested and loaded into an automated cargo pod bound for the port where they'd be shot into space to a processing station on New Mars on the other side of a wormhole, to be put into energy bars or jolt-shakes to feed Marines and sailors—at least that was who he hoped would consume them. His berries could just as easily—and more probably—be made into food for the civilian masses, but he chose to assume for the tenuous connection to his previous military life.

Colby could return to the house, pop a holo in the player, and waste away the morning on the couch, but that wasn't in him. Instead, followed by Duke, he wandered down a meticulously manicured path to the field where the berries were to be harvested. It wasn't that he maintained the path. No non-commercial vegetation had been allowed to be established on

Vasquez, so weeds and other superfluous plants were non-existent.

Colby's three-month old HRI-30 harvester hadn't yet begun by the time the two of them arrived. The micro-sensors were reading the moisture content on the berries, and at exactly the right moment, the harvester would begin its task. Colby knelt beside one of the plants at the outer edge of the field, picked a berry, and again made a show of rolling it between his fingers though Duke couldn't have been less interested. He popped it into his mouth, bit, and almost as quickly spit it back out, grimacing at the rotten-corpse taste. It still amazed him that the berries tasted so nasty, yet could be transformed into delicious jolt-shakes and hundreds of other delectable and nearly addictive snacks.

"Yep, Duke, they're ready," he said as the dog lay down, put her head on her crossed front paws, and went to sleep.

With a whir, the squat "Henry" harvester started into motion. Colby was still fascinated at how the meter-wide bot could advance down the field, looking like it was going to crush his plants, yet leave each one standing undamaged, but minus its crop. The type of plant didn't seem to matter. Whether that was Wasabia japonica, pyro berries, corn, or anything else on his farm, the same harvester did the job.

Colby blinked up his implant. As a Marine general, he'd had the highest-level implant available to man, and when he'd resigned his commission, it hadn't been military policy to try swap it out for a civilian model. Instead he'd simply undergone a quick procedure to deactivate the secure access function. Now, with the same 500,000-credit implant that would have allowed him to command a division in combat, he pulled up the harvest readouts. The numbers were excellent, both in production and quality of the berries. If the harvest continued with the same results, he'd be in for a quality bonus.

Not that I need it, he told himself. *What am I going to spend it on here?*

Colby had never married. The demands of the service had been too great. He'd dated a few times as a junior officer, but women quickly realized that his dedication was to the Corps, and not to them. Now, on Vasquez, with its extremely sparse population, there wasn't much potential on the horizon. He had a handful of nieces, nephews, and their children, but none had paid much attention to him in the past, so they could go suck on an egg, for all he cared.

"If you outlive me, girl, you're going to be one rich dog."

Duke whumped her tail twice on the dirt, then went back to sleep.

Colby's stomach rumbled.

While he'd fed Duke after waking, not wanting to feel her accusing eyes on him, he hadn't eaten himself, and he wouldn't eat until after his workout. He was still young and fit at 73 Standard Years, but he wouldn't be if he let his body go to hell. He had a good fifty or so more years left to him, and he'd be damned if he'd do that sitting on a couch and simply observing the universe pass him by. Six days a week, he went through his Marine Corps PT program.

"OK, girl, Henry's got this in hand. Let's get back."

Ten minutes later, he was back on his porch in just running shoes and shorts, no shirt. In the Corps, he'd run in whatever was the official PT gear at the time, and despite keeping up with his Marine grooming regs, he felt a little guilty at this small act of rebellion. He'd even once run stark naked, the ultimate rebel, until he realized that wasn't the most practical way in which to jog. So, now a pair of shocking pink shorts and civilian running shoes were the most obvious manifestation of his rebellion.

"You coming?" he asked Duke as he stretched.

She watched him with what looked to be interest, but he knew she'd just lay on the porch as he ran around the farm, waiting for him to give her a second breakfast while he ate his.

He easily jumped over the four steps leading off the porch and broke into a comfortable lope as he warmed up. As he reached the southeast corner of the farm, down by the winter melon patch, he picked up the pace. Within 500 meters, the sweat was forming and rolling down his chest as the machine of his body started humming. He might not be 25 any longer, but he felt like he was, and he reveled in how easily he ran along the perimeter path.

After eight klicks, he gave a salute to Henry as he ran around the lowest 20 hectares, then sped up as he climbed back up to the house, sprinting the final 200 meters. It didn't look as if Duke had moved since he'd taken off, but she sat up as he came to a stop, bent over at the waist, hands on his knees, to catch his breath.

"Just give me a moment, girl," he said, chest heaving like bellows.

He grabbed the towel he'd placed on the porch rail and wiped his face. It took a moment, but something hit him as odd. He gave the towel a sniff, and it smelled, well, *green,* if a color could smell. He took another sniff, then looked closely at it. Instead of just Colby-sweat, he could see small specks of something. It wasn't until that moment that he realized that his skin felt different, too. Wiping his hand on his chest, he could feel something rough and almost gritty. It wasn't dirt, he could see as he examined his hand. Whatever it was looked organic to him.

He immediately looked up to the north. One of the old terraforming projectors was in that direction, about 20 klicks away. Vasquez was a Class 1 world, fully terraformed. It shouldn't need any more adjustment to the environment.

Maybe there is something they're doing and I missed the announcement?

From beside him, Duke whined, putting her right paw on his thigh.

"OK, OK, girl, I get the message."

He opened the door and let her in, then stripped and went into the shower. As the water jets scoured his skin, he couldn't help but note the surprisingly large number of specks, or whatever they were, flowing off his body to swirl down the drain.

It was rare for the small residual TF office on the planet to do even minor tweaks, but if they were doing something, that could affect his farm.. . . He'd have to check to find out.

"After chow, though. I'm pretty hungry," he said to himself, and his stomach rumbled again in agreement.

****

Colby let out a satisfied, and completely non-reg, burp as he climbed up on his Number 3 wind turbine, the taste of bacon coming back for a second time. One of the advantages of living on Vasquez was the readily available meat products, not the least being thick, applewood-smoked bacon. Even as a Marine general, most of his protein, and much of his other food, was fabricated in huge food factories, the kind to which the bulk of his crops provided the raw materials. Despite the scientists swearing that their factory-grown slabs of meat could not be distinguished from the real thing, no one believed that. And while Colby only grew crops, there were more than a few ranchers who raised chickens, turkeys, pigs, and cows for the rich and powerful, those men and women at the top of the Republic's corporate and government ladders.

Cost for moving foodstuffs out of the gravity well had come down significantly over the last 30 years, but still, it wasn't cheap. Along with the specialty vegetables (such as Colby's winter melons), meat couldn't be preprocessed at Vasquez' ag station, so the cost to transport it was high. That meant the costs were relatively low on the planet, and he had arrangements with several ranchers to barter winter melons, pomegranates, and densuke melons for beef, pork, and chicken.

He reached above his head and tried to twist the offending vane into place. It didn't' budge. Colby's farm was completely self-reliant for power. Solar panels, four wind turbines, and a methane digester provided for all his energy needs. With the single automated hover rail that took his products to the port and delivered what he needed, Colby rarely had to leave the farm let alone interact with another human being.

It looked like he would be having a guest over to the farm, however. Number 3 was only producing at 94 percent. That wouldn't affect his operations, but 51 years in the military had ingrained in him to be prepared for any eventuality. If other systems went down, then that missing six percent from Number 3 would be felt. The problem was that while the turbine's analytics pinpointed the issue, it could not correct the physical problem, and none of Colby's tugging was having any effect. He'd have to put in a service call to get one of the techs out to fix it. With four techs on the entire planet (and only one on the continent), that might take a while.

Admitting defeat, he climbed down off the structure, placing the request through his implant. He received an immediate response, and as he expected, an appointment was scheduled in four weeks time.

"Come on, Duke, let's get back to the house," he said.

To his surprise, Duke seemed more interested in something by the hop-beans, another high-caloric base crop for the factories.

"Let's go girl. Lunch!"

Instead, Duke barked, then pawed at something. Curious, Colby knelt beside the dog, wondering what had gotten her worked up. On his home planet of Tiergarten Delta, rabbits and other small animals had been released into the wild, so there were things for a dog to chase. But this was Vasquez. There weren't animals on the planet that had no commercial value. Earthworms, bees, and livestock, yes. Rabbits or other small mammals that could eat the precious crops, no.

But it wasn't a mammal that had caught Duke's attention. To his surprise, Colby saw several small plant-like. . . *things*. . . under the broad leaves of the hop-beans. He used the term "plant-like" because while they looked like vegetation of some sort, they were not anything he'd seen before. Naturally meticulous and with time on his hands, Colby had studied every crop and plant that had been introduced on the planet. Whatever these were, they were not on the list.

It was possible that these were some sort of nitrogen-fixing genmod that was being introduced, but when Colby had queried the net for info right after breakfast, he'd come up blank. For a Class 1 world to have something else introduced, there would have been tons of forums and debate, days and days of documentation and recordings to wade through. It was inconceivable that the planet's inhabitants would not have been part of the process. Things like this, usually fueled by corporate greed or governmental experiments, had occurred before, almost always with disastrous results.

And whatever the small, five-centimeter-tall things were, they didn't look like normal plants. They had a central stalk, a leafy, compact crown, and what looked like thick, ropy roots splayed under them. Weirder still, they seemed oriented to Duke and him, as if they were watching them. He slowly moved to his right, and while he couldn't be sure, it seemed like they were following him.

Come on, Colby, get ahold of yourself. You've been alone too long. It's bad enough that you talk to Duke like she's human, but this. . . ?

Whatever the things were, they bothered him. Plants, even genmodded plants with who knows what genes spliced into them, didn't grow this fast. If they had, in fact, come from the specks that had landed on him during this run, they were way too big a mere three hours later.

"Let's go, Duke, now!" he said, pulling back on her neck scruff.

He shuddered, then quickly walked back up the path to his vault. He could see more of the plant-things along the way, and he could have sworn that some actually moved off the path as he approached.

But that's impossible, right?

The door whooshed open as he approached. He grabbed a hand-sprayer and he went straight to the rack of cylinders, where 20 were on three offset shelves, tubes sprouting from the tops like crazy Medusas. It took him a moment to find the right one, then by bypassing the main feed tube, he managed to fill his sprayer with RU-22. He gave it a tentative spray, and it emitted a fine mist. The vault's air evac system sucked it up and away into a catch-vent.

Duke had jumped at the mist, but as it didn't seem to hurt her, she poked her nose forward, sniffing the sprayer.

"No, you don't want that," he told her, holding it higher, out of her reach.

All of the RU products were certified safe for animal life, but if it killed plants that easily, Colby wasn't sure it was totally harmless. He grabbed a mask out of the dispenser by the door, put it on, then went forth to do battle.

He didn't have to go all the way to the perimeter fields. Field 2A, which was also a pyro berry field, was in the middle of the eastern sector. He thought he saw movement, so he stopped and crouched down. There, under the bushes, were close to a hundred of the small plants. He held the sprayer forward, close to them, and sprayed. A fine mist coated them and the nearest berry bushes. He hated to sacrifice the half-dozen bushes, but the invading plants gave him the creeps.

Almost immediately, the plants reacted, as if trying to evade the spray. RU-22 worked quickly, but not that quickly. The berry bushes were already wilting as the spray broke down their cellular walls, but the small plants were writhing—actually writhing—as the spray touched them. Colby knew this had to be caused by their cellulose walls contracting unevenly, but it was still disconcerting.

"Well, at least we know it works, huh Duke?"

She barked in response, then pawed at the nearest of the plants. Colby had to jerk the dog back.

The movement ceased, and the small plant bodies started to decompose. Within five minutes, there was nothing left of them, along with the six berry plants that the mist had touched. With a final nod, he stood and went back into the vault.

RU-22 was an amazingly high-tech herbicide. It was designed to break down plant matter and let it seep back into the soil. This was far more efficient and timely, if more expensive, than the ancient method of plowing plants back into the ground. The problem with earlier versions of the herbicide was that it decomposed in a broad spectrum. Winter melon vines were alive for only one fruiting, and if the RU-20, the older version of the herbicide, was used to decompose the melon field drifted to, say his pyro berry field, where the bushes lasted two to three years before yields began to fail, then it would kill the berry bushes as well. Monsanto's solution was to have genetic blockers mixed in with the RU-22 that made it harmless to targeted crops. If he'd targeted the RU-22 in his sprayer for pyro berries, then they wouldn't have died when he'd sprayed the invading plants.

Colby gave the instructions to his ag AI. He wanted his entire farm sprayed, but he didn't want to lose his crops in the process. The AI gave him a price for the operation. He blanched at the cost, knowing it would more than eat up the bonus, and the next ten bonuses, for his bumper crop of pyro berries. He hesitated, then gave the go-ahead. The ag AI started its work, mixing the outgoing RU-22 with the correct genetic blocker for a given field, then sending the spray out. Colby waited for the 30 minutes, afraid the AI would make a mistake and wipe out a field of densuke melons. As usual, however, the AI did its job, and the entire farm was sprayed.

Colby didn't know why he bothered to open the door a crack and peek out first as if checking for an enemy lying in wait. Laughing at his caution, he sauntered down to 2A. The ground was littered with what was left of the tiny plants, the berry plants were untouched. He moved over to 2B, then 2C. It was the same there. He checked each and every field, and by the time he was done, all traces of the invading plant had disappeared into the soil.

Breathing a huge sigh of relief, he turned to go back into the house. He needed to report this to the central office, 3000 klicks away in Freesome City. He knew he should have kept a sample of the plant, but if they wanted one, all he had to do was go outside his farm and gather a couple.

"Well, girl, I think we did a good job," he said as he plopped down into his kitchen chair. "Nobody, or I guess, *nothing*, is going to invade my farm."

****

Colby lay on his bed, Duke fast asleep and sprawled across his lap. The dog gently snored, a string of drool soaking through the light blanket and onto his thigh.

"At least one of us can sleep, girl."

He hadn't been able to drop off, and he'd ended up binge-watching the final five episodes of "The Beltov Boys." He hated the show. In typical Hollybolly fashion, the writers had just about everything wrong about the military and warfare. Despite this, and despite the fact that he kept pointing out all of the mistakes to the uncaring Duke, he watched every episode. And while he'd deny it until the end of time, he'd had a tear or two form when Anton slipped into death's embrace.

He checked the time. Dawn had just broken, and while he could pull up the next season, his day would begin soon enough. He might as well get a start on things. Carefully sliding Duke off his lap, he got out of bed and dialed up a coffee. Taking the steaming mug, he stood over his display, checking the readouts. As usual, nothing was out of the ordinary. Every reading was within standards.

Colby had lived an eventful life with no less than seven combat tours. Sure, most of his career had not been as exciting, either in desk jobs or in training for combat. But even then, there was always the potential for combat that made the training relevant and gripping. Those days were over, however. Nothing exciting was ever going to happen to him again. Every day, for the rest of his life, he'd check his readouts to see them the same as the day before, the year before, the decade before. Sometimes, he wished that something new would happen, anything to break the monotony.

The gods of war, farms, and just about everything else, are a capricious lot, and as if listening to his thoughts, they chose that moment for one of his motion sensors to go off. Colby's farm was a long way from any of the ranches in the district, too far for a wandering cow to happen by and eye his crops, and this was the first time the alarm had been activated. He tapped the screen a few times, but it remained on. Frowning, he stepped out onto his porch, clad in only his boxers, and looked out towards field 4D at the far eastern edge of his property. He couldn't see anything, not that he expected to. The alarm had to be a bug in the system, which meant his AI could be acting up in more ways than just false motion detector alarms.

That could be catastrophic, and he felt a surge of, well not panic, but concern. For all that he wanted to be in control of the decisions made to run his farm, the thought of actually being forced to make those decisions left him apprehensive.

He looked back through the open door to Duke, still happily asleep, leg twitching as she chased dream rabbits. With a shrug, Colby walked off the porch, barefoot and still in only his underwear, and down one of the paths to 4D. He was sure there wasn't anything there and that this was a glitch, but his military mind wanted to confirm that before he put in a priority call for a tech to check out his AI.

4D was a good 900 meters from the farmhouse, and as he walked, the exertion, coupled with the morning sun, caused him to sweat. Vasquez' sun, a relatively old star as stars go, was heavy in the red-to-blue wavelengths, which made the planet such a good place to grow Earth crops. The standing joke was that a farmer could plant a seed but would have to jump back before the plant sprang out of the ground and hit him in the face.

The morning's rays felt good on his skin. Like all Marines, Colby was extremely self-conscious about letting the sun, any sun, shine on his unprotected skin. On Poulson's World, he'd been terribly burned by the planet's young sun. It hadn't seemed to be generating much heat, but its ultraviolet output had been more than enough to crisp his bare chest and back and land him in the hospital for regeneration for two full weeks. Here on Vasquez, however, the sun put out relatively little ultraviolet light, which was good for plants and human skin alike.

He reached 4D, and as he expected, there wasn't a lone cow on a walkabout eyeing his corn. He was just about to return to the house when something else caught his attention. The plot of land to the east of his was still owned by the government, and it had been planted with sawgrass as a means of erosion control as well as providing ethanol for vehicles. It looked to him as if the sawgrass moved. Except there was no wind at the moment to account for any movement. He took a couple of steps farther down the path, and things came into focus. It wasn't the sawgrass that was moving, but rather something else, something that looked like larger versions of the plant he'd eradicated the night before. About half-a-meter high now, they were definitely moving—slowly to be sure, but moving.

Colby hadn't imagined that the only place the invasive species had landed was on his farm, of course, but seeing as how large the things had grown in the last 15 hours, he was glad he'd killed each of the pests on his property. He wasn't even sure they would harm his crops, but something had his nerves itching much as he used to have before going into battle. He just knew they were bad news.

He squatted right at the edge of his property, peering into the sawgrass at the hundreds, if not thousands, of the plants. He could have sworn that the nearest of them swiveled to him, although if to face him or turn away, he sure couldn't tell.

If these were an invasive species, he really had to report them. He activated the record function on his implant, which pulled the images from his optic nerve. On impulse, he reached over and grabbed one of the plants, expecting to pull its roots out of the ground so he could get a clear recording of it. Two surprising things happened. First, the roots were barely attached into the dirt, if at all. Second, a searing pain shot through his hand and up his arm. He dropped the plant and jumped back. This time, there was no mistake about it; the plant dragged itself back to the sawgrass, its leaves acting as arms.

Colby instinctively started to stomp on the plant, but he pulled back at the last moment as he realized he was still barefoot, almost naked, in fact. His hand was still burning, and suddenly, he felt very vulnerable. He stumbled back five meters, then stood there, watching the plant join the others, then pull itself upright.

I've got to report this.

He tried to connect to Central Ag, but his call wouldn't go through. The channels were jammed. He queued up his recording and left a message, knowing that the call would be received when there was some available bandwidth.

4D was just on the west side of a slight rise on the government land. As Colby stood there, wondering what he should do next, the sun's rays rose enough to illuminate the ground. Almost immediately, there was an increase in activity among the invading plants. He felt an ominous foreboding that something bad was about to happen.

After a few moments of direct sunlight, the plants started walking across the boundary path, their "roots" working like octopus tentacles to move them along. At the edge of the field, the first few plants stopped, leafy arms reaching out to touch the stalks of corn, almost tentatively.

"Got you now, you bastards," he muttered.

He'd sprayed the field with RU-22, which had a two-day period of efficacy. The herbicide would still be more than powerful enough to manage the invasion. A squad of the things was now on the path, but not pushing forward into the corn.

Until they were.

With a sudden surge, the entire mass pushed forward. Leafy green arms reached forward to pull down the corn stalks.

"Oh, no, you don't!" Colby yelled, taking a step forward before common sense again took over.

He was still standing in his underwear, after all, and the things had proven that they had a bite to them. He spun and bolted back up the path, not bothering to watch his field laid to waste. Three minutes later, he burst into the vault.

Evidently, the RU-22 had weakened enough overnight so that the plants could stand up to it. But he'd wiped out the baby plants before, so he was pretty sure he could take care of their bigger siblings. He gave his AI direct orders to initiate the same herbicide sequence as the day before, but starting with 4D. A few moments later, RU-22 was being dispensed.

With a huge sigh of relief, Colby went back to the door and looked down the slope in the direction of the field. He couldn't see much, but he knew the plants would be disintegrating. He wondered if they were screaming tiny plant screams as their plans were foiled. If they were, he didn't care.

It was obvious by now that these were no ordinary plants, but whether the products of some ag lab gone mad or an alien species, he hadn't a clue. Nor did he really care. If they wanted to take his farm, they'd suffer the consequences.

He checked his message, but it was still in the queue. He couldn't be sure, of course, but he had the sinking suspicion that this invasion was not something isolated to the local region.

Colby was not the most sociable neighbor, but on sparsely-populated planets, people helped each other. He gave Gabrielle and Tonsor, his nearest neighbors, a call to warn them. The local nets were not jammed, and the call went through, the visuals opening up to show what had to be their living room in the background. He waited patiently for either of the two to appear. Neither did. He guessed they could be asleep, but farm folk tended to wake up early, and it was already past 7:30 in the morning. If they were out in their vault, their implants would patch them through.

If they were asleep, he had no way to wake them, so he left a message for when they woke up. Hopefully, they'd still have crops by that time. He was about to cut the connection when movement on the screen caught his eye.

"Hey, about time—" he started, before he realized that he hadn't seen Gabrielle or Tonsor.

A plant invader, followed by two more, moved past the pickup. There was a crashing sound, then more of the plants passed into view before the pickup was knocked to the floor, and the connection was cut.

"Holy shit," he said quietly as what he'd seen sunk in.

This was getting serious.

He checked the status of the spraying. 4D and E were completed with five more fields commencing. His entire farm would be covered within 20 minutes. He doubted the plants would be able to reach the farmhouse by then, given what he'd seen.

Suddenly, he felt very vulnerable standing there in his underwear. Ancient warriors might have girded their loins before battle in what was their version of Bryson Mills boxers, but this wasn't then. He bolted for the house and to his closet, pulling out his old Marine Corps camouflaged utilities. He hadn't worn them since his resignation, but they now gave him a sense of purpose. Out came his boots, and as the wraparounds tightened on his feet, it was as if he'd never left. His hand strayed to the armor activation, but that was too much. The RU-22 was killing off the invaders, so it wasn't as if he was going into battle against the Borealis Pact.

"Wake up, Duke," he yelled as he started out the door again. "I said, come, girl," he added while the dog whumped her tail on the bed, but not getting up.

He rolled his eyes and ran to the vault, eager to check the progress. About a third of the farm was sprayed. The motion sensors were still screaming their warnings.

Let them come. As soon as they step on my property, it's mush for them, and I'll grow my crops on their dead bodies.

Satisfied that everything was going according to plan, he tried to call Ag Central one more time, but there was still no connection. Hesitating more than a combat vet should, he tried to get ahold of Gabrielle and Tonsor, but that connection was dead. He knew he should have called them yesterday when he'd first noticed the baby invaders. If he had, they might have had a chance.

He stepped to the doorway and looked out down the slope. It was almost a klick to 4D, so he couldn't be sure, but it looked as if more of his corn was on the ground and the vast swath of sawgrass on the next plot was flattened. The sawgrass made sense. If these things were attacking Earth vegetation, then the sawgrass had no protection. But his fields were being sprayed. They should be stopped in their tracks.

I need to get a closer look.

He may not have the X55 carbine he'd favored while on active duty, but simply being in his utilities gave him a sense of confidence. The plants weren't very large, after all, and his boots made for good stomping if it came to that.

Colby didn't get far. Halfway there, he could see the last of his corn topple to the ground. The RU-22 should be working, but the evidence was right there before his eyes. He turned around and ran back up the hill and into the vault. Checking the readings, he confirmed that the herbicide had indeed been dispensed. He switched the display, and four of his fields were now essentially dead, the numbers showing zero growth.

"Son-of-a-bitch!"

He wasn't sure what to do, so he queried the AI. It recommended increasing the concentration of the RU-22. He hesitated. The first spraying didn't work, so he wasn't sure a second one would, either. But he had nothing else, so he approved the course of action. Within moments, the higher-strength herbicide was being dispensed. Colby watched the readouts, but the damage continued to mount. Eighteen percent of his crops had been destroyed so far, and the damage showed no signs of slowing down. He had to do something.

"Ralph, dispense RU-20 to rows three and four," he ordered the AI, using the name assigned to it when he'd taken over the farm. "Maximum strength."

"RU-20 will destroy all crops," the AI responded. "Please confirm instructions."

No one wanted to employ slash and burn as a strategy, but it was becoming clear that he was fighting a losing battle, and the only thing that made any sense was that somehow the invading plants were being protected by the same genetic blockers that kept his crops safe from the RU-22. It was better to lose half of his crops than all of them. Not just crops, either. The image of the invaders inside Gabrielle and Tonsor's home was gnawing at him. RU-20 was a merciless herbicide, and it would stop the bastards in their tracks.

As the RU-20 made its way down the lines to the fields, Colby tried Ag Central again. This time, he didn't get the full bandwidth error message but rather the "cannot connect" message. He didn't even want to contemplate what that meant, but his military mind wouldn't let it go. The enemy, as he now thought of the plants, had seemingly begun a full-scale invasion. What he didn't know was whether the plants themselves were doing the invading or if they were merely biological weapons employed by another species. Mankind had never yet encountered an intelligent life, but the universe was a vast place, and he was not willing to dismiss any possibility out of hand.

I've got to see what's happening. He opened the door to the vault.

The enemy had cost him half his crops, and that would cripple any hope of profit for the year. He wanted, no, he *needed* to see them destroyed. Once he secured what remained of his farm, he could worry about the rest of the sector.

Standing at the top of the hill, he could see crops disappear as the herbicide did its work. Colby had lost troops in battle. He'd lost friends. Watching his crops being destroyed wasn't the same thing, but it was close. He knew that was a ridiculous sentiment, but he couldn't help the feeling.

Field 3C was the closest of the targeted fields to him, and he watched the hop-beans first shrivel before collapsing onto the dirt. As the beans dropped, they revealed 4C behind it, and hundreds of the enemy plants, each continuing the march forward, seemingly unaffected by Monsanto's best.

"Shit!" he shouted, rushing back into the vault.

"I said maximum strength, Ralph," he told the AI.

"Affirmative. RU-20 was dispensed at the maximum legal strength."

"I don't care about legal or not. I want the max possible."

"Civil Code 4002.3.12 expressly forbids any Class 4 herbicide to be applied above 40 percent concentration without a special use permit."

"I don't give a fuck about Civil Code 4002-whatever. We're under attack. I order you to dispense pure RU-20, no dilution!"

"Your illegal command has been duly noted and forwarded to Ag Central."

"There is no Ag Central anymore, you idiot, Ralph" he yelled.

Colby didn't know if Ag Central still existed or not, but it seemed like a good guess that was the reason he could not connect with them. Not that his AI cared. It was programmed one way, and the end of the universe would not sway the stupid thing. He could scream and shout at it, but that would be beating his head against the wall.

"Dispense RU-20 to all rows," he ordered the AI. "Maximum strength."

"RU-20 will destroy all crops. Please confirm instructions."

You already told me that, he thought, but just before he gave the confirmation, another thought hit him, and he said, "Wait one."

Running back outside, he could see waves of the enemy crossing the now denuded Rows 3 and 4. As they reached Row 2, the invaders started to tear into his crops. Colby was sure that the things had killed his neighbors, and now they were marching towards him. If he cleared the way by destroying his own crops, they would get to him that much sooner.

"You've got to get out of here, Edson," he said aloud.

He wanted to protect his farm, but it wasn't worth his life. He ran to the house where Duke greeted him with a whomp of her tail on the bed.

"Come on, girl. No time for this," he said, snapping a leash around her neck.

Duke resisted, pulling back, but Colby was having none of it. He dragged her to the door and grabbed his bugout bag, a holdover habit from his service days. He turned to give the small house a once over, then pulled the dog outside.

"Pay attention, Duke! Don't give me any shit!"

He started to the west in a slow run, only speeding up when Duke gave into the inevitable and began to lope beside him. As he ran, he tried to think of his options. The local spaceport was 40 klicks away. He wasn't in his fighting prime anymore, but he could make it in five hours at a steady jog. He wasn't sure Duke could, though, and he wasn't going to abandon her. If they had to stop and rest her, so be it.

So engrossed in his calculations was he that he almost made a second lieutenant mistake—he lost track of the bigger picture. He rounded the bend in the middle path as it approached Row 8 where the bulk of the pyro berries were grown, and came to a dead stop. Ahead of him, was the Gustavsons' farm, or more accurately, what was left of it. Their single-crop fields of corn were flattened, almost every stalk gone. Attacking the last few meters had to be thousands of the enemy plants. Within a few minutes, they would be crossing over into his property. Either these plants were larger cousins of the ones he'd seen on his property earlier or they had grown. These had to be a meter tall.

Duke whined beside him as he lifted his gaze. He didn't know the reclusive Gustavsons well, but their house was visible from his farm. It took him a moment to find it, or what was left of it. Half of a single wall still stood. The rest was a jumble of rubble.

How the hell. . . ?

The enemy plants, which were uprooting the Gustavsons' corn, weren't that big. If this was all there was to them, if they didn't have some sort of tools, how could they have destroyed a house? It didn't seem possible.

Ever the practical soldier, Colby had to accept what his eyes told him, even if his mind protested the impossibility. Their house was gone. And if the enemy could destroy their house, it could destroy his.

Colby started running back, this time with Duke pulling forward on her leash. At the corner of Row 6, he took a left and ran to the high point of the western half of the property. It didn't give him a panoramic view, but in every direction he could see a mass of enemy plants advancing on him.

"Looks like we're surrounded, girl," he said in a matter-of-fact voice.

This wasn't the first time this had happened to him. On Proclyn 301, his battalion had been surrounded by a division of the Gannon Imperial Army. It had taken the Marines 42 days and 73 percent casualties to break the siege, but break it they had.

"And you're no Imperial Cybotroopers," he shouted out before turning to Duke and saying, "Let's go see what we can do about this."

He ran back up to the compound. The enemy had already reached Row 3, some 400 or so meters away. He could hear them tearing into his crops.

Bolting into the vault, he stopped and ordered his thoughts. He had to figure out a way to stage a breakout, to get beyond the line of advancing plants. As a commissioned officer, Colby had been infantry, but he'd also been prior-enlisted with a combat engineer Military Occupational Specialty. As a combat engineer, he knew how to blow things up.

With his engineer kit, he had dozens of ways to pulp the enemy. Unfortunately, kits like that were not available to civilians, not even retired generals.

No problem, Edson, you'll just have to gyver it. OK, first what to make?

Combat engineers used a variety of explosives on their missions. Low explosives were used to move thing like dirt, high explosives to shatter and destroy objects. Colby would like nothing better than to use HE to destroy all the enemy in an area, giving Duke and him a clear path, but as he looked around the vault, he didn't have the time nor ready materials to create an HE bomb. What he did have, however, was fertilizer.

An ANFO it is, then.

The primary ingredient in an ANFO is ammonium nitrate, and that was also a main ingredient in fertilizer. He stepped up to the corn mixture and read the text under the red skull and crossbones on the side.

There! Ammonium nitrate, his pulse raced with excitement until he read the rest of the ingredients. *Fuck! Urea!*

Ammonium nitrate will not explode if it is mixed with common ingredients such as urea or ammonium sulfate, two typical additives to AN-based fertilizers for just that reason. He quickly checked the next cylinder, the one for pyro-berries. It wasn't any good, either. Each mixture had the needed AN, but not in a high enough concentration or without the additives that made it useless as an explosive.

He stepped back, hands on his hips, trying to figure out a solution. Then, he remembered his two specialty fields, the ones in which he grew the winter melons, raspberries, and other rare foods for his own consumption and to trade for meats. He didn't have one single cylinder for each of those—his fertilizer was mixed in the magnetic agitator and applied by a man-packed sprayer. He opened the pantry and pulled out a pack of Señor Fukimaru's Wonder Grow. The ingredient list started off with aluminum nitrate salts—and without any of the other ingredients that would render them inert. With a thrill, Colby grabbed another 5kg pack and put them on his workbench.

Now, he needed fuel and a detonator. Normally, the fuel would be a carbon-based liquid, such as gasoline or diesel. His farm, though, ran on electricity. He didn't have liquid fuel.

But I do have photovoltaic cells, though. And what do I paint on the back of the new ones? Aluminum powder paste! Aluminum powder and aluminum nitrate makes ammonal. Boom!

The cells that produced electricity were pretty foolproof, but they could be damaged by weather. Because he was a long way from a tech he had a small stock of the cells on hand for repairs. They'd been ready to go before he took over the property, so he hoped he still had the paste that had been used to paint the backs. He returned to the house and rummaged around the pantry shelves, trying to find some. He'd just about given up when he found a stained can which had obviously been opened previously. He carefully pried up the lid, and to his relief, there was at least half a can of the powder remaining.

Better still, he could use the can as a body for his bomb. What he didn't know was the proper percentage of AN to aluminum powder. He automatically tried pulling up the information on the net, but it was still down. His implant, however, contained some 10 terabytes of information, everything for the Marine seeking to perform almost any mission. Within moments, not only did he have the numbers, but a nice recording on how to mix the two. Minutes later, he had what he hoped was a working ammonal bomb.

Except for a detonator. This won't go off without one.

That might be a little more difficult, he realized. His farm had long been terrascaped to maximize productivity, so there wasn't a need for construction equipment. But the fuel and explosive needed something to set them off. He searched the vault, racking his brain for a solution, all the time noting that time was running out. He considered running out to the silos; grain silos have been known to explode and had dampening systems installed to prevent that. but he had no idea as to what mechanism in them set them off.

There's got to be something here I can use, but what?

He queried his implant, scanning through a list of military detonators until he came to field expedient measures. There were at least twenty, but all took time to prepare, time he didn't have. Finally, one caught his eye. If the tolerances were not too tight, it might work. He grabbed a small glass bottle of sulfuric acid, his half-made bomb, and bolted out the door. . .

. . . and came to a stop. To the east, the enemy plants had almost reached his house.

"Come on, Duke! No time to waste."

Duke whined, then ran back into the vault while Colby bolted back to the house and to the kitchen.

Please, please, be enough, he begged as he reached for the matches he kept above the stove.

The power in the house was electric, but he'd grown fond of grilling meat outside, and for that, he needed old fashioned matches—and friction matches used potassium chlorate to ignite. He had about 30 left in the box.

I hope it's enough.

Snapping off the heads, he placed them in a small plastic bag before dumping a cup of sugar in as well, shaking it up. It was crude, and it probably wouldn't work, but he was running out of options.

Turning to his liquor cabinet, he carefully removed a highly polished wooden box, flipping open the lid. Nestled in a form-fitting silk-covered pad was a small 250ml flask of 2402 Martell Cognac. The bottle had cost him three weeks salary, and he'd been saving it for a special occasion. Without hesitation, he opened the flask and dumped the golden liquid down his sink. It was the flask he wanted. Handblown by retro-craftsmen in Iberia back on Earth, it was delicate, almost insubstantial, crystal. He carefully filled the flask one quarter of the way with the sulfuric acid, then started to place it in his bomb, intending to surround it with the sugar-potassium chlorate mixture. Despite how fragile the flask was, however, it was possible that the aluminum nitrate and aluminum powder mixture would cushion it after he threw it. He needed to make sure the flask broke, causing the sugar mixture to explode, thereby setting off the rest of the bomb.

He opened the cabinet with his kitchenware and spotted his small salad bowl. It looked about right, and it just fit inside the aluminum powder can. Colby put in the sugar and match heads next, then lay the flask with the acid on top. The bowl was hard, the sides of the can were hard. He was sure that when it hit the ground, the flask would break. Whether the match heads would ignite and explode was another story, but this was the best he could do. He carefully closed the can, sealing the ingredients inside.

Colby ran back outside. The plants were in the compound, a dozen or so up against the east wall of his house, their leafy branches hugging the walls like nature-lovers communing with trees. He ran to the north side of the compound, ready to blast a hole in the incoming horde, but stopped. Duke had left him to run back to the vault, but he couldn't leave her. With a sigh, he ran back. The dog was cowering behind the cylinders, and he had to drag her out using the still attached leach. She put up a fight, but he simply overpowered her.

There was a cracking sound as he dragged Duke back to the north side of the compound. A chunk of his house broke off under the assault of the plants. They might be much slower than him, but like a tree buckling pavement with their roots, they evidently had immense power.

More had entered the compound, but for the moment, they seemed to be ignoring Duke and him. He wasn't going to test them, however, and stayed as far away as he could as he got into position, ready to blast a path to freedom.

As he took in the sheer numbers of the enemy, though, he began having second thoughts. His little homemade bomb didn't seem like enough. But it was all he had.

Duke was jerking wildly at her leash, whining and barking. Colby jerked back, almost knocking her off her feet. He didn't need a panicking dog while he had a homemade bomb in his hands.

"He who will not risk, cannot win," he said, quoting an ancient wet-water navy hero, one of the many quotes that adorned the walls of the Officer Training School auditorium back on New Mars.

There was one more thing he could do. His Marine Corps utilities were sturdy, able to take a lot of punishment in addition to normal wear and tear. When the bullets were flying, however, they needed the body armor that was intertwined with the uniform's cloth. With a quick command, a tiny current activated that caused the armor fibers to align, making them impenetrable to small arms fire. He felt a little foolish activating the armor when faced with plants, but he was of the better-safe-than-sorry school of thinking.

He shifted the leash to his left hand, transferring the handle of the bomb to his right. He swung it around, building momentum until he released it to arc up in the air. Like an idiot, he stood there, feeling elation as it flew straight for the densest concentration of the plants he could see. He really didn't think it would work, and so was surprised that as it hit, there was a huge explosion, strong enough to blow him back on his ass.

"Ooh-rah!" he shouted, scrambling back up to his feet, ears ringing, but none the worse for the shock wave.

Below him, pieces of green littered the area around a 15-meter-wide hole in what had been hop-beans. Chunks of the enemy had reached him, torn apart by the blast. His little bomb might not have the brisance of a military HE bomb, but it had packed a lot of power. As strong as the enemy seemed to be, they couldn't stand up to pure brute force.

"Let's go," he shouted at Duke, pulling at her and starting down into the blast zone.

He didn't get far, pulling up into a stop as beyond the zone, enemy plants were rising from where they'd been blown flat. Colby had once seen a time-lapse video of sunflowers back on Earth following the sun, turning to keep their faces oriented to it. This was what he was seeing right then. The plants didn't have a flower, but there was no doubt in his military mind that they were turning to face him. If they had been ignoring him before, he was certainly the center of their attention now. As they started converging on him, he knew he wasn't about to break through to the north—or to any direction.

"Shit, Duke, back to the vault!"

The dog didn't need any encouragement. She bolted, almost pulling him along with her. They passed the silos, but as they approached the vault, the plants surged forward to cut them off. Colby let go of the leash, and Duke darted ahead, just out of reach of the forward edge of the plants. A couple of steps behind her, he wasn't going to be so lucky.

He wasn't going down without a fight, however. As the first plant moved to block him, he leveled a kick that sent the plant flying ten meters. He felt his warrior take over as he leveled a second kick, breaking leafy branches off another.

"I'm going to make it," he said as he broke through, and darted just ahead of the advancing line.

Ten meters away from the door, something tripped him, and he ate a facefull of dirt. He twisted around, and one of the plants had wrapped its arm-like branches around his left ankle. He tried to kick it off him, but the branches started squeezing. Colby immediately understood how the things had started to take apart his house. It was like being caught in a compression vice. Without his body armor, he was sure his leg would be crushed, and whatever the first tiny plant had done to his hand when he'd picked it up would be repeated. He pushed with his right leg and managed to scoot forward, dragging his attacker with him as the pain mounted. He pushed off again, then four or five of the plants grabbed his attacker. Their combined effort started to pull him back. Colby clawed the ground for purchase, but he was being overpowered.

A flash of gold shot past his face. With a growl worthy of a wolf, Duke sunk her teeth in the main stalk of the plant latched on his leg. To his immense, but welcomed surprise, the plant released him, recoiling to about half of its length.

Colby jumped to his feet, grabbed Duke's leash, and bolted for the vault door as the rest of the plants rallied to converge on him. He darted though the door, then slammed it shut, bolting it.

Duke looked up at him, tail wagging.

"I owe you, girl, big time," he said as he tried to catch his breath, adrenaline flowing through him.

He'd tried to create an egress route, but all it seemed to do was to piss off the plants, assuming they even had the capability for that emotion. The way they'd reacted, especially when several of them had tried to help the one on his leg, had convinced him they were not mindless automatons, much more than simple biological weapons. He'd bet on the fact that they were individuals of some sort, at least.

"At least they're not invincible," he said. "We sure blew the crap out of some of them. Now I've just got to figure out how to do that again, but on a larger scale."

There was a thump from outside the vault. Duke growled as the hair on the back of Colby's neck stood on end. He'd seen the plants starting to tear apart his house. There was a big difference between his home and the vault, however. The house was built from Mennyboard, which was essentially compressed cellulose. Cheap and easy to make, it was sturdy enough for most purposes and could stand up to routine weather, but the building was hardly a fortress. The vault, on the other hand, was built to withstand a possible explosion of any of the chemicals it contained, and it was a shelter from extreme weather conditions. It would take quite a bit more effort to tear it down. He turned his attention back to trying to make a bigger bomb— although not before finding a long-handled shovel to keep readily at hand.

He went through the entire vault, comparing the ingredients and materials at hand to what his implant fed him about making explosives. Given six or seven hours, if the vault held up, he should be able to create a more powerful explosive, but would it be big enough to wipe out the plants? He didn't think so. He could make a type of napalm, but he had no way to deliver it.

Too bad. I bet they'd burn like old Christmas trees.

The image of the thousands of meter-tall plants going up in flames was appealing, and while he searched for a response, his mind kept drifting back to that image. But there was no way to bring flames to them. The farm had the heaters, of course, to protect the crops from cold snaps, but while each heater put out about 600,000 BTU per hectare/hour, which was pretty hefty, it was hardly a conflagration. Unless he could convince the plants to march into each heater in turn, they wouldn't do much. He couldn't even let the methane that powered the heating units build up. The gas-activated sensors on the heater automatically fired the ignitors when the methane first reached them.

But what if I could deactivate the sensors somehow?

"Ralph, can I run methane through the lines but deactivate the heating units?"

"Negative. Doing so would cause a dangerous buildup of gas with possible catastrophic consequences."

That's what I'm trying to do, idiot.

"I want to override that. Deactivate the heating units."

"I'm sorry, but Civil Code 4008.4.10 expressly forbids that while the system is online. Tampering with the heating units carries a 100,000 credit fine."

"So, it's possible to do it?" he asked, his interest rising.

"Affirmative. Each heating unit has a manual cut-off switch. The valve can then be opened to flush the system."

His excitement dropped off. In order to do that, he'd have to go out among the fields, something he doubted the plants would let him do.

"So, there is no way to do it from here?"

"Technically, yes, there is. But Civil Code 4008—"

"Stop," he ordered, not wanting to hear the AI continue.

"Can you override the farm AI?" he subvocalized to his implant.

A normal civilian implant wouldn't be able to force an AI to break a law, but high-level military units had more capabilities.

"Yes, that is possible," it replied.

"Do it. I want the heating units deactivated."

A moment later, his implant said, "Three of sixty-four units deactivated."

Colby's heart fell.

"Only three?"

"The remaining units are no longer receiving signals. The probability is high that they no longer have unit integrity."

"You mean they're destroyed?"

"Yes."

Colby could ask his implant for more details, but it was programmed to give them only when queried. If it said the probability was "high," then that was good enough for him. And it was good news. If the units were destroyed, then they couldn't set off the gas before enough had built up to be effective. With only three units still intact, his plan, half-formed as it was, might have a chance at success.

The real question in his mind now was if the methane could actually be concentrated enough to take the farm up in flames. He checked the weather outside. With winds at 5 kph, that might be enough to blow the methane off the property before it could build up. He needed to somehow transform the gas into something "stickier," for lack of a better term.

He queried his implant, not expecting a solution, but one popped up, something far easier than he'd expected: magnesium stearate. The substance was essentially a soap, the same thing that caused soap scum in his tub. The farm used it to coat the inside of all the cylinders and tubing to ensure the ingredients, especially the powders, didn't stick to the containers. It was also a general lubricant for much of the farm's pieces of equipment.

If the stearate kept materials separated, it didn't make sense that he could mix it with a gas, but his implant instructed him to run it through the agitator, giving him the percentages of each substance. With more than a little trepidation, he put in the commands to run the methane and magnesium stearate through the agitator and out through the lines to flood the farm.

"Distribution lines are not intact," the AI informed him.

"Pull up a diagram."

He leaned forward to study the schematic. The bulk of the lines were still in place, but all were damaged to some extent or the other. Some indicated leaks while others had huge chunks of line torn out.

"The bastards have been busy," he muttered before asking his AI, "Ralph, how can I achieve the most coverage?"

A moment later, the schematic changed with the selected lines highlighted in blue. The AI had bypassed several lines that had been torn out close to the compound while leaving others in the distribution plan. The resultant coverage was complete, even if the concentration varied.

A large cracking sound filled the vault, and Colby grabbed the shovel, holding it aloft as Duke let out a throaty growl. There was another crack coming from the east wall, but nothing penetrated into the building.

Yet.

Still holding the shovel, he ordered the AI to start the distribution, half-expecting to hear another protest that doing so violated some civil code, but Ralph acknowledged the order. He looked back to make sure the flow of both methane and magnesium stearate had begun, and the readouts on the control suite confirmed that. A green feed light indicated the mixture was being pushed down the lines.

Colby had learned more than he'd wanted to about explosions over the last half-an-hour. He'd never heard of the term "stoichiometric proportion," which was the concentration of the flammable material in the air at a given temperature and pressure that gave the most bang-for-the-buck. What he did know was that he wasn't going to achieve that with his gyvered system. He needed to reach the LEL, or Lower Explosive limit. For methane, that was 5 percent. Despite the huge repository of data in his implant, he couldn't find what the LEL was for a methane-stearate mix. He didn't even understand what the 5 percent LEL meant; it was not something as simple as meaning 5 percent of the atmosphere. He tried to follow the math before giving up. He didn't need to know what it meant. If the sensors on the remaining three heating units worked, all he had to know was when the meters read 5 percent. Or in this case, 10 percent, the buffer he was giving himself to take into consideration the addition of the magnesium stearate.

There were more cracking sounds from the walls. The plants were making progress even on the vault. Colby just hoped the building could hold out.

"There we go, Duke. It's working," he said when Unit 14 indicated a jump in methane. It was only at .5 percent, but it was a start.

Duke whomped her tail on the floor.

More to keep busy than anything else, Colby gathered the materials to make a Molotov Cocktail, something he could have done in his sleep. He intended on using the three heating units to set off the explosion, but it was always a good idea to have a back-up.

Slowly, the methane concentration started to rise. Unit 14 hit 5 percent within ten minutes, with 23 at 3 percent. There was no feedback at all from Unit 33. With 14 and 23 covering a third of the farm at best, he wouldn't know how well the coverage was getting to be on the rest of the property.

He waited, one hand on Duke's back and chewing the fingernails of the other, trying to will the readouts of the two working sensors to rise faster, but after reaching 8 percent, Unit 14 seemed stuck. Unit 23 kept rising, but at a glacially slow pace.

There was a louder crack in the wall, and pieces of the inner wall broke free. Colby jumped to his feet while Duke stood beside him, her head held low while she fiercely growled. He slowly stalked forward, shovel held out, until he stood before the wall. Poking it, he knocked away the inner wall covering. He was now staring at the structural body of the wall, a solid-looking piece of some metallic alloy. As he watched, it warped, twisting before his eyes. He wasn't an engineer, but that had to be a tremendous amount of force to actually warp it. Suddenly, whatever feeling of security he had vanished. He knew that if he merely tried to wait the enemy out, he'd fail. They would break into his fortress. His plan had to work if he and Duke were going to get out alive.

He went back to the display. Unit 14 was still stuck on 8 percent, but 23 was at 7 percent. Unit 23 was at the third highest piece of property on the farm, a good 15 meters higher than the lowest point. Even "thickened" gas would tend to flow downhill, so common sense told him that the concentrations were probably higher at the other points.

*But the Gustavsons' farm is lower than min*e, he realized in a flash. *I bet I'm losing methane to them.*

He checked his methane supply. He was down to 23 percent. The methane was produced in-house in the digestion tank behind the vault. It was still being fermented, but it was draining at a far greater rate. He'd be out soon.

A rending screech filled the vault, and the entire building shook. Colby ran back to the east wall, tearing away the inner coverings. At the northeast corner, behind the racks of cylinders, four rivets had popped out. He couldn't see daylight, but it was only a matter of time now, a very short time.

Shit. I've got to give it a shot now.

He took a deep breath, then said, "Ralph, turn on the heater ignitors."

His AI might have had a problem with turning the ignitors off, but it didn't have one with turning them on.

"Confirm," it said as Colby held his breath, drawing Duke into his arms.

And nothing happened.

There was no explosion, no anything.

"Ralph, did you initiate the ignition."

"Affirmative. There was no confirmation return to indicate compliance."

"So, they didn't go off?"

"That is a possibility. Another possibility is that the confirmation circuits are down."

"What's the probability that it was the ignitors that malfunctioned rather than there being a problem with the circuits?"

"There isn't enough data to calculate an acceptable figure."

The noise coming in from the outside grew louder, but he pushed it out of his mind. He had to make a decision. There had been no explosion of fire. That could be because his plan was faulty, because it was a good plan but the concentration of methane was not great enough, or because the ignitor failed to set off the initial explosion. He had two options: wait until the concentration increased (or he ran out of methane) or try his Molotov Cocktail. He checked the display; he was at 19 percent of his methane supply. As the supply decreased, so would the flow out the lines. Too slow, and the methane hugging the ground out there would flow or be blown off the property faster than it was being replenished.

"Molotov it is, girl," he said.

He picked up the bomb, checking it over one more time. It seemed to be in order. The wick, which was a twisted rag, should burn long enough for the bomb to hit the ground and burst open. If there was enough methane out there, it would ignite. It was that simple.

With it in one hand, the shovel in the other, he walked up to the door, leaning the shovel up against the wall and placing that hand's palm against the door itself. He could feel vibrations. He didn't know whether that meant the plants were attacking the door or the vibrations were transmitted from the attacks on the east and north side of the building.

"Only one way to find out, girl," he said, placing the Molotov Cocktail on the ground at his feet and putting his shoulder to the door.

One... two... three, he counted to himself before hitting the latch and pushing with all his might.

And he hit resistance. He got the door opened halfway, shoving several of the plants to the side. He knew nothing of the enemy's physiology, but he could have sworn that the things registered surprise for a moment before they reacted.

Colby reacted quicker, though. He grabbed the shovel and stepped forward, swinging it like the Grim Reaper's scythe. He cut down two of the plant creatures, toppling them, and knocked back several more, clearing a small space for himself. He lunged back for the Molotov Cocktail, lit the wick, and with two hops forward, launched it towards the west, trying for the lowest section of the farm he could reach. As the bomb arched up in the air, the rotten egg smell of the odorant added to methane registered in his brain. He hadn't purposefully released any methane around the house, but enough had flowed in for him to smell it. If it had been above the LEL right there, he'd have just blown himself up.

If he could smell it, then a big enough explosion could ignite the compound. He jumped back and grabbed the door, hoping to slam it shut, but several of the plants had other ideas. Green branches reached forward to hold the edge of the door. One branch latched onto his arm while Duke started to dart forward, teeth bared.

And the world exploded. A huge fist hit the door, slamming it shut and sending Colby flying across the floor on his ass. He hit the base of the first cylinder rack and lay there, stunned. The door to the outside started to swing open a crack as heat and smoke poured into the vault. Still dazed, he managed to get to his feet and stumble to the door, pulling it shut and locking it. Bits and pieces of plant arms, cut off when the door shut, lay on the floor. One larger chunk was slowly moving. Without much thought, he picked up the shovel, put the blade against the meatier part of the plant, and stepped on it, cutting the piece in two. Green goo squirted out, but it lay still.

"You OK, girl?" he asked, his voice sounding as if he was underwater.

Duke gave out a plaintive whine, but thumped her tail on the floor.

Colby knew that his plan had worked, but to what extent? He had no eyes on the farm, and given the temperatures being recorded from the vault's roof sensors, the entire place was on fire. He and Duke weren't going anywhere for the time being.

Ever the pragmatist, and still somewhat dazed, he lay down for a nap, Duke's head across his stomach. He knew people who'd had concussions weren't supposed to sleep, but there wasn't anyone around to scold him for that. He awoke a few hours later, his mind feeling much clearer. Immediately, he tried the net again, but once more, he couldn't connect. For all he knew, the planet could be razed and he and Duke the only survivors.

He stood up and checked the temperature outside. While still a few degrees higher than normal, he knew he could survive. With Duke on his heels, he went back to the door, kicking the pieces of enemy plants to the side. He put an ear to the door, not knowing what to expect, but he heard nothing.

"Might as well get this over," he told Duke as he pushed open the door.

"Son-of-a-bitch," he said as he surveyed the charred landscape.

The entire compound was blackened and covered with what had to be plant corpses. He shifted his gaze over to what were the remains of his house. He couldn't tell if the plants had destroyed it or the fire, but it was definitely gone. With Duke following, he walked down the line of silos, the twisted remains telling him the plant creatures had destroyed them before the fires had done their work.

The enemy remains became less substantial as he wandered to the western side of the compound where utterly devastated fields stretched below him, the ashes of enemy plants and pyro berry bushes indistinguishable from each other. The destruction didn't end at his property line. Flames had made their way across the Gustavsons' fields to their house, which still smoked. Beyond that, black smoke of an active fire rose into the air.

Colby knew that his methane mixture couldn't have flowed that far, and if it had, the LEL would have been too small to ignite. But sometimes wildfires grew from the tiniest of sparks, and if each farm's firefighting system was knocked out, then they could grow unchecked.

Without a word, Colby turned and walked back to the rubble that had been his house. He paused for a moment at what had been the front door, then with a sigh, stepped over the jam. There was nothing left. Duke bounded past him and started nosing around what had been the kitchen. He started to call her back, but then stopped. If she found something to eat, all the more power to her, and she was smart enough to avoid anything hot enough to burn her.

He kicked a partially melted support beam out of the way and walked to the back of the house. This had been where his I Love Me wall had been, the culmination of his long career as a Marine. All of it was gone, now, and it felt as if that career had only been a dream. His eye caught a rectangular object on the ground, and he bent over to pick it up. It was a plaque from his first battalion as a second lieutenant. The top of the plaque had burned away, but enough of the bottom had survived that he could read "Second Lieutenant Colby Edson, Fair Winds and Following Seas from the Magnificent Bastards."

Half of a burned plaque wasn't much to show for 51 years of service. With a shrug, he dropped it to the ground with the rest of the junk.

Interlude I: Spores, Before and After

Like a dormant seed within its pod, the Gardener dreamed. It waited in its vessel high above the planet, lost in contemplation as it luxuriated in the steady stream of data carried up from the atmosphere below. No slightest glint or gleam of energies spilled from within the vessel. No signal slipped out from its shell. The Gardener itself had designed the meta-cellulose that enclosed its home in space so as to render the vessel undetectable by its own kind, leaving it free to work without interruption. With visionary intensity it had painstakingly shaped the code underlying every gene for both optimization and aesthetics. The vessel could sense, react, absorb, ignore, and otherwise respond to both minimal and extreme gravimetric forces, as well as a broad range of hostile radiation. Out of a sense of ambition, it had nurtured the specifications to endure encounters in proximity to a gas giant, though of course it would never venture to such a world. What need for a Gardener where no garden could grow? But this world, a planet it had only visited twice before, most recently some two hundred of its revolutions ago, this world offered its vessel neither threats nor challenges.

Or so the Gardener had presumed.

Passive mappings had flowed into the vessel as the planet completed several rotations below, revealing crude, right-angled distributions of vegetation, the sort of blocky plantings that a newly sprouted child might make, in stark contrast to the graceful fractal distributions the Gardener had seeded during its last visit. But children were not permitted to stray into the gardens of adults, let alone possess the experience to create a vessel to take them so far from home.

Other problematic signs had demanded its attention as well. Patterns of erosion, oceanic oxygen levels, and historic indications of rain density—each individually improbable but nonetheless plausible particulars—combined to hint that one or more other beings had come and placed their imprint upon this world. Imbeciles, judging by the data. Or worse, a Gardener who had put forth its own sense of the artistic instead of creating in tune to the universe's whispers. Such things occurred, albeit rarely. It had caught word of just this sort of radical movement when it last tasted the soil of home. There were few enough Gardeners, and fewer still who chose to share their work in space, that even a pod's worth could produce unsavory excuses for gardens amidst the otherwise barren planets and moons of the galaxy. And yet, surely, even such radicals would not presume to intervene on a claimed world.

No, another factor was in play here. Over the span of several more rotations, the Gardener had turned its attention to gathering preliminary chromatography data. It had even repeated the initial analysis, but the outcome remained unchanged. The perfect garden it had seeded during its last visit now exhibited the presence of complex toxins that could not exist in nature. They ruled out the possibility of even the most extreme and iconoclastic of Gardeners or even any of the weak imitators scattered among the lesser races of the galaxy. Only a single explanation existed: Meat.

Every Gardener knew that a certain amount of meat was necessary to maintain proper atmospheric balance. Anaerobic gardens were certainly possible, some portions were actually elegant, but real complexity and biodiversity required a synergy of gases, and one could only go so far with plankton. It was the classic tradeoff, allowing larger and more complex invertebrates—and even vertebrates—into a garden could lead to a lush outcome, but time and again animal life proved itself a nuisance. The Gardener had observed similar patterns among its peers' creations, some pesky vertebrate evolving over the course of millennia until it achieved a pathetic proto-sapience, and with it, invariably, a compulsion to either alter the perfection of the environment or simply overbreed until it poisoned its habitat with its own wastes.

But this was different. Millennia had not passed, barely two hundred revolutions. Animal evolution did not advance at such rates, even in as idyllic an environment as it had put in motion before leaving. Moreover, the other signs of proto-sapient pests—alteration and degradation of the landscape in pursuit of mineral resources, erection of crude and short-lived structures, pollution of rivers as a consequence of early industry—none of these had occurred in significant density or frequency, or so the vessel's passive scans suggested.

Data would continue to pour in the longer it remained in orbit, but even at this stage it had detected only a single, major, artificial structure where none should exist. Enhanced optics might well reveal smaller constructions in the vicinity of the crude patches that marred its carefully designed plantings, and indeed, patterns and concentrations among the air vectors had implied these locations were the source for the toxins that had been introduced to its world.

Was it possible? Had the Meat despoiling its garden arrived from outside? Could Meat ever achieve sufficient sophistication as to travel between worlds? Fantastic as the idea might be, the stuff of nightmares and madness, how else to account for the data?

Deep within the husk of its navigational locker, the Gardener had stirred. Left to its own tendencies, vegetable nature preferred patience and slow change. Its own species evolution into motility had been weighed and discussed for ages before embracing the opportunities of choice and direction it afforded. Yes, they could now venture off world, travel into space and apply their vision to craft new gardens, but even so, all Gardeners sought stillness. In this next phase of gardening this planet, it had expected to spend fifty or more revolutions tweaking and pruning, and never having to physically move. Already the Meat had pushed it out from its comfort zone.

In response to a pulsed signal, its husk had split and the Gardener had emerged. Green tendrils shot forth from its core forming ropey limbs, reinventing the motility it had shed upon entering the navigation locker. Even as carefully grown a thing as its vessel could not be allowed to handle all operations remotely; some few tasks required direction attention. It had slid and sloped its way to a subsection of the vessel, triggering long dormant processes.

The Meat would have to be eradicated. Whatever flawed plantings it had devised would be razed to make way for the resumption of the original design. The crude shelters that Meat always seemed so fond of would be pulled apart, sundered down to constituent pieces, and these pieces further reduced to their basic elements with the help of a few revolutions of erosion until they were reclaimed by the soil. And the offending toxins would be absorbed by carefully designed vegetable tools programmed to encapsulate every molecule, removing it from interaction with the rest of the environment until the Gardener could deploy other tools to spirit the foulness away. If the Meat happened to be razed or sundered or otherwise destroyed in the process, that, too, would be just a part of weeding one's garden.

The Gardener had consulted its records of past work, made adjustments, and instructed its vessel to manufacture and disperse several loads of spores strategically so the prevailing air patterns would carry them to the Meat's locations of disruption during the planet's dark cycle. The basic resources needed by all organic life existed in abundance on this world, even in those places where Meat had gained hold. With the warmth of morning the spores had sprouted into purge agents, quickly achieved sufficient mass to acquire a rudimentary motility, and begun carrying out the directives the Gardener had encoded in them.

By the end of the next day cycle, its garden was back on track, leaving only a single, major structure with which to deal. An additional rotation's worth of data indicated electromagnetic concentrations that did not belong in its garden, suggesting the possibility of an incursion of Mechanical pseudo-life. Irritating as that might prove, such an outcome made more sense than postulating the mysterious arrival of proto-sapient Meat. Moreover, the protocols for disabling mechanicals were well established. The Gardener keyed the creation and programming of a few billion additional spores, similar to purge agents but with combinatorial capabilities. Their insertion into the atmosphere would land them in a tight ring around the offending structure. As they quickened and took form, they'd encircle the target, establishing containment, and then advance, rending any inorganics in their path. Meat or Mechanical, all would be purged, the offending structure dismantled, and the insufferable electromagnetics eliminated.

Afterwards, the Gardener would need to allocate time to study the data in order to learn the origin of such an affront, but best to resolve it first. And too, time was always on vegetation's side, a concept Mechanicals could not appreciate and which Meat would never be able to grasp. Pleased with its efforts, the Gardener perambulated back to its navigation locker and drew the walls tight around itself, bonding once more with the living green of its vessel. Leaving the spores to do their work, it returned to the pleasures of contemplation.

Part II: Reinforcements and Retreat

"Come on, Erin, I really need to talk to the Dickhead," Colby said.

"You shouldn't call the vice minister that, General. You know that. But I told you, he isn't taking your call."

"Did you ask him face-to-face? And what did he say?"

There was a pause, then, "I don't want to repeat it."

"Tell me, Erin."

"It wasn't nice, General."

"I'm a big boy. Tell me."

"Well, OK. He said he that you are a worthless piece of shit who should rot in hell."

It took a moment for that to sink in. He knew that Vice Minister Asahi Salinas Greenstein hated him, but this went beyond the pale. This was a matter of security, not petty politics. Besides, the vice minister had won. He wasn't the one exiled to a backwater agricultural planet at the edge of human space.

When Colby had uncovered the corruption at the highest levels, the siphoning of war supplies to personal accounts, he'd thought the vice minister would have led the pack to throw the criminals into prison. He hadn't realized the depth of the corruption or how high it went. When he'd been given the choice between resigning or being court-martialed over trumped up charges, he'd wanted to fight. It wasn't until the threat of levying charges against his loyal subordinates that he'd given in and taken the poison pill.

He took a deep breath to calm himself. He couldn't afford to get the vice minister's personal secretary upset with him as well.

"Erin, I'm going to record what I've observed here, all of it. If I've still got the connection, I'll upload it to you. Please, please, get that to the Di. . . to the vice minister, or if not him, to General Tybor. This is important."

"I'll forward it up, General. But with the resumption of hostilities with the Borealis Pact, some agricultural pest isn't going to be high on anyone's priorities."

Colby wanted to scream his frustration, but he damped that down.

"Just do what you can, Erin, OK? I've got to go now."

He cut the connection, fuming. He was trying to report an invasion, because after examining what little was left of the marauding plants, he was convinced that they were not some lab experiment gone wrong but a full-scale alien attack.

He'd been lucky just to make it through to his old boss. Communications, both on Vasquez and off-planet, had been cut. With the full capabilities of his implant, that wouldn't have been a problem, but his implant had been stripped of those when he'd left the service. It had only been through some convoluted routing and hacking that his implant had been able to route the call through the local wormhole's comms bot and back to New Mars, and then only to Erin's public line. His implant estimated that he had fewer than 400 seconds before the bot's AI caught up to his implant's machinations, realized there had been a hack, and closed off the pipeline. Colby's call had taken 405 seconds before he cut it off. Now, his best course of action was to record everything he'd seen, send it up as a pulse upload, then trust Erin to get it to the right person.

He'd stood up to go back into the vault, and Duke jumped to her feet, tail wagging as she looked up at him.

"Sorry, girl. I'll try to find you something to eat, but I want to check the progress on the precipitate."

Colby hadn't simply sat around all night in the vault. He'd known he'd been lucky with both his ANFO bombs and the methane. They'd been made on the fly, and the fact that they'd worked was nothing short of a miracle. He might have beaten back the assault, but that was only a battle, and the war might still be ongoing. If that was the case, he needed to be better prepared, so with his implant's guidance, he'd been busy preparing better and stronger weapons. He'd already produced a better flammable jelly-substance that now filled two cylinders, complete with jury-rigged dispensers. They were bulky and heavy, but he thought they'd make passable flamethrowers. One task that took time, however, was to precipitate pure potassium chlorate from bleach. He'd been too lucky with the match heads setting off the detonator, so he needed to improve that.

The process required to produce the potassium chlorate he needed released chlorine, so he wanted to precipitate the crystals outside, but he didn't have a power source out there, and he'd had to do it inside the vault, but under the hood. This was actually the second step in the process, what his implant termed "fractional crystallization," and he was more than pleased to see that the reaction looked to be completed. With the pure crystals, he could finish detonators for the almost-completed bombs he had prepared. An hour later, he had 30 powerful grenades lined up, ready to use. He carefully packed them into empty storage cases, then stacked them up by the door.

He felt a sense of accomplishment, something he hadn't experienced since he'd arrived on the planet.

Let the bastards come again! I'm ready!

Duke had been sitting alongside the wall, watching his every move. He felt guilty. The old girl had come to his defense, and he'd been ignoring her. His house was destroyed, but he should be able to scrounge up some food for her.

"Come on, girl, let's go see what we can find."

With her on his heels, he left the vault. As he crossed the compound, he opened the planetary comms net, more from routine over the last 15 hours than from any hope of hearing from anyone, so he was surprised when a voice said, "Mayday, Mayday, is anyone receiving this?"

"I am," he said automatically, then instantly regretted it.

In time of war, communications had to be limited. Even with scrambling messages, the mere fact that there was a transmission might give the enemy AIs information that they could use.

"Who is this?" the female voice asked.

Colby hesitated, but as he realized that this was obviously a human and not an invading plant, he said, "Colby Edson. I've got a farm in Guernsey. Thirty-one F."

"Oh, thank god! Are you OK? Were you attacked?"

"Affirmative," he answered, snapping into military-speak. "Who are you?"

"I'm Topeka Watanabe, assistant launch coordinator, and I need help."

Colby knew the name, of course. All of his crops, all of the crops in the continent, were slung into space from Blair de Staffney Station, and he'd seen her tagline on most of his receipts.

"What kind of help?"

"We've been attacked by the plant things. They killed Sestus, and Riordan's been hurt."

Riordan was the station director, but Colby had never heard of Sestus.

"We've been hit pretty hard out here in Guernsey, too. I don't think my neighbors made it, either. It looks like the attacks have stopped, though."

It was true. Colby had gone on a quick recon of the area that morning after emerging from spending the night in the vault. There wasn't any sign of the plants, at least not living ones. This wasn't only in the burned area of his farm; it was everywhere. All of the vegetation within sight had been destroyed, as had all buildings and windmills, leaving only his vault intact— damaged, but intact. Outside of the scorched area he'd burned, there were rapidly decomposing bodies of the invaders, but nothing living.

"They've stopped for now, but there's a ship above us in orbit, and it isn't one of ours."

For a split second, Colby felt relief. A ship could take them off the planet. A ship would have comms back to New Mars or even Earth. But he also knew that no ship was scheduled for another two months, and Ms. Watanabe wouldn't be telling him she needed help if it was a human ship. Still, he had to ask.

"Is it alien?"

"You'd better fucking believe it. It matches nothing on the scans."

"So, you've got power?" he asked.

"I'm on back-up. Most of the station was destroyed. I've got the processing station and the cannon, and a few of the buildings are left. They did a number on us."

"I was a Marine Corps general—"

"I know who you are. And I need you here. It's your duty."

"Well, just hold on a minute. You're 30 klicks away, and I don't know if the way between us is clear of the enemy."

"It's clear."

"How can you be sure, Ms. Watanbe?"

"Because I saw them stop in the middle of their attack, then go off to die. Why don't you know that, I mean if you're alive, you must have seen it, too. They're dead there, right?"

"I've been in my vault since yesterday afternoon."

"And they let you alone? That's weird. I saw the monitors of what they did to the outlying farms around here. It wasn't pretty. The Pavonis, when the bastards came in their house, and Hermes tried to fight them, that was. . ." she said, trailing off.

"I beat them back," he interrupted, sensing she was getting into visuals that were better forgotten for the moment. "I burned them."

"No shit? You burned them? With what?"

"I made a kind of napalm," he said, not without a bit of pride.

"Then I really need you here, like now."

"But you said they're all dead. Why the urgency?"

"Because, that ship up there? It launched landers, thousands of them, and all are heading right here to the station!"

****

Two hours later, Colby brought the cargo pod to a halt as the station came into view. He'd loaded the pod with with his two flame throwers, his grenades, some extra chemicals, and, of course, Duke. The pods were designed to transport crops to the station and bring back supplies, not for personal transport. It was awkward and snug, but it beat walking, which he'd assumed he'd have to do before he'd been able to repair one of the dead-lined pods. It had just enough power in the batteries to follow the inert telltales buried in the hover track to the station.

Even at this distance, he could see through the front-mounted cam that the enemy plants were already at the station, what had been a collection of four warehouses, a processing station, and the launch facility. Three of the warehouses had been broken down into rubble, and the plants looked to be swarming the processing station and the launch cannon. He couldn't be sure over the distance, and the damaged structures were of little use for comparison, but the enemy seemed bigger today.

"I'm at D2, Topeka," he passed over the comms, using her first name as she insisted. "How're you holding out?"

"About fucking time, General," she answered. "They've still got hard-ons for the cannon and factory."

The cannon was essentially a rail gun that launched the cargo pods into space and on an intercept course for the wormhole that took them to the huge distribution network on New Mars. Although it wasn't designed for personnel, it could be used as a last-ditch emergency evacuation system in specially designed cargo pods. If the plants managed to take the cannon out of action, then neither of the two surviving humans (three, if you counted Riordan locked away in his medical chamber) was going to get off the planet until and if someone came charging to the rescue.

"I think they're keying in on the cannon and irradiation units in the factory," she added.

"Why do you think that?"

"It makes sense. What's the cannon but a big electromagnetic field? And the irradiation units, what powers them? It makes friggin' sense. I think they can detect them, 'cause that's right where they headed. I about crapped myself when they landed, seeing as you were taking your sweet time to get here, but they walked right on past me."

Colby ignored the not-so-subtle jab. Topeka might be outspoken and crude, but she'd been through a lot, and what she'd said about the plants made sense.

"Have you seen any movement to the south of your position?"

"My position? You mean in the house?"

"Where you're at now. At the launch facility."

The three station personnel's living quarters were above the facility's office and control center, so it made sense that they simply called it their "house," but he couldn't assume anything, not with these stakes.

"I'm not sure. I can't really just go for a stroll to see, you know. But I think it's probably clear."

He took a moment to observe the station compound. On the north side of the building, the cannon's rail lay on an east-west axis to take advantage of the clockwise rotation of the planet. He couldn't see too much detail from well over a klick away, but while the plant soldiers were all over the rail, the south side of the building looked clear.

"OK, this is what I'm going to do. I've got some weapons with me, and I'm not going to abandon them. I'm going to take my pod to Charlie's loading docks," he said, referring to the lone warehouse still standing."

"Can't," Topeka interrupted him. "The road's been too torn up. Your pod won't make it through. Just come here to the house, and I'll let you in."

That was getting too close to the enemy for comfort, but he had a bigger concern.

"No hover pads to take me there."

"Don't need them none. Get to D1, then uncouple your pod. You can trolley it from there to here."

"Uncouple it?" he asked, more than a little confused.

Once locked into the track, the pods followed the designated path, internal controls keeping them on course.

"Geez! You've been here how long, and you don't even know your equipment? Uncouple it. Just hit externals, then your pin, then 'Break Lock.'"

Colby hadn't known he could do that. In all fairness, he'd never had to. Once his pods left the farm, they were out of sight and out of mind. But if he could unlock the pod, then he should be able to guide it as it hovered over the ground.

"OK, I'm on my way," he said.

"Make it quick, General."

He didn't respond but started the pod up again. He was in plain sight of the enemy fighters, if they even had sight as he knew it, but he couldn't detect any sign that they were paying attention to him. At the farm, they hadn't focused on him until he'd tossed the ANFO bomb. Before that, it was as if he didn't exist, or as if he wasn't considered as important as pulling up his crops. That made no sense to him, but part of his training had been to try to understand his enemies. He could not accept that ignoring him was some random act. For the plants, there had to be a reason he'd been ignored until he'd revealed himself as someone who could cause them harm.

I hope the ones at the farm haven't been in contact with these guys, passing around my mugshot.

He reached D1 and stopped the pod. Following Topeka's instructions, he uncoupled it from the track.

"Here goes," he said to Duke, then popped the cover and stepped out.

He half expected some of the plants would turn towards him, but once again, it was as if he wasn't there. Just as well; these plants were indeed bigger, nearly his own height. He shrugged, thankful for their disinterest, and gave the pod a tug. The thing had to mass 3,000 kg, but it followed him like a puppy as he slowly made his way off the track and down to the footpath that led into the station. He passed a destroyed junction box of some kind, the twisted wreck and smashed foundation a testament to the raw strength of the plants.

Duke whined from inside the pod, but he ignored her. He didn't want her running around and drawing attention to him. He was too exposed as it was, and he kept his eyes scanning, ready to bolt and run at the first sign he was on the things' radar. They may be immensely strong, but he was quicker, and he was ready to put that quickness to use if needed.

But it wasn't needed. He made his way to the facility unopposed. The most difficult thing was to control the pod. It moved easily enough, but it packed a lot of momentum, and off the hover track, he crashed the thing into the remains of Warehouse B and the facility before he reached the door and called Topeka.

"About friggin' time, General," she said as she opened the door.

Colby didn't know what he expected based on her somewhat rough and in-your-face language, but whatever that was, she wasn't it. Petite with long black hair, she was young, possibly not even 50 years old. She looked like a school teacher, maybe, or a programmer. But there was a fire to her that almost danced out of her eyes. This woman meant business.

"So, what do you got in there that was so damned important?" she asked.

"Let's get it inside, and I'll show you," he said, ever conscious of the teeming plants bent on destruction just on the other side of the building.

She stepped back, sizing up the pod, then said, "I don't think so. It ain't gonna fit. No reason for a cargo pod to come in here, you know. We gotta unload it here."

He realized she was right, so he opened the top. Duke immediately jumped out, tail wagging.

"Shit, a dog? What the hell do you have a dog for?"

Colby immediately bristled and said, "She saved my ass back on the farm. I wasn't going to leave her."

Topeka shrugged, then said, "Fine, but what else do you got? What's with the feed cylinders?"

"I made them into flame throwers. The plants don't like fire," he said, feeling proud of his ingenuity.

She shrugged again, then said, "I hope they work. Let's get them unloaded." She grabbed one and tried to lift it, then said, "Holy shit! What's in them?"

"You take the boxes, but be careful. They're bombs. Grenades, more like, and I don't know how stable they are."

"Hell, I didn't call him here to blow me up," she muttered as she lifted the first box and took it inside.

Colby rolled the first flamethrower to the edge of the pod, then with a grunt, lifted it and lowered it to the deck. It was heavy, no lie, and he looked to see if Topeka had seen him lift it. He wasn't used to anyone giving him orders, and the young woman had a take-charge personality. A show of physical strength was in order, he thought, to reassert his position as a Marine general and in charge. She didn't seem to notice as she brushed past him to pick up another box.

He about popped a gut lifting the second flamethrower, but they had the pod unloaded within a couple of minutes. Topeka gave it a hard shove with her leg, and it drifted out of the way.

"OK," he said, trying to take charge. "If we let them destroy the cannon, we're stuck here. So, we have to take the fight to them. Either that, or we retreat and wait for rescue."

He didn't like the second option, but he felt obligated to mention it. She wasn't a Marine, and he didn't feel like he could order her into what would probably be a futile fight.

"If we retreat, Riordan's a dead man," she said bitterly. "We can't move him in the chamber, and if we take him out, he's a goner. Those fucking plant-things will tear this place down, chamber too. I can't leave him."

Colby felt a rush of respect. She understood the situation, and loyalty was more important than her own safety. He understood the sentiment—he just hadn't expected to see it in a government civilian.

"Those flamethrowers," she said, tilting her chin to point at them. "They gonna work?"

"They should, at least as long as the pressure stays high enough. The jelly, it'll stick to anything and burn like Hades' fire, but I had to use compressed air to load them. Once that runs out, well, we don't want the fire to back up into the cylinders now, do we."

She nodded, then said, "That'd not be a good idea."

"But until then, I think they'll work fine."

"Kinda heavy, though. In case you haven't noticed, I'm a bit on the small side. But, I think I got an idea. Can you wait here?"

"Where're you going?"

"Just wait. Five minutes, tops," she said before she opened the door, peeked in both directions, then slipped out.

What the hell? Where's she going?

He shook it off and started opening the cases with the ANFO grenades. He was very confident as to the 2.0 versions he'd made. Not only were they closer to foolproof, they should have a much bigger bang.

When that was finished, he looked around the room. Through a clear window in the back, he could see lights. Walking over, he saw the lights were from displays. This was the control room. There had to be at least internal power still running as five of the displays were active. A red light was flashing on the second display. Colby entered the room for a closer look, and his heart sank when he realized what was on the screen.

The plant soldiers, much larger than the ones that had attacked his farm, had managed to damage the immensely strong ceramalloy rails of the cannon. The display indicated that the entire cannon was on the verge of failure.

The outer door opened, and Colby spun around, ready for battle, but it was Topeka sticking in her head.

"Come take a look and tell me what you think," she said. "Can we use these for your flame-thrower contraptions?"

With a last glance at the display screen, he went to the door and looked out. Topeka had rustled up a forklift, one of several that must have been used at the station. Carried in the forks was a personal lift-assist.

"We had this in the repair shop right here," she said, pointing to a roll-up door further down the side of the building.

"That might work," Colby said, moving to sit in the lift.

"Have you used one of these?" she asked, blocking his way.

"Well, no. But how hard—"

"Doesn't matter if you can learn to use it. I can, so this is mine. You get the Daihatsu," she said, pointing to the personal lifting yoke.

He started to argue, but she was right.

"The cannon's about to fail," he said, changing the subject. "Anything we can do about it?"

"Shit, I thought it'd hold out longer," she said, as she dashed back into the control center, Colby on her tail.

"Well, I guess it's time," she said, more to herself, Colby thought, than to him.

"Time for what?"

"Time to make me some green mash," she said as she flowed into the control chair. Her hands flew over the switches as she vocalized some orders that made no sense to him. Several other displays came to life, and on one of the screens, a door opened.

"Is that a space pod?" Colby asked, despite recognizing it for what it was.

"Yep. It's been in the breach and ready for launch since the bastards attacked. We had eight more on deck, but they got themselves destroyed by our friends out there. So, this is it."

Colby immediately realized what she was going to do.

"What about the rail?" he asked, pointing to the monitor with the red flashing light.

She shrugged and said, "It'll work or not. But for sure, we're going to crush some of the fuckers."

"And if the damage to the rails is bad enough?"

"Then this baby's gonna be smashed all over the landscape," she said.

Which doesn't matter now, does it?

"Have at it," he said.

He watched the countdown, alarms deafening the control room while Topeka overrode each attempted shutdown.

"Here she goes!" she said as the charge released, sending the pod accelerating down the rail.

The plant soldiers had been working on the center of the rail, right in front of the control facility. By the short time the pod had reached the plants, it was already at nine kilometers per second. With over 3000 kgs of mass, that was an unstoppable force, and the air above the rail exploded into a green mist.

"Ooh-rah!" Colby shouted, unable to contain himself as he pounded on Topeka's back.

He didn't even notice that the space pod continued past the damaged area and made it to the ramp at escape velocity. Vasquez's last pod to go out would deliver its cargo as it was designed to do.

"I think that's green ick," Topeka said, reaching to the screen and touching an out-of-focus green spot that was on the cam lens.

"And I think you're right. You exploded the suckers!"

"Oh, and now I think we might have their attention."

Colby looked at the displays. The singular focus of the plant soldiers had been broken. A good number seemed to swing to the west towards the loading ramp. What was more troubling was that some of them had swung towards the facility itself. One started to move toward the building, then others followed.

"What the hell is that?" Topeka asked, pointing at the screen.

In the foreground, plant-things were heading to the facility, but she was pointing to the background. Colby bent over to get a closer look. The pod had crushed the plants on the rails into mush, but not all of them. Many, probably those on the edges, had simply been torn apart. As Colby watched, the parts, scattered over the landscape, started to twitch. To his utter amazement, a torn leafy branch pulled itself to what had been a central stalk and hugged it. He couldn't tell for sure with the display's resolution, but it looked like it melded into the stalk.

"Oh, hell, they're reanimating!" Topeka said.

The branch pulled itself and the stalk to the side where another chunk of stalk lay and pulled it in. After a few moments, that second chunk was absorbed into the first.

Colby felt a deep misgiving. If they could reanimate, then that changed the rules of the game. He and Topeka had to do something now. If they waited, they'd be in much deeper shit.

"Get ready," he said, wishing he'd had time to discuss a plan of action with her first.

Even with Marines, men and women who put in immense amount of time training in the deadly arts, there should be operations orders and rehearsals. Topeka, who was evidently quite capable at her work, was still a civilian, and the best he could do with her was to simply say "Get ready?"

He pulled her by the arm to the cases of ANFO grenades. He'd made these to detonate upon impact, so it was simply a matter of throwing them. The flamethrower took a few more minutes to teach her to work it. The air had to be released first, then once the stream of jelly was being shot out, then, and only then, could it be lit off. The flame was a very simple device, the spark caused by touching a naked piece of wire to a tiny fuel cell.

She assured him she had it as there was a crash against the back of the building. The plant soldiers had reached them.

Colby rolled the cylinder forward, and Topeka picked it up with her forks. He ran the ignition wire back to her, then slapped the fuel cell to the vertical strut of the cage. Taking a roll of duct tape, the ubiquitous must-have for any shop for the last millennium, he affixed the wand to one of the forks. She'd have to control the direction of the fire with the lift.

"Remember, don't touch off the ignition—"

". . . until the air is releasing, I know, I know."

Colby slapped the cylinder, then grabbed the lift yoke. It was a standard model, used to lift up to 500 kg. He'd never liked the loss of mobility the leg braces created, but he'd be a lot more mobile than if he was horsing the cylinder on his own.

He picked up his cylinder, locking it into the harness. This left an arm free to hold the wand. Grabbing six grenades, he slipped each one into a separate compartment.

There was a loud crash as the back wall gave in.

"You ready?" he asked Topeka.

"It's go-go time," she shouted, using the pet phrase of Major Mountie, Space Explorer.

He managed not to roll his eyes. He hated that asinine, juvenile series.

"You're not maneuverable enough to stay inside here. Go outside, then move to the left to engage. I'll take care of these," he said, wheeling to face the back of the control room.

She nodded, then drove her little forklift out the door.

Colby readied his wand, then stepped forward to join the battle.

When Colby was a young lieutenant, zombie flicks had been popular, with mindless undead pursuing dwindling numbers of the living. As the plant soldiers pulled themselves through the wall with green leafy arms, he was struck by how close the image looked like old zombies breaking into houses, singularly intent on devouring brains.

He shook his head to clear the vision, then opened up the compressed air. A moment later, the jet caught the flammable jelly, sending it out to splash on the enemy. He thought he saw a few of the plant-things flinch, but before he could contemplate the significance of that, he touched off the jelly. Immediately, a rush of flame reached out, so hot the heat against his face made him flinch.

The plants went up most satisfyingly. Within ten seconds, every one of them was on fire, a few staggering, but most slumped to the floor, rapidly disintegrating under the onslaught.

"Get some!' he shouted, stepping forward to give him a better field of fire to outside the broken wall.

More of the plants walked forward into the flame, and Colby felt a rush of exultation. His flamethrower was working, and the stupid things were helpless before him.

And then there were none in view. He kept the stream going for a moment, but he didn't have an unlimited amount of fuel or compressed air, so he cut off the flow. The floor in front of him, as well as the inner walls near the break, were still on fire, the acrid smoke making his eyes burn.

For a moment, he thought he might have defeated the enemy, but through tearing eyes, he could still see masses of green just out of reach of his flamethrower. He edged to the side to give himself a better angle, and suddenly, the attention of the plants seemed to shift away from him. Almost in unison, the mass started to the right.

Topeka!

He'd told her to take her forklift in that direction, and he knew she was engaging. Taking one of his grenades, he armed and tossed it out through the break in the wall, almost hitting the edge and bouncing it back to his feet, but the grenade landed outside with a satisfying explosion, blowing bits of green into the air. The mass continued to move, though, and Colby knew he couldn't do much from inside the building. He needed broader fields of fire.

"Come on, Duke!" he shouted, wheeling around, pushing against the inertia of his flamethrower.

The dog was nowhere in sight, but he didn't have time to look for her. He almost stumbled out the door, then turned right. With Topeka on the other side of the building, he wanted to hit the mass of plant soldiers from their rear.

It was taking him a bit of effort to deal with the Daihatsu lifter. The 100-kg flamethrower might feel like it weighed 15 or 20 kg, but like the cargo pod, the mass was the mass. That didn't change. Colby had to lean into the turn to horse the thing around the corner of the building, then sprint along the side and to the front. He could see plant soldiers moving as a single unit towards the south and where Topeka would be hitting them. As soon as he was in range, he opened the air, igniting the flames once the slightly pink jelly shot out.

And, of course, he forgot about his momentum. Not only was turning difficult, but so was stopping. He was barely able to nudge his direction to the side in order to avoid the burning jelly and plant-soldiers on the ground as he rushed forward. His unprotected face blistered in the heat.

He forced the pain from his mind as he spun around, swinging his wand to lay down sheets of fire. Ahead of him, near the far side of the building, ropes of flame revealed where Topeka engaged the plants.

There had to be hundreds of the enemy between them, and for a moment, Colby thought the two humans had them trapped, but as he swung his wand to the right, he caught a glimpse of hundreds more of the plant-soldiers peeling off around the launch terminal.

At that moment, it sunk in. He'd assumed that the slower-moving enemy were mindless, automatons like the zombies in the flicks. But that had been a mistake. What he was seeing was tactics, pure and simple. The enemy between Topeka and him were a fixing force while the main body was maneuvering to envelope her. Coming up from behind her, she couldn't fire in two directions at once, and she'd be engulfed.

Never underestimate your enemy, Edson! he reminded himself.

Topeka wouldn't know she was in deep shit, and he was not about to let her be overrun. With his right hand controlling the flames, he tossed each of his remaining grenades in front of him, sending up gouts of plant tissue and green mist.

"I'm coming in for you!" he shouted, trying to get her attention so she didn't crisp him in her battle fury.

He could just see the top of the forklift, but the wall of flame that had been swinging towards him reversed course. Leaning forward, he pushed ahead, gaining speed and momentum, keeping his own flame to Topeka's left. He crashed through a line three deep of the plant soldiers, almost breaking into the clear beside her. One plant had managed to grasp the edge of his lifter, and amazingly, started to bodily pivot Colby around. He could sense he was getting dragged back, and he tried to bring his wand to bear, but the thing was too close, and the flames were shooting over it.

Colby was about to shuck the lifting harness when a string of fire, much depleted from what it should be, splashed the plant, and it recoiled, letting him go.

Topeka had come to his rescue, but in doing so, had opened her back, just as the flanking plant soldiers rounded the launch terminal.

"Behind you!" he shouted, unable to engage with her between the enemy and him.

Topeka's look of jubilation at having saved his ass turned to fear as she saw the enemy converge on her. She swung her wand, but barely a dribble of flame shot out for five meters, well short of the threat. Colby's flamethrower still had a good charge, but either she'd expended much more of her air then he had or he'd just not put as much into hers.

With a sweep to his left, he bolted forward to her, shouting, "I've got your six. Now, back out of here."

She didn't argue, which was a relief. With a curt nod, she put the forklift into reverse. Colby followed, back to her as he sprayed one swipe after the other, trying to slow down the onslaught.

He couldn't keep it up. The plant soldiers moved slower than a human could, but they were fast enough to close the distance with him walking backwards.

"Can't that thing go any faster?" he asked her.

"This is about it," she answered, her voice cracking from the stress.

She tried another shot, but the flame quit after only a second. She was out of either fuel or compressed air.

Colby flamed five of the closest enemy, then looked back. They were about to be cut off, with only a tight seven or eight-meter lane alongside the eastern wall of the building. Then something else caught his eyes. Beyond the attackers, over where the other plants had looked to be somehow merging their bodies, two green figures rose, and his stomach churned. They had to be standing ten meters tall. As he watched a huge leafy hand reached down out of his line of sight, then reappeared with a piece of plant-part. It stuck the part to its side, held it for a moment, then released. The piece of plant was absorbed into the huge body. The other giant rummaged in the remains for additional parts as well. If those two joined the fight, Colby's little flamethrower wasn't going to do him much good.

He didn't try and analyze the situation. He didn't weigh the pros and cons of various courses of action. He made the decision before he really thought through the problem.

"Get out of the lift and run for it!" he shouted in his best voice of command, one that brooked no dissent.

With a smooth movement, he shucked his lift assist, clamping down the wand release and pushing it forward. The stream of flame acted like a tug-bot motor, slowly rotating it back towards him. He didn't try and correct it. Either he was fast enough to make it clear or he wasn't, and hesitating would seal the deal. He bolted after Topeka, watching out of the corner of his eyes as the flame slowly moved to intercept him.

It also incinerated the plant soldiers that were reaching out for him as he sprinted. He expected either the grasp of green strength or the kiss of fire to bring him down, but somehow, with only centimeters to spare, he managed to avoid death. The hair on the back of his head felt as if it'd been singed, but he was in the clear, pelting after a surprisingly quick Topeka.

And then he remembered his remaining grenades.

"Wait!" he shouted, but she wasn't slowing down.

He'd managed to open up some space around him, so he turned to the right and ran down the length of the back wall. Stopping just short of the door, he peeked inside. The front wall and the control room had been destroyed, and he could see movement all the way through the building, but otherwise the room was empty. He darted in, then swept the grenades back into the carrying case.

"Easy, boy. Don't set them off now."

He knew he didn't have time, but he'd be naked without a weapon. Poking his head out of the door, he could see that twenty or thirty of the enemy had cleared the corner of the building. From this side of the building, he didn't see the two giants, but knew they would be coming.

"This way!" Topeka shouted at him. "We've got to lead them the fuck away from here."

She was standing by the ruined shell of Warehouse B, frantically waving her arm for him to join her. He didn't know where she was heading, but anyplace had to be better than where he was.

Marines never liked to retreat. It wasn't in their DNA. But sometimes, discretion was the better part of valor, and with Riordan in the med chamber somewhere in the building, she was right. If the man was going to survive, the two of them had to clear the area. Without any more flames, they had to act the rabbit.

I might as well get their attention, he told himself as he lowered the case and took out one of the grenades.

He arched it in a beautiful throw, landing it right at the leading edge of the oncoming enemy. Colby knew that the plant soldiers were latched onto them and he hadn't needed the grenade, but it sure felt good to see salad being made before he took off to follow Topeka. The plant bastards would follow at their own pace.

Interlude II: Harvest

Telemetry flowed to the Gardener's vessel, chemical signals released by the mature plants resulting from the second wave of spores it had unleashed during the previous dark cycle. The vessel processed them without judgment, collating and compiling information and feeding it to the roots of the Gardener's navigation locker. Information could be a form of nourishment, but these reports soured rather than fueled the Gardener. Despite its earlier suppositions, its unleashed tools had not encountered any Mechanicals. The remnants of their limited visual processing described only a handful of pathetic, right-angled structures, the sort of boxes that Meat created when given the chance. That, and a single massive structure that had somehow launched a pod of its own through the atmosphere and into the surrounding space. The Gardener's own craft had lost track of the thing. One moment it had been clearing the world's exosphere and when scans next swept that location where it should have been, it had vanished. The Gardener spared a few cycles to review the pod's trajectory and extrapolate its location in space, but further scans were fruitless. It couldn't be found anywhere. Strange.

Stranger still, the force it had planted to dismantle those offending structures had failed. A significant portion had expired prematurely, releasing chemo-signatures into the air tallying their demise. Mechanicals would never have bothered engaging vegetation and Meat lacked the sophistication to offer a challenge to such a degree. Strangest of all though was that the remainder of its tools had turned from their task, the destruction of the structure responsible for the now-missing pod. Instead of completing the disassembly, the survivors had abandoned the converging ring formation the Gardener had encoded into their spores and reformed into a ragged line that hurtled across an open plain toward the edge of a forest. Pointless. This planting, even more than the first one, had limited resources of strength and duration. More than half would exhaust themselves before they had crossed even half the distance. Worse still, those that endured and entered the forest would be lost to its sensors, their chemical telemetry absorbed and blocked by the trees above them.

Something had gone wrong. A string of somethings, in fact, and two rounds of purge agents had not resolved the discrepancies. The second planting would not, could not, deviate from their coded tropism without a compelling stimulus. Another something even now led them into the forest, subverting the mindlessness that should have been sufficient to the task at hand.

The Gardner roused itself to fuller wakefulness within its navigation pod. It considered the imperfection of its results. Perhaps it had erred, reacting too directly to the intrusion in its garden. A literal perspective rarely served. After all, its art thrived on the figurative. It opened itself to the memories of past cycles of growth and found a metaphor from its earliest teacher, a memory it had tucked away in ages past for just such a need as it now felt.

Where the branches cannot reach, the roots must dive deeper.

Then too, perhaps not quite so figurative after all. The Gardener released chemical signals to the receptors of its navigation locker. The vessel responded to the commands and slipped from orbit, spiraling soundlessly downward into the atmosphere, targeting the same copse of trees that had captivated the remnant of the second planting. To understand the situation, the Gardener would have to descend to the planet's surface and resolve the matter within the forest itself. Only then could it return to tending the garden it planned for this world.

Part III: Resolution and Threat

"Are they still following?" Topeka asked, her breath coming hard.

"You just keep moving," Colby told her, "And let me worry about them."

Duke yipped with an enthusiasm she'd never displayed before. Apparently fleeing an alien invasion had inspired her. She had rejoined them as they ran through the rubble just ahead of the plants. Together, the three had crossed the open area surrounding the station, pulling farther ahead of their pursuers. That had started to change. Topeka was struggling, now. She'd proven herself to be a hardass during the fight, but too many hours sitting in her control seat had cut into her fitness. Despite having at least 30 years on her, his daily exercise routine had kept him in excellent shape, and he'd barely broken a sweat.

"Can we stop for a minute?" Topeka asked, barely getting the words out as they reached the far treeline, about four klicks from the station.

Colby wanted to keep running, but slowed. He'd lose her otherwise.

"OK, but just for a minute," he said as she came to a stop and bent over, hands on her knees.

Duke ran up to her and licked her face.

Colby looked back along the way they'd come. The mass of smaller plants had actually followed them out of the station complex, away from Riordan in his med chamber. Even with Topeka huffing and puffing, they'd opened up at least a two-klick gap between them and the pursuers. But something had changed. The main body of plants chasing them had thinned out. Those in the front continued in their pursuit, but those towards the rear were barely moving. Some of those had fallen, and through the gaps in the front line, Colby could see them lay prone on the ground. Even as he watched, more of those in the front ranks started to fall back. Colby wondered if the plants had varying degrees of fitness just as the two humans had.

Towards the rear of the pack, the two giants had slowed as well, but remained clearly focused on them. Then, with no warning, one ponderously turned and lumbered back the way it had come, returning to the station. The other one kept oriented towards them for a long 20 seconds. At the risk of anthropomorphizing the things, Colby thought it reluctantly turned to join the other, heedlessly smashing some of its smaller brethren. But where the small ones were dropping like flies, the giants didn't move as if they were fatigued.

"You doing OK?" he asked Topeka as he watched the giants walk back into the station.

"Yeah. No. Shit, just give me another minute," she said, anger dripping from her voice.

Colby watched her, evaluating her as he had many soldiers over the years. Was her anger at the plants or aimed at herself for not being able to keep up? Probably a bit of both. Anger was usually a liability in a battle, but if he could use it to keep her moving, he would.

"Those bastards. . ." he started, then stopped, looking out over the broken ranks of pursuing plants.

"Those bastards what?"

"Look at that. Some of them, they look like they're decomposing," he said.

It was true. While the closest few plants were still pursuing them, the ones farthest back, the ones that had fallen, were flattening out. Maybe a few had been smashed flat by the retreating giant, but most seemed to be wilting and breaking down. Wisps of green mist rose above the plant corpses before being dissipated by the breeze. Even the nearer plants that were still coming at them didn't look healthy.

"Fuck them," Topeka said, straightening. Still, she looked back, stepping around Colby for a better view. "You're right. They're going straight into compost."

With the chase petering out, Colby didn't see a need to push on, and Topeka could use the break, so he watched what was happening. He wished he had a pair of binos to see better, but even with his naked eyes, he could see more and more of them staggering as the roots they walked on gave way.

But not with the giants. They had made it back to the launcher and tore into it, their leafy arms twisting and tearing the ceramalloy like so much tissue paper. If they could do that, then the launch facility, with Riordan inside, wouldn't stand a chance if they turned their attention to it.

As if on cue, Topeka asked, "How does the house look?"

Colby shifted his gaze. The building in which she'd stashed Riordan was one of the few still standing. But it was only a matter of time. If a pair of plant giants could completely demolish a launch mechanism designed to withstand the stressors associated with payloads at gravity-defying velocities and last a hundred years doing so, he knew they could make short work of any building on the planet. And there was nothing they could do about it.

Topeka had to have come to the same conclusion, but she just stood there, saying nothing.

Colby was a general—a disgraced general, true, but a general nonetheless. Marines didn't earn their stars unless they had that take-charge attitude needed to fight their Marines. He stood there with only a civilian and a dog, but his mind kept churning on how he could turn the three of them into a task force that could defeat the enemy.

No miracle plan popped into his mind.

"I sure wish I knew what was going on everywhere else," Topeka said, as she stared back toward the station.

Colby hit himself in the forehead. The local net had been knocked out and Topeka might be cut off, but he had his military implant. He'd largely forgotten about it after calling Erin. Ralph, the farm AI, was connected to the local repeaters and was now silent with them knocked out, but the implant was connected to the hadron comms ecosystem. It didn't need to rely on planet-based repeaters and could create networks almost out of thin air.

He activated the implant, feeling the familiar surge as it hugged his brain. The implant was downloading terabytes of information from thousands, if not tens of thousands of sources, from any PA on the planet still transmitting to satellites in orbit. The shared volume of information pouring in threatened to overwhelm him. The key in getting something useful from all that data was knowing how to manage it in usable forms, and Colby had years of practice doing that.

He immediately created a filter to isolate inputs into a series of categories. The first one was for human transmissions, hoping to see if anyone else had survived and was trying to contact others. That folder was empty.

His implant had flagged another folder with a red alert message. This one was for vehicular movement, which might mean someone was trying to come to the station. Colby quickly opened it, but was confused. No surface movement had been identified, but rather something high in the sky.

What the hell is that? It looked to be coming in from outside the planet's atmosphere.

He narrowed his search parameters, and the explanation came into focus. Something was heading to the planet's surface.

"We've got company coming," he told Topeka.

"What do you mean?"

"I mean, something is coming in for a landing, something not in any database. You told me there was a ship in orbit that was the source of the plants we've been fighting. If I had to guess, I'd say the plant boss is coming to take a look at what's happening here."

"How do you know that?" she asked. "The system's down, and my PA ain't working for shit."

"I've still got my implant," he told her, pointing to his temple.

"So? I've got mine, too."

"Uh. . . mine. . . well, it's got a few more capabilities than yours. I'm connected to the hadron ecosystem."

"So, can you order up a navy battleship or something?"

"Not exactly. I already attempted to get us some help, but I sort of got the door slammed in my face."

She let that sink in, then said, "General, you must have fucked up royally. We always wondered why you were here on this shithole in the ass end of the galaxy, and if they won't even talk to you. . ."

Colby ignored the dig and ran a landing trajectory. He wasn't surprised that the ship was going to land nearby. If this was the general calling the shots, or even just some version of an inspector, it would want to be near the troops.

He turned to look back at the plant soldiers again. A few were still advancing, even more slowly than before, but most were down and becoming compost.

Pretty lousy soldiers, if they can't even pursue us, he thought, forgetting for the moment at how easy they'd demolished his farm and the station.

"So, where's this motherfucker landing?" Topeka asked.

"Unless it alters its course, about 800 meters thataway," he answered, pointing deeper into the trees.

Topeka pulled a machete out of her pack and said, "Then I say we go meet this piece of shit and teach it a fucking lesson."

✳✳✳✳✳✳✳✳✳✳✳✳✳✳✳

"Remember, we're only trying to gather some intel," he told Topeka as they crept forward through the trees.

"You already told me that, like ten times, already, too," Topeka snarled.

If the whitening of her hands around the handle of her machete was any indication, she wanted, no, needed, to kick some ass. And that could be a disaster. Until he knew exactly what they faced, any rash action might screw things up.

Colby understood Topeka's emotional state, however. He was a Marine, and he'd lost friends, leaders, and his troops in combat. No warrior could ever forget that. Topeka had lost her friends as well, and Riordan was back in a med chamber right now, at risk from some giant broccoli. She was angry, and she wanted revenge. It was up to Colby to hold her back until he had a better grasp of the situation.

Behind Topeka, Duke started whining.

"Quiet, girl," he said, kneeling with his hands out to her.

She ignored him, her attention riveted to the front. It was evident that she did not want to go any further.

"Wait here," he told Topeka before grabbing Duke's collar and leading her back 20 meters.

He hadn't thought to bring a leash, and there weren't any handy vines that every hero in any Hollybolly flick seemed to find when they needed a rope. With a sense of resignation, he pulled off his belt, looped it through her collar, and tied it off on a low branch.

"Stay here, girl. And please, don't bark," he said, cradling her head in his hands.

Her brown eyes looked up at him. He wondered what was going on in her little dog mind. She understood something was very wrong, that much was certain. She'd been whining at something, after all. He rubbed her belly for a few moments, and with an almost human sigh, she lay down and rolled onto her back. He kept it up for a full minute, feeling her fur through his fingers, hoping this wouldn't be the last time he'd be doing it. He'd inherited Duke, and she'd grown on him. Him. General Colby Meritt Edson. A dog lover?

"That's enough, girl. I've got to go."

She whumped her tail once on the ground, but didn't bark. With a last pat on her head and a pull to hitch up his pants, he left her there.

"What did you do with her?" Topeka asked as he caught up with her again.

"What? I tied her to a tree so she won't get hurt. Why, what do you think I did?" he asked confused.

"Oh, I don't know. I'm not a soldier," she said, her voice restrained and emotionless.

What the hell does she think I am?

He almost demanded that she come back with him to see Duke for herself, but he shook it off. Up ahead was the enemy. She'd see Duke soon enough.

"OK, let's move up, but slowly. We don't want to be picked up by any pickets."

"Pickets? You mean a fence?"

"No, pickets. Uh. . . sentries. Soldiers sent out to make sure no one like us sneaks up on them."

"Why didn't you just say 'sentries' in the first place," she muttered under her breath.

Colby chose to ignore the comment. She wasn't a Marine, and he wasn't her commander. Still, it took a force of will to turn away.

The thought of pickets gave him pause, though. He wanted to conduct a quick recon, find out what was there, then get back unseen to decide their next course of action. But if there was a picket, then they might be spotted, and they'd have to defend themselves—and they didn't have all that much with which to do it. Sure, they still had a few grenades, but no direct fire weapons.

But, relatively speaking, rifles and beamers were only the more recent weapons man had ever used.

He held his hand out for the machete, which Topeka reluctantly gave him. They were in a fir forest, a common terraforming tree. A fast growing, renewable resource with a million and one uses. Firs were not the best for what he had in mind, but not the worst by any stretch of the imagination, either.

With Topeka looking at him as if he were crazy, he selected four young trees, each about three-to-four meters tall. A few whacks with the machete, and they were down. Working quickly, he stripped the branches, leaving the central shaft bare. He hefted one to his shoulder and balanced it for a moment. Satisfied with the feel, he laid them down and cut each shaft to about two meters in length.

He was so caught up in what he was doing, it was a few moments before he remembered that Topeka was much smaller than him. Looking up at her, he mentally measured her height and arm length, then lopped off another half-meter from two of them. A few more chops with the extremely sharp machete, and he had pointed tips.

If I had more time, I'd fire harden the tips.

If I had more time, I'd fit a metal head on each of these, he admonished himself. *Or requisition a meson beamer. Hell, might as well go for broke and call in a Navy battleship.*

These were not the best spears ever made, but they could use them in a pinch, not waiting for a grenade to go off. There were too many unknowns ahead of them, and a few seconds might make the difference between life and death.

There was one more easy thing he could do to improve the crude spears' effectiveness. Colby searched the detritus on the ground until he found a piece of wood that would serve. With a few more cuts of his trusty machete, he fashioned an atlatl. Colby had employed them many times during Escape and Evasion exercises, and they were surprisingly easy to use.

"Are you done farting around, General?" Topeka asked.

"Have you ever used one of these?"

"Used one? I don't know what the hell it is."

Colby frowned. He'd expected her to at least know that much.

"These are your spears," he said, handing her the two shorter ones.

"I'll take the machete," she said, hand out. "And I've got the grenades you gave me."

He gave it back, but added, "The grenades have about a ten-meter ECR. . . uh, that means, Effective Casualty Radius. Any nearer, they'll get you, too. And you'll have to close in with one of them to use your machete."

"Close with who? We don't even know what we're facing."

"That's my point," said Colby, shaking one of the spears to bring her attention back to them. "With these babies you can hold them off. Given the right opportunity you can even throw them."

"Throw them? You only made two for me."

"Right, which is why you should avoid doing that, if you can help it. But if you do have to throw, this atlatl will put more power into it. Here, try it."

He showed Topeka how to use the atlatl and had her practice half-a-dozen throws at the trunk of a large tree ten meters away. She missed each time and was getting frustrated.

"OK, don't throw if you have to. Just stab anything that comes close."

"Stupid *at-lat-all*," she muttered and she slipped it through her belt.

"OK, then, I think we're ready. Let's go find our spaceship."

They didn't have to advance far. Within 50 meters, they reached a small opening in the trees. Smack-dab in the middle of the opening was what looked like nothing more than a 20-meter long, mottled greenish-black seed pod. There was no doubt, however, that this was a ship, a huge, space-faring zucchini.

Topeka stopped for a moment, then reached for one of her grenades, taking a step forward before Colby grabbed her and pulled her to the ground.

"We're here to observe, now," he hissed through clenched teeth.

She glared daggers at him, but nodded.

Around the spaceship, several small plants moved about, poking rope-like tendrils into the ground and holding feathery-looking branches into the air. Colby didn't need anyone to tell him that they were taking measurements.

"They're taking measurements," Topeka said anyway.

Colby shushed her.

The side of the ship split open with a one-meter fissure, and a squat plant trundled out. The front elongated into a flat blade, which it used to scoop up some soil before turning back and reentering the ship. The opening sealed shut with nary a sign it had even existed.

"What now?" Topeka asked.

"Now we wait and observe."

He could feel Topeka's frustration, but he wasn't going to rush things. Too much depended on them not going half-cocked.

Sun Tzu had dictated that a soldier had to know his enemy, and there were just too many things that he didn't understand about these plant things. They didn't act like any human enemy he'd known.

First, they hadn't initially attacked him. Their offensive had been aimed at his crops. They'd only moved to him when he'd tried to intervene. That made no sense. Why attack stationary crops when a mobile human, who had the ability to take action, was left alone. The conclusion he'd reached was that the crops themselves were the focus of the mission. They'd attacked him when he tried to interfere with that.

Even at the station, they were focused on the facilities, not the people. He had to wonder, if no one had opposed the plants, would they have still attacked? Would all those people, with their farms destroyed around them, still be alive?

Colby let the hours pass, and as the morning turned to afternoon, there still wasn't any action around the ship to reflect a military operation of conquest. It looked more like a science expedition than anything else. During his military career, he'd seen more than a few boffins in action, overly concerned with taking samples and spinning hypotheses and beyond clueless when it came to strategy and tactics.

The plants had killed people, true. But the more he watched, the more this didn't feel like a war of conquest. Just what it was, he didn't know yet.

All he could do was to observe and hope things became clearer.

****

Late afternoon, and Colby was no closer to an answer. He didn't even know what was in the ship. Nothing over a meter tall had emerged.

Beside him, Topeka had gone beyond antsy and advanced all the way to agitated. If they didn't do something soon, he knew she would explode. But it wasn't clear what, if anything, they could do. They had his grenades, but even if that was the right course of action to take, Colby doubted they held sufficient power to disable the ship. He'd taken retinal-shots of everything in the clearing, and had them queued up for his implant to send to headquarters. But, given his last reception, he knew he needed more.

Like one of them to bring back, alive and whole and not broken down into compost. Which meant *not* waiting around for HQ to send a ship, but bringing the thing directly to them.

Of course, that supposed he had a ship fueled and sitting on the apron, ready to go. Which he didn't. Yes, there might be some fuel stored back at the station, but the only ships on Vasquez were sub-orbital continent hoppers, and if his growing suspicions were right, none of those would have survived the plants' attack any more than his farm had.

While he mourned the lack of a vessel, another fissure opened on the ship in the clearing. This one a little bigger than the others, but otherwise the same. He watched as a slender plant emerged, a woodier variation than any he'd seen before. It had squeezed out of the fissure and then unfolded and unfolded again to a full two meters in height. Colby wondered if it was the ship's operator, but it went to the far side of the clearing and extended a proboscis of sorts and bored into the tree.

Just another lab tech.

"Fuck this shit, I'm going in," Topeka said from beside him.

She jumped to her feet. Colby lunged for her as she bolted, fingers brushing the heel of her boots as she darted across the open area.

It was only then that he saw the last opening had not closed, and he knew that was Topeka's target. He jumped up and chased her, one hand holding up his pants, the other holding a spear. Colby knew he'd be too late. He almost hoped that the two plants between her and the ship would interfere—not hurt her, just delay her down enough for him to catch her, but they ignored her.

Topeka didn't even slow down. Machete in hand, she dove into the opening. Her feet were visible for a moment, then with a kick, they disappeared just as Colby reached the ship.

He hesitated a moment, running through his options. For all he knew, the ship's atmosphere could be poisonous to human life. And what internal or automatic defenses did it possess, ready to spring into action at the first sign of an intruder. And they had defenses. Just touching one of the smaller plants when they'd first arrived at his farm had caused him pain. Topeka's rash action could already have killed her.

But he really had no choice. He had to follow. Taking a big breath of air and leading with a spear still in his hand, he pushed his head and shoulders through the opening. It was tight, very tight, and the walls themselves seemed to push him back. With a grunt, he set his feet, still outside, and pushed, gaining some ground. His legs churned, toes tearing up the dirt, as centimeter by centimeter, he gained ground. His shoulders, then his arms, made it past, and he grabbed at the floor of the entrance, trying to pull himself forward.

He couldn't hold his breath any longer, and he let it out with a gasp, followed by a desperate inhalation. He didn't die. He could breathe. The air smelled funky, a rich, loamy scent that was somehow undercut with the tang of ozone, but he wasn't suffocating or choking out his life. His lungs weren't burning.

The walls of the opening remained tight on him, and as he pushed and pulled himself forward, his pants began slipping. With his arms inside, he couldn't do much about that, so he ignored them.

It took a few more moments of struggle, but he finally made it into the ship—sans pants. It had been like crawling back up the birth canal. The thought made him shudder as he looked around to get his bearings, spear at the ready.

No plant soldiers rushed to attack. There was nothing except for a featureless tunnel, a meter-and-a-half high. Crouched over, Colby crept forward to the end, about four or five meters away. The floor gave way slightly under his feet, which only raised his anxiety.

The tunnel ended in a gate of some sort. He couldn't see any controls, but Topeka had to have gone this way, so holding the spear out, he pushed himself through.

Any lingering doubts vanished. He was in a ship of some sort. It looked nothing like any Navy ship he'd seen, but there was enough organization and instrumentation to register in his mind as something recognizable. Some of the Hollybolly scifi flicks he'd watched had ship bridges far more outlandish.

He spared only a second to let that thought sink in before his attention locked onto Topeka. She stood in the middle of the compartment, machete raised. And on the other side of her was what had to be the general/captain/big boss/whatever of the ship.

It was a plant, but not like any that Colby had seen before. A meter and a quarter tall, it was rounded and symmetrical, having no discernible front or back. It resembled a torpedo more than a man, if someone had painted that torpedo a slick, greenish black and festooned it with dozens of thick, ropey tendrils that began a fifth of the way from the top, just beneath a slight narrowing of its core, a neck of sorts, beneath a rounded pointed "head." The tendrils continued in irregular groupings on down until the ends of the lowest of them pooled out onto the floor around it.

It half stood, half leaned against a depression in the wall where some of its tendrils had reached out and connected to the ship itself, piercing or plugging in, at what on a short human might have corresponded to knee- and waist- and elbow-height.

Another grouping at the highest point had splayed out on the side facing Topeka, lining up vertically, side by side. It took Colby a moment before he realized what it looked like—like a man raising both hands in a warding gesture, almost pleading, having backed itself away as far as it could.

It wasn't just fearful, it was scared. Scared for its life.

This wasn't a general, and if it was the ship's captain it was probably only by virtue of being the only sapient being on the ship at all. It hadn't come to fight, that much was clear. Just as Colby could see that Topeka couldn't care less.

"Stop, Topeka! We need to capture it!" he shouted.

She turned to him, and the honest pain on her face underscored her words as she said simply, "It killed my friends."

Before she could turn back, the plant opened a sphincter and let out a puff of air that blew Topeka's hair about, and stopped her in her tracks. Colby froze, expecting to see her collapse or start melting like in the horror flicks, but she slowly wiped her forehead and looked at her arm.

"Is that the best you've got? A fart?" she asked, taking another step forward.

"Wait, what's that?" Colby said, grabbing her by the shoulder and pointing to the small beads that had been smeared around her face when she wiped it.

"Don't know," she said, wiping the back of one hand across the opposing sleeve. "They felt like a sandstorm for a moment when it shot them at me, but they're nothing now."

"They could be poisonous."

"All the more reason to end this shit now!"

She pulled out of his grasp and stepped forward, machete raised.

The plant-thing shambled to its left with surprising speed, eager to put some distance between the small woman and itself. Colby took the opportunity to dart forward, stepping between the two. That probably wasn't the smartest thing to do, what with a creature of unknown capabilities on one side and a crazed woman armed with a machete and hungry for revenge on the other, but he needed to capture the plant, not kill it.

At least the plant wasn't shooting him with some kind of death ray. In fact, it still looked like it was trying to escape from the two of them. Keeping in front of Topeka, he advanced on the thing. Colby had been the Combined Military *Atarashi Karate* champion back when he was a lieutenant. He'd kept up his fitness, but he wasn't sure his training translated into subduing an alien plant.

As if he was still in competition, his body memory pulled him into his *kokutsu-dachi* stance, body back over his rear leg, left foot thrust forward as he tried to analyze his opponent.

How do you analyze a giant artichoke?

He couldn't just stand there. That would invite attack or let Topeka get around him. He stepped forward to deliver a *mai geri* kick. . . and the plant shot a tendril at one of the little helper plants along the bulkhead and threw it at him, smacking Colby in the face before he could block it.

There wasn't much power behind the throw, but it stung, like getting slapped in the face. The plant's many tendrils started picking up everything in its reach and throwing them. Colby ducked several more, and from the curses from behind him, he knew some were connecting with Topeka.

"Get out of my way!" she yelled as she pushed past him just as a small, ropy plant hit her square in the face, making her stumble.

She fell into the wall with a thud and collapsed, the machete clattering across the deck and making him jump to avoid the razor-sharp blade.

Colby couldn't tell if she was seriously hurt, but the berserker in him rose to take over in a wave of anger. Forgetting all the niceties of *Atarashi Karate*, he let out a bellow and charged. The plant threw two more small plants, each missing as it panicked, then tried to hit him with another blast of rancid, fetid air.

None of that fazed Colby as he slammed into the plant, knocking it to the ground. He tried to grab anything he could to control it, but it was immensely strong as it struggled to get away. He got both arms around one of the stalks and pulled back with his entire body, arms, legs, and back straining, as he tried to rip it off of the thing.

The result wasn't what he'd expected. Instead of tearing the plant apart, it made an ear-shattering squeal, then went still. Colby didn't know if he'd killed it, if it was surrendering, or if it was trying to trick him. He held on for a few more moments as the plant quivered beneath him. Hesitantly, he started to ease up.

The plant remained still, so he let go and sat back. As soon as it was released, the plant started to inch away, and Colby reached back up to grab the stalk again. It froze immediately.

It knows if it moves, I'll tear it apart. That proves it's intelligent, he told himself.

"Hell, of course it's intelligent. It's got a freaking spaceship!" he said aloud. "Use your brain, Edson!"

He had to secure the plant, and if he'd still had his belt, that would be a start. He might even have made do with the legs from his pants, but he was down to his BVDs. He looked back to Topeka for a moment, who was starting to stir. She had a belt, but he wasn't going to start disrobing a half-conscious woman.

There wasn't much else he could see. The interior of the ship was not cluttered like a tramp steamer. There wasn't a handy coil of monofilament lying around. The only long ropy thing was the. . .

Colby reached up one more time as if to grab the plants stalk, and it shrunk away from him, but didn't try to escape. He stood up and grabbed one of the small plants the alien had thrown at them. The tendril-like arms were rubbery, not like real rope, but it would have to do. Pulling the first tendril to its full length, he wrapped it around two of the big plant's stalks, bringing them together. With a quick clove hitch, he secured it shut. The small plant had five such tendrils. He was tempted to just pull them free and use them as individual sections of rope, but he didn't know how his prisoner would react. Better to keep it calm. There were three more of the ropy plants he could see: a total of 19 more arms.

He didn't need them all. After ten, it was obvious that their adversary was trussed up like a pig ready for the spit. It wasn't going anywhere.

Colby looked down at the big plant, breathing heavily. They'd done it. They'd captured the thing. This was the proof he needed to convince the government of the threat, and unlike the spores and the plants it had unleashed on Vasquez, his gut told him this thing wasn't going to decompose on him any time soon.

"Can you understand me?" he asked.

The thing didn't respond, not that he'd expected it to. It would have been asking too much for it to have responded with any variation on the "Take me to your leader" trope in crisp Standard.

But a spaceship, even one operated by a sapient plant, was too complex a piece of equipment to operate by hand. It had to possess computers, or plant analogs to computers, and Colby's implant was one of the most advanced pieces of technology ever developed. He didn't need to be able to talk directly to his vegetable adversary, not if his implant could communicate with the ship, then he could use that to query the plant. And he needed answers. The battle was over and done. The casualties had yet to be tallied and assessing the full extent of the damage and its impact on provisioning the war effort would take time. But all of that was secondary. He had to find out why it had attacked the planet.

Colby reached out to his implant, opening its access paths to their broadest capacity and giving it a free hand to scan up and down the electromagnetic, mass, energy, and discrete spectra for anything that might carry a signal or provide a path way to communication. "Can you interface with this ship?" There was a delay of almost six seconds, which was centuries in implant time.

"Yes, in a fashion. I have made contact, but there is yet to be a full interface."

"Keep trying. I want to be able to talk with this thing."

He turned to Topeka, who was only now sitting up. He hurried over to her, helping her to her feet, and asked, "Are you OK? You hit the wall pretty hard."

"Yeah, I'm fine," she asked. "Is it dead?"

"No, I've got it restrained. It's missing a few parts, and its hurt, but it isn't dead."

She shook off his arm and stood on her own. She'd dropped the machete when she'd been flung across the tiny space, and now with real deliberation she walked over to it and picked it up again. Her eyes blazed with anger as she hefted it.

"Topeka," he said, not liking her look. "Remember, we need to get it back to the government. They need to interrogate it."

"Interrogate it my ass. That thing killed Sestus."

"No!" Colby shouted, but in letting her retrieve the blade he'd mistakenly allowed her to get between him and the plant.

With a lunge, Topeka closed the distance with the plant. She gripped the machete with both hands, and with one quick stroke its molecularly-sharp edge cut right through what Colby assumed served as the thing's neck. The head plopped onto the floor with a sound like a crashing watermelon as the rest of the body slumped in the restraints he'd fashioned.

"What they hell have you done?" Colby cried as he rushed forward.

He pulled the machete from her unresisting fingers, too little, too late.

"Revenge, General. I got my revenge."

****

"Yeah. I've got to see to Riordan."

They stood outside the ship. Topeka had squirmed back through the way they'd come and Colby had followed more slowly. She'd left his pants for him and went off to retrieve Duke while he pulled himself through the fissure and reclothed himself. Duke had come running into the clearing, tail wagging with more enthusiasm than she'd ever managed for breakfast before. Topeka handed him his belt.

"What if the giants breached the part of the station where you stashed him? We don't even know if they're still out there."

"Yeah, so? You think my odds are worse than your plan to somehow take this alien piece of shit through the wormhole?"

She had a point. His implant was still going through trillions of queries and responses with the plant's ship, trying to create a communications matrix. Colby was confident that he could lift the ship off the planet's surface now, but navigating it through a wormhole in order to make his way back to HQ and present the proof of his claims was in no way a done deal. Even if he could aim it at the wormhole, the plant's ship might not be able to withstand the trip through. His implant had yet to identify anything that might be the vegetable analog of an escape pod. If the ship's integrity failed, he'd die in the nonspace between. No one would ever find his body. He'd uplinked as much data as he could, but with headquarters alerted to his implant's previous hack, he had no doubt that the vice minister had since erected barriers to its efforts. His reports might be queued up in a buffer that no one would ever access. If they did get through, Greenstein might not believe him. The man had made a career from lying on paper and that's how he'd see Colby's outlandish claims of a planetary attack by an intelligent, alien vegetable. No, Colby needed to present the ship and the body of the plant back to the government. He might have been cashiered, but he still knew enough people who would act upon what was right in front of their faces.

He had assumed that Topeka would come with him, but with the plant-thing dead, she seemed to have lost her fire. It had all happened so fast. A day ago she'd been fighting for her life, and when she'd survived, healthy and whole, alone among everyone she knew, she'd been consumed by the need for revenge. After she killed the alien plant-creature, nothing remained to drive her, and the enormity of her losses sunk in. Now, she only wanted to get back to Riordan and begin the process of rebuilding.

There was absolutely nothing she could do for her friend. He had to remain in the med chamber if he was ever going to survive. Colby doubted she could do much in the way of rebuilding. Clean up some of the debris, assemble some solar cells to keep the power going to Riordan's chamber, maybe bring a few of the systems back online, but little more. The launch rails could not be repaired without outside help. But the scheduled shipments had stopped coming, and headquarters would send someone through to investigate, with or without Colby's reports. Still, he understood to some degree her desire to stay busy on the planet, to work at righting some of the wrongs.

Colby's own situation was different. He'd been exiled to the planet, so he had no attachment at all. Sure, he might die trying to get the ship and dead alien back, but he'd faced death in battle countless times before. This would be no different.

"Well, good luck," Colby said, suddenly feeling awkward.

She had driven him crazy, and he was still pissed that she'd killed the plant, but she'd been a good wingman. As good as any Marine he'd served with.

"OK, you too," she said, turning away before she wheeled around and rushed Colby, almost crushing him in a hug.

Colby didn't quite know what to do, but of their own accord, his arms enfolded around her, taking her in.

"And come back for me, General, or I'll come find you and kick your ass," she whispered into his chest.

"I'm sure you would, Topeka. Don't worry, though. We'll get you and Riordan off this mudball."

They held each other for a moment longer before Topeka shifted her hands to his chest and pushed away.

"OK, now, let me get out of here before you destroy the whole forest trying to take off in this thing." Without another look backward she walked out of the clearing.

Colby turned, and with a command to his implant, caused the ship to reluctantly widen the opening that he'd already begun thinking of as the airlock entry.

"C'mon, Duke, inside." For once, the dog did as she was told and clambered into the ship. Colby followed, the entry shaft already dwindling and shoving him forward in a manner all too reminiscent of peristalsis. He strode down the corridor to the spot where he'd encountered the plant creature, the spot that his implant assured him was the nexus of all of the ship's command functions. There was no command chair as humans had, just a rounded depression in the wall, a shallow alcove of sorts. He leaned his back into it and smiled as Duke settled herself on top of his feet.

"Are you ready?" he queried his implant.

"Waiting your command."

"How about you, Duke? You ready?" he asked, reaching down to pat her head.

She whomped her tail on the floor. Whatever else had happened over the last couple of days, he and the dog had finally bonded. For a brief moment, he'd thought about sending her back with Topeka, but he knew that wasn't really an option. She wouldn't have gone, not now, probably not ever.

And truth be told, he was damned happy to have her with him.

"OK, then, let's punch out of this one-horse planet."

He gave the command to his implant, and slowly, the alien spacecraft rose into the sky.

END OF BOOK ONE

Schoen & Brazee

Book 2

SCORCHED EARTH

Part I: Any Landing You Can Walk Away From

You never forget your first taste of combat. That first low orbit insertion where you plunge from the belly of a spacecraft and plummet like a fireball, your battlesuit ready to take on any opposition. Every mission is different, as is every world—the feel of the gravity, the taste of the air—but the planet of your first fight with the enemy gets imprinted on your brain, good or bad. For Lieutenant General Colby Merritt Edson, Republic Marine Corps (Retired), that world had been New Mars, more than fifty years ago.

It had also been the site of his greatest failure, a battle of politics and misplaced trust. He'd tried to do what was right for the Corps, tracking down and ferreting out the bastards sending substandard equipment and ordnance to the men and women who were risking their lives for the Republic, only to be screwed over by politicians and corporate ladder climbers eager to make money without regard for the damage they did along the way. But those bastards enjoyed the wealth they had skimmed, and they had power. Colby had been willing to risk his career for the good of the Corps, but in the end they had won by threatening his people. He could walk away or watch as they destroyed the lives of men and women like Jonas Venango and Li Siniang Greensboro, whose only crime was being extraordinary Marines. For their sake Colby accepted "voluntary retirement."

To avoid unfavorable optics they'd pushed him through one of the many wormholes on the elliptic above New Mars and dropped him on Vasquez, a nearly empty agricultural world. He had a farm, an agcomputer that did all the work, an old dog, and a kit full of recriminations and regrets.

And now he was heading back again, albeit not in any fashion anyone could have ever imagined. Alien plant soldiers had destroyed almost everything and everyone on Vasquez. As proof, Colby had hotwired the boss alien's ship for his ride.

The absurdity of sitting on the deck of an alien vessel felt oddly calming after the last couple of days of fighting plants. He absent-mindedly rubbed Duke's head as the ship continued its climb into the space surrounding Vasquez. His command-grade implant had managed to connect with what was a one-level vegetable control system. It wasn't a perfect interface, though; there were many blank areas his implant could not interpret. Colby had been able to take off from the planet's surface, however, as that was nothing more than feeding the engines power and pointing it in the right general direction. Trying to make it through the wormhole and then back to New Mars would not be so easy. A slight miscalculation, a slight gap in the ability to work the controls, and instead of easing smoothly over the event horizon of transition, he and Duke could nick the perimeter of the wormhole and be rendered nothing more than pink mush by tidal forces beyond the explanation of physics.

Assuming that didn't happen, they'd either get there or they wouldn't; there was no chance of ending up somewhere else. Vasquez's star system was no different from eighty percent of systems with wormholes, which is to say it only had one. Fly a vessel into it without bouncing off the edge and you came out the other end, sometimes hundreds of light years away. Sol system was one of those which filled most of the remaining twenty percent by boasting two different wormholes, one on the ecliptic above the orbit of path of the asteroid belt—and there was no shortage of boffins and squints who thought one had a lot to do with the other—and one further out above the Kuiper Belt.

But a fraction of a percent of star systems had more than two wormholes. Ninety-eight percent of these had between three and six, providing not just gateways between worlds, but interstellar highway interchanges. And the remaining two percent of that original fraction had stupid numbers of wormholes. No one knew why. There was no pattern. It didn't seem to relate to the type of star, the number or kind of planets (if any), moons or not, or anything else. It was just the luck of the draw. To date, the Republic had identified seventeen star systems with an excess of ten wormholes each. The system containing New Mars had thirty-three, the fourth most of any of them, and all of them clustered in the ecliptic above the one planet. It wasn't an interstellar highway, it was a freaking hub of endless high-volume traffic with well-regulated guidelines and time tables for what could come through which wormhole when, which despite a fleet of AIs still saw the occasional collision at speeds where even a small nudge or graze was deadly, and none of the objects coming through any of the holes in space were anywhere near small.

He would be arriving above New Mars without benefit of the schedule for when something was expected to emerge from the Vasquez system transit. Space is vast, but the sheer amount of traffic—both manned and automated—coming and going above New Mars made it seem snug. There was a very real chance that he would collide with something before the traffic control AIs could do anything to stop it. It didn't matter how fast their dedicated brains could calculate, some things just came down to mass, velocity, and distance.

Colby chose not to think about that.

The ship didn't have anything that looked like seats, so he sat on the deck, back up against the rubbery bulkhead. Duke was lying beside him, head on his lap as he petted her. She was calm, happy to be with him. She wasn't thinking about the wormhole. She didn't have the imagination to picture what could happen, what could go horribly wrong.

No, I'm not going to think of that. Think of happy thoughts, Edson, like just being alive.

Most of the people on the planet had evidently been killed during the plant invasion. For all he knew, Topeka was the last human left on the planet—well, she and Riordan, stuck in his med chamber. Staying behind as she had done was probably the smart thing to do. Eventually, someone would come to find out what happened, why the agricultural shipments had ceased.

Colby didn't have that luxury. He had to report back to the government reps on New Mars so they could get word back to Earth. He had to prove to Vice-Minister Greenstein and the rest that there was a threat out here in the far reaches of human space, that aliens had arrived at Vasquez without benefit of any wormhole. Which in turn suggested technology beyond anything humanity possessed. And if aliens had stumbled upon Vasquez, then how long before they noticed the wormhole to New Mars and its cornucopia of routes to dozens of other human-inhabited worlds? Fifty years before, Colby had helped wrest control of the system from a fringe government, back when they'd only discovered five wormholes there. He'd damned well do all he could to ensure aliens didn't get their hands on it now. Before lifting off from Vasquez, he'd downloaded a complete account of the plant invasion and sent that forward. He couldn't be sure it'd be read, or if anyone would believe him.

In a way, he couldn't blame them. It was pretty fantastic. A sentient plant had invaded Vasquez with millions of plant minions that had destroyed everything in their path. He wouldn't have believed it if he hadn't seen it with his own eyes.

"How about you, Duke? Would you have believed it?"

Her eyes remained closed, but her tail gave a weak thump on the deck.

He looked around the ship. It was somewhat sparse, but with the help of his implant, he'd worked out which mossy patches and which knobs and roots were actually instrumentation, enough to let him know he was inside a ship. Instead of control seats with harnesses, there were ropy, vine-like arms that were pressed against the bulkheads. Several had been connected to the king plant when he and Topeka had entered the bridge, but they had released it once the fight commenced. These tendrils still slowly reached out, as if wanting to embrace him. Colby wasn't up with that, which was why he'd settled on the deck just out of their reach.

With dampeners that were not as effective as in human ships, the gentle shifts in pressure were evidence enough that they were in motion. He contemplated querying his implant to find out how long before they entered the wormhole, but after a moment, he decided against it. Better to be like Duke and remain blissfully in the dark.

He couldn't just sit there, though. He gently slid Duke's head off his lap, then stood up, looking around the bridge. He wandered over to the so-called instrument panels and tried to make some sense of the displays, noting the vines and keeping away from the leafy ends.

"What's this?" he asked his implant, touching one of them at random.

"That displays the atmospheric content inside the ship."

When he'd first followed Topeka and her machete-wielding charge into the ship, he'd worried whether the atmosphere was even breathable. After taking his first breath, he'd forgotten about it. Now, his curiosity was piqued.

"What is the oxygen level in here?" he asked.

"O2 level is 17.9 percent."

That was a little light for most terraformed worlds, but well within human tolerance. Some of the Phase 2 worlds, already inhabited, had far lower percentages while the terraforming process continued.

He was about to ask what other traces were in the ship's atmosphere, but he realized he didn't care. He was breathing. Duke was breathing. That was enough. He asked because he was trying to keep his mind off of the wormhole.

Nope, I'm not going to think about that.

He turned away from the displays, ran his hand across the bulkheads, and wondered as to their structure. They weren't metal or any of the substances used in human ships, but they didn't quite feel organic. They were clearly made from some sort of vegetative matter.

Maybe a plant alloy? Is that even possible?

Whatever it was, it would keep the scientists busy for years— if he got it back in one piece. If he didn't wreck the thing by clipping the edge of the wormhole or smashing into other traffic once he reached the other side.

For God's sake, Edson! Get your mind off of it. You've faced death before, so put on your big boy pants!

And he had faced death—more than once. This time, though, was different. He didn't have much control over what was happening. He could fly the ship, but not well. He was essentially a piece of cargo, an unexpected shipment that wasn't on anyone's schedule.

It was what it was.

One of the vines reached his boot, and he spun around and strode to the back of the bridge in search of another distraction. He pressed the side of the slit along the bulkhead. Nothing happened. He raised his hand higher, pressed again, and was rewarded when the slit opened up to a small cold storage locker. There, trussed up on the deck, was the headless body of the dead plant-thing, with its head jammed between the body and the bulkhead at the back of the locker. Inside, several vines had emerged to encase the body, but he thought it was a little late for whatever they could do for it.

"Sorry," he said, poking the body with his finger. "But maybe you'd prefer this than to be a lab sample."

He'd wanted to keep the thing alive, and he'd had it restrained when Topeka, angry at losing her co-worker Sestus, had taken the thing's head off with her machete. If that was its head, that is. For all he knew, its brain was deep inside the torso. One thing was for sure, though—it was stone-cold dead.

Colby didn't know how long it would take to navigate the alien ship. He was gambling that once he emerged from the Vasquez wormhole, an AI traffic controller would send a cargo drone to tow him safely planetside. He wanted to make sure the alien didn't decompose like the plant soldiers had on Vasquez, so he had his implant query the ship's control system. There wasn't anything that could act as a morgue on board, but the locker/alcove/whatever in the back could be kept at a cooler temperature. That had to be better than nothing, and even if the thing did decompose, whatever was left would be easier for the science-types to scrape out.

It had taken a good five minutes to horse the thing into the locker. Its limp, dead weight had not been easy to handle. But he managed to stuff it in, Duke looking on in frank confusion as he did so.

With a sigh, he touched the other side of the opening, this time hitting it correctly, and the locker closed.

Now what?

He hadn't explored the rest of the ship yet. The bridge took up at least a third of the ship's length, but that meant there was still two-thirds that he could explore. He doubted that he could learn much, but it was better than just sitting around with his thumb up his ass.

"You coming?" he asked Duke.

She opened her eyes, wagging her tail twice, before she got up and padded over to him. He reached down and petted her head.

"Yeah, who's a good girl, huh?"

A ripple passed through Colby's body, as if his insides were trying to become his outsides and then back again.

Duke shook herself once, twice.

"Did we pass through the wormhole?" he queried his implant, standing up and looking around as if he expected the ship to be coming apart.

"Affirmative."

"And, are we. . . are we OK?"

"Wormhole insertion accomplished within standard parameters."

"Well, hell, girl. That wasn't bad at all," he told Duke, who wagged her tail in response. "A little more topsy-turvy than usual, but what the heck, right?"

Duke thumped her tail. Good enough. But they wouldn't remain in the wormhole for long. Time inside was relativistic. Some claimed it lasted days, others just seconds. After what seemed only a minute another ripple ran through the ship. They were back in normal space.

"And. . . uh, where are we?"

Colby had the coordinate inputs to get back to New Mars, courtesy of Topeka, but that didn't mean they'd entered the wormhole at the slender window to arrive at a known location.

"We are within the RS402 funnel."

Colby gave a sigh of relief. Every wormhole had an active outer rim where piloted vessels emerged and a narrower, inner funnel used by automated cargo pods and similar craft.

"Are we within range of a cargo drone?"

"Affirmative. I have activated the transponder, and it is aligning for an intercept."

Getting through the wormhole to the RS402 funnel had been the hard part. Between his own implant and the transponder codes that Topeka had provided he anticipated no difficulty in getting the funnel's designated AI to assign a cargo drone to react and capture it. They were still a long ways from the planet, and by surrendering control to the drone Colby wouldn't have to rely on his limited skill with piloting the alien ship in order to get there on his own. If the drone could grab the alien ship, then it would carry them to New Mars without any more action on his part.

He wandered back to the control panel. Surely there had to be some form of video display.

"Can you show me the cargo drone?" he asked.

"Affirmative. It is on the display now."

Colby didn't see anything that looked like a view of space, and certainly, he couldn't see a drone.

"I can't see anything."

"The feedback circuits indicate that it is being displayed."

Colby could swear that his implant sounded a little peeved— but that was impossible, right?

"Upload a visual."

Colby gave the mental command, then blinked three times, taking a biological snapshot that his implant could analyze. Controlling his beta waves like that was beyond most people, and most implants didn't have the capability, but he'd had years of practice, so it was almost second nature to him.

"The feed is not visible," his implant told him.

No shit.

"As I said. I guess the interface isn't perfect. But, you're sure the drone is on its way to us?"

"Affirmative. ETA in eight minutes, forty-two seconds."

Unless your interface is screwing up.

Colby chose to assume the drone was approaching. If it wasn't, he'd figure out how to navigate the plant ship to New Mars under its own power.

"Well, Duke, we'll just see what happens now, huh, girl?" he said, patting her on the head again.

She leaned into his leg and wagged her tail, forehead pressed up against his hand. He was suddenly struck by how much she trusted him. He'd never had a pet while on active duty, and he'd taken care of her at the farm more out of responsibility than anything else. Yet here she was, on an alien ship, trusting him to keep her safe.

And he was glad she was with him.

"Give me a countdown on the drone's arrival," he said, still petting Duke.

"Five minutes, twelve seconds."

He took a seat, out of reach of the vines, and Duke snuggled her head in his lap. Unlike the last time he was sitting, he was now totally relaxed. What could go wrong now? It was nice to be able to simply sit back, petting his dog. As soon as he landed, he'd have to jump into action, forcing Greenstein and the command to understand the threat. Hostile first contact, right on the doorstep of one of humanity's most critical systems. Assuming they believed him.

It's going to be hard for them to ignore this ship, though, and the dead broccoli man in the locker.

"Four minutes," his implant told him as he closed his eyes.

He'd been up and running almost since the plant soldiers had attacked his farm. He didn't know how long it would take the drone to get him to New Mars, didn't know where the RS402 funnel was in relation to the planet in its orbit. Surely there'd be time to get some shut-eye once they were on their way.

"One minute."

Heck, that seemed like five seconds.

He knew he'd fallen asleep, so he opened his eyes, slid a protesting Duke off his lap, then stood up.

"Plenty of time to sleep as soon as we've been grabbed, girl."

He waited for confirmation, his nerves stepping up a bit. There were thousands of the drones around New Mars at any given time handling the many shipments coming in from dozens of wormholes. Transponder codes indicated which were to be sent down to the planet's surface to one of many depots for handling and processing, and which had to be rerouted on to one of the many other wormholes for the next stage of their journeys across space. A hundred AI traffic controllers routed ships from ingress to egress with rarely an exception that had business down on New Mars itself.

A jolt well beyond the capacity of the ship's dampeners staggered Colby and knocked Duke off her feet.

What the hell?

Most of the cargo arriving from Vasquez was agricultural, but some of the specialty foods were easy to bruise. He couldn't imagine that the cargo pods would be manhandled like that. Another jolt almost sent him to the floor, and from behind him, Colby heard a sound no one in space ever wants to hear: a hissing.

All of the vines connected to the bulkheads lifted up in unison.

Colby spun around, trying to pinpoint the hissing, but it wasn't in the bridge.

"Stay here, girl!" he shouted, bolting for the passage leading to the ship's rear. The hissing grew louder, and he could feel the movement of air. And then he saw it. The tip of a cerralloy blade had cut into the ship. Air whistled around it.

Tiny, overlapping, green scales flowed along the ship's walls trying to seal around the puncture, some kind of automated algae that struggled to coat the cargo drone's arms and immobilize them. They failed when, as if shifting its grip, the prong moved, making the hole a little larger. What had been a soft hissing became a roar, pulling at Colby. If the drone's grasping arm moved again, there would be an explosive decompression.

"Duke!"

Colby turned and ran back, fighting the rush of air. Duke was whining, her voice sounding tinny as the air became thinner. She ran up to him, trying to jump into his arms.

Even without a catastrophic evacuation, he knew his time was limited. He had a minute, maybe a little more, to figure their way out of this mess. The ship jolted again, almost knocking him down.

The locker!

Colby grabbed the struggling Duke, then dragged her to the locker. If he could get inside and close it, then he'd at least have that much O2 to breathe, which was a heck of a lot better than trying to breathe vacuum.

He hit the door release three, four times, as dark spots danced across his vision. Finally, the door opened. There wasn't enough room for him and Duke with the alien's body there. He put Duke down, then yanked the body with all his might, pulling it out, tearing it free of the vines that had held it and flailed to continue in that purpose. Gasping, he fell on his ass in the process, the plant carcass sprawled on top of him. He lay there a moment dazed.

Get with it, Edson!

He pushed the body off him, then grabbed Duke by the scruff of her neck and threw her into the locker. He pulled the boss plant's severed head out and tossed it to the deck, then jumped in, pushing Duke to the back.

"Close, damn you!" he gasped, punching every square centimeter near the opening.

He was entering hypoxia. He recognized the signs: confusion, sweating, wheezing. If there'd been a reflective surface anywhere on this damn ship he didn't doubt that it would show his skin color somewhere between blue and cherry red. Like all Marines, he'd undergone vacuum training, and as part of that, he'd been sent into never-never-land in a training chamber. He'd hoped he'd never feel that again.

The ship lurched, more powerfully then before, and Colby was thrown and pinned against the back of the locker, face first in a mass of leafy vegetation. His body ached in a familiar way as gee forces reminded him of the difference between weight and mass. The ship was accelerating. His dog whimpered, though whether from her own hypoxia or the extra gees he couldn't tell.

"Sorry Duke," he coughed, feeling her warm body at his feet. "The drone must be dragging us downward, for all the good it'll do us."

She stopped whining and hugged him back, which made him feel good. They were going to go out together.

She hugged me?

He managed to turn despite the forces holding him to the wall. It wasn't Duke. The same vines that had wrapped around the alien's corpse had now latched onto to him and were holding him fast. He knew he should fight them, but he couldn't. His mouth opened as he gasped for air, but there just wasn't any. He straightened back up and feebly pushed at the opening, trying once more to close the door.

And then he was out of energy. This was the end, he knew.

Surprisingly, he wasn't angry, he wasn't panicking. He felt a wave of lassitude sweep over him as he gave up.

In his last moments, he started hallucinating. Sergeant Warshowki, his first DI, appeared, yelling at him to get up. Colby just giggled. The head of the alien scurried across the floor towards the control panels, dozens of tiny plant fingers having emerged from its neck to carry it along. He giggled again and his world went dark.

Interlude I: Per Capita Perspective

A frigid torpor gripped the Gardener, a lethargy it only understood as it broke through the edge of it like a questing root easing through clay soil. Bits of memory—glimpses somewhere between acquisition and true consolidation—taunted its awareness. Meat had entered its vessel. Meat with tools and weapons. They had attacked. Its attempt to neutralize the pair of primitives had failed and. . . one of them. . . severed its cranium from the ambulatory caudex it had fashioned rotations earlier. That accounted for both the disjuncture of memory and the torpor. The brutality of their incursion had shocked the Gardener into quiescence. Before it could recover, whether by design or random chance or simple Meat destiny, they had returned the pieces to the cold storage of the craft's navigation locker where the waiting vines exuded much-needed and healing oxygen even as the lower temperatures slowed its restoration and pushed its awareness into oblivion.

Until it hadn't. Circumstances had altered, and quickly. Its recovering sensorium as yet possessed only limited visual processing, like seeing through a thick layer of unremitting cellulose, which coupled with the steady warming of its core was enough to recognize that it no longer lay within the alcove. A silhouette, possibly that of one of the Meat creatures, wrestled a smaller, quadruped form into the space, batting at the indiscriminate vines that sought to embrace them both.

Audition returned and brought the whistle of escaping air. Escaping to where? Its elegant vessel rested comfortably in a forest clearing. And yet. . . as more and more of its cognitive processing came back to it, the Gardener understood. The vessel was not at rest, not on the planet at all, was in fact in space and damaged, possibly hulled.

It strained and pushed at the ganglia bundle that had once connected it with a functional trunk and limbs. They descended from the slit just above the point of its neck wound, trembling as they adapted to serve as ambulatory roots. By whatever fluke, the Meat had managed to launch its ship into space. Necessity demanded it interface with controls, initiate repairs, and expunge the pests.

The vessel jerked, rolling on an axis that should never have known rotation, and accelerated along a vector that was impossible for it. The Gardener skittered across the floor, re-evaluating priorities and aiming itself toward one of the ship's backup seed supply compartments along the edge of the far wall. The compartment served double duty as an emergency pod, existing to launch an assortment of supplies in the event of absolute catastrophe. Under such contingencies the Gardener's own navigation pod could also launch as a life pod. As the rising cry of dwindling air demonstrated, the situation had reached that extreme, but there was insufficient time to eject the Meat from its escape route. Nor did it require such action. In its current form, the supply pod would serve.

Pressing a root ganglion into the wall, it accessed the vessel's systems to open a slit into its intended destination.

The access was granted, but even as the Gardener slipped within an alien clamor reverberated through it. An outside force had accessed the vessel's systems!

«Impossible!»

The system had been tainted, and yet the telltales of a Mechanical infestation were not present—which explained why the defenses it had crafted against such an attack had not activated. No, it was unthinkable. There was only Meat on the vessel. Meat did not possess the sophistication or technical savvy to communicate with spacecraft. And yet. . . as the Gardener communed with the vessel it had nurtured from a seed, it read the evidence that they had lifted from the planet's surface, exited its gravity well, and passed through some spacial anomaly that had left it in an uncharted *location before it had been attacked by a robotic tool of limited intellectual capacity.*

«Meat. Meat capable of space travel, capable of movement between stellar bodies. Impossible!»

And yet. . . clearly possible. The Gardener compiled the horrifying ramifications, bracing itself against the cushioned sleeves of supplies making up the pod's emergency seedbank. It abandoned any possibility of saving its vessel even as it abandoned the vessel itself. The greater need was to get away, determine its location, and get word back to its people. Meat was loose in the galaxy, with the full range and promise of ruination that Meat delivered on any world where it evolved.

Indifferent to increased acceleration, it launched the newly purposed life pod, bringing its rudimentary navigation systems to life, relieved to find no taint of Meat present. Crude visual sensors showed the shattered shape of its once beautiful vessel gripped and pinched by a robotic tool that dragged it toward a distant mud-red sphere at speed.

The Gardener consulted a manifest of its supplies and allowed itself a moment of relief. Assuming the planet wasn't too distant, assuming it held even a modicum of friendly soil, it could grow the tools it would need, fashion a body appropriate to its demands, and do what had to be done.

The desire to tend its own garden could wait. Meat, thinking Meat, threatened everything that set down roots or yearned for simple sunshine. That threat would be eliminated first and foremost.

Part II: Home is Where They Have to Take You In

A fractal of frames slowly formed in Colby's mind. Each tiny image revealed a progression towards an immense facility of some sort, but from a slightly different perspective. Each frame moved independently from all of the others, in different vectors, spins, and rotations that weren't limited to three dimensions. Colby knew it was a dream, but it still made him nauseous, and he thought he was going to lose the emergency rations he'd eaten with Topeka before leaving Vasquez.

Two sounds started to register as well: a low moaning and a higher pitched whining. With his growing discomfort, it took a moment to realize that the moaning was coming from him. And that meant the whining was. . .

Duke?

He tried to reach out to her, but couldn't move. A million hands conspired to restrain him. They held him back, keeping him from her for no purpose he could fathom. As a young lieutenant, he'd often had nightmares of being in an assault on an enemy position, with his Marines leading the way, only to feel as if he was trying to run through quicksand. He feared not being able to make it to the assault and being branded a coward, but no matter how hard he tried, he could not break free from the quicksand's grip.

Now, the same feeling of frustration and fear swept over him. Duke needed him, and he wasn't able to get to her. The thousands of images, most of the fuzzily out-of-focus building, relentlessly pounded into his brain, too much for him to take. The dream demons were not going to let him comfort his dog.

Even in his sleep, his body revolted. His stomach heaved, the acidic bile burning his throat. He wasn't sure if he dream-vomited, or if it had been real. He struggled to turn his head, afraid of suffocating in his sleep, but his brain simply shut down, and he sunk back into the welcome embrace of oblivion.

****

Oblivion ended. Time resumed with little indication of how long it had been held in abeyance. As Colby started to resurface from the depths of darkness, the myriad of images appeared again. As before, most of them centered on a large structure, as if each was a feed created by a tiny camera on an independently operated bot of some sort. Like he was a security guard monitoring a building at night, but instead of 20 wall-mounted spy-eyes showing different areas in a building, he had thousands of aerial feeds, all showing the same thing, each from a slightly different angle or distance.

The images themselves were odd, with deeper, more vivid colors in the blues and purples, with a lack of reds and yellows. Colby was familiar with the full range of military scanners, and the images reminded him of what ultra-violet surveillance gear produced.

Nausea threatened him again, but he fought that back down. His mouth and throat still burned from before.

Wait a minute. Did I really puke? Or am I back in the same dream?

Colby had been subject to recurring dreams since his forced resignation from the Corps, but not like this. It was as if whatever he was dreaming before had just picked up where he'd left it. He didn't understand what was going on, and it was hard to concentrate while being bombarded with sensory overload.

Control yourself, Edson.

The sheer number of inputs was overwhelming, but the overall concept of controlling different inputs was not anything new. As a leader of Marines, he'd had to manage individual inputs from his Marines as well as scanners and comms with higher headquarters. It had been difficult at first, even with only the thirty-nine Marines and corpsmen in his platoon. But with the help of his command implant and hours of practice, his mind learned how to make sense of everything. As he became more senior and had more Marines in his command, he'd increased his capacity for comprehension. But the thousands of inputs coming at him now was an order of magnitude more than he'd ever had to monitor before. And yet. . . once he'd awakened enough to understand what was happening—if not actually what he was receiving—it was clear that his unconscious mind had clued in sooner. Based on his familiarity with the general concept, it had begun rewiring the patterns of his synapses, rerouting the organization of the feeds so that, with the help of his implant, he started to have a sense of the overall picture.

He was treating this as reality, not a dream, and that insight provided the final push, letting him focus on only a few inputs chosen at random, flicking from one subset to another and another. The building in the images had the Spartan look of a commercial processing center, like the—

Hell, I'm on New Mars.

It came rushing back to him. He'd taken the alien ship through the wormhole. The cargo drone had damaged the ship, and it had bled air. His last-ditch effort to save Duke and himself had worked, somehow, but while he was out cold, the drone had taken the ship to one of the planet's processing centers, along with what were probably hundreds, if not thousands, of other cargo containers.

Colby opened his eyes—to nothingness. He felt a moment of panic, but ironically, it was the onslaught of other images that kept him grounded. With a mental flipping of the switch, a trick he'd mastered over the years of battlesuit telemetry, he compartmentalized the inputs, shoving them to the side to focus on his own senses. He still couldn't see anything, but it was now simply darkness, not a loss of vision. Which in turn allowed him to register his other senses again.

Nearby, Duke softly whined, and she struggled, pressing herself against his side.

"Easy, girl. I'm here with you. It's going to be OK."

She seemed to quiet down, but that could have been his imagination. What wasn't his imagination was the itch that started to take over his senses, threatening to shut them down much as the visual inputs had before.

Or maybe it was—he didn't know. It didn't matter if it was real or his imagination, it was driving him batty. It was as if a horde of cockroaches were crawling over him. He tried to lift his arm to scratch, which in turn reminded him that he was still being held fast.

He heaved, struggling with all his strength, but while there was some give, he couldn't manage any real movement. After two solid minutes of effort, he gave up. His body was still trying to make sense of everything, and he didn't want to waste energy on a futile attempt to break free.

"I've been immobilized and I've got who knows what being shot into my mind," he said aloud, a technique he'd picked up when first learning to use his implant and feeds as a lieutenant.

When faced with too much input, it helped to verbalize his thoughts. His voice was working fine, and as it had so many years ago, speaking allowed him to hone in on the specifics that defined a situation.

"I'm on the ship, probably on New Mars. I'm getting feeds from somewhere, too many of them to handle."

The feeds started encroaching again, and he hurriedly continued, "Most of all, I'm still alive, so I can affect what is going on. First thing first is to figure out why I'm getting the feeds."

He tried to focus on a single input, but then the bulk of them started pressing down on his soul.

"One at a time, Edson, one at a time. That one, right there. I'm only looking at you, so reveal your secrets. I'm ignoring the rest for now, so only you."

His implant was second nature to him after so many years, and even if it had been a long time since he'd pushed its capabilities to full operation mode, his mind slipped into it like a pair of well-worn shoes. The rest of the feeds remained, as did the sounds of Duke's and his breathing, the itch on his skin, even the sound of his voice, but his chosen feed seemed to expand and come into focus.

119

"Shit, it's more of the plants!" he said, as everything whirled back into the jumble of impressions.

"Bring it back, Edson." He forced everything into place and brought his chosen feed back to the fore.

When first confronted with the thousands of images, the large building had been all he'd noticed. But now, with his attention on just one feed, while the structure still occupied the foreground of the image he could make out details in the background, a background that resolved into a sea of plant soldiers. The colors were off from what he'd seen on Vasquez, but there was no mistaking the shape and movement. With a mental command, he released the feed, and it retreated to join the rest of the confusing mass.

"I did this," he said. "I brought them back through the wormhole with me. Somehow, they were in the ship, and now they're loose."

An image? Memory? of the boss plant's head scuttling across the deck on tiny legs came to his mind. He thought it had been a hallucination brought on by hypoxia, like Sergeant Warshowki yelling at him, but what if it had been real? Was the thing somehow alive and now waging war on New Mars?

If so, that made Colby a traitor to humankind. Sure, he'd been railroaded into resigning his commission, but if he'd just abetted an alien invasion, he deserved whatever punishment would be meted out.

"I've got to fix this."

His own fate was the hangman's noose, but that was irrelevant in the big picture. He was still a Marine, a loyal servant of mankind, and he was going to do anything he could to avert this catastrophe.

He pulled another of the feeds to the fore, this time not having to speak. A mental shrug was his only acknowledgment that this was getting easier. His implant excelled at adapting, filling in gaps to make the system work.

His new point of view was at the wall of the building itself. Leafy green tendrils reached up, attached themselves with a wet click to the walls, and started to pull.

"Click?" he said. "Did I feel that or hear that?"

A crack opened up in the wall, grabbing his attention. Within moments, the crack was a gap, and his *host?* slipped in. With a start he realized what he should have known all along: the feeds were coming from the plants. He was seeing the world through the horde of plant soldiers. Colby understood what he was experiencing, although he'd only known it on a much smaller scale. When he hitched a ride with a Marine in a battlesuit, it was through the Marine's sensors and cam feeds. This wasn't so different. If he concentrated, he could sense everything around the plant soldier, a full three-sixty. No, more than a three-sixty, a complete sphere around it.

He started to get nauseous again and had to pull back. It had been bad enough when faced with a bee eye's kaleidoscope of thousands of views, but now, he had full environmental awareness from a multitude of sources, and worse still, they all that overlapped one another.

He threw up again, a poor effort that was mostly stomach acid. He spit several times, clearing his mouth. A moment later, he could feel the spit drop back down on his neck from where it had fallen from the locker's ceiling.

If he was going to do anything, he had to find a way to block some of the sensory input. Even with his implant integrating better, there was just too much for him to process. He just didn't know how to do that.

"Maybe the security shields?" he asked, his burning throat turning his words into a rasp.

His implant was the pinnacle of current technology, an amazing piece of gear, powered by a tiny long-life battery implanted in his sinuses. As tiny as the current draw was, however, it was possible for a sophisticated enemy to hack his implant, which could obviously have terrible consequences in a battle. That was why implants like his were not only heavily shielded, but he could erect firewalls at will.

He pulled up his collection of firewalls and selected FC-90, which had an hourglass neck that allowed the passage of a limited amount of data. He slapped the firewall over the feeds, then hesitantly opened the flow. It wasn't perfect, but it helped. The onslaught dropped from overwhelming to barely manageable.

Feeling a little more confident, he found another plant soldier already inside the building and zeroed in on it. Within a split second, he *was* the soldier. It was his arms that were tearing apart a piece of machinery, ripping pressure rollers right off of their cradle. Another plant pulled one of the heavy cerasteel pieces out of its grasp and started to bend it in two.

His plant reached for a control, and a spark jumped across, zapping it.

"Yow!" Colby yelled. "Wait, how the hell did that happen?"

Colby was not feeling everything the plant touched, but he experienced that shock. At least, he thought he did. His fingers were still tingling, and it sure felt real.

His implant had high-level haptic controls imbedded into it. With enough practice—and Colby had had more than enough over the course of his career—he could control machines with what was essentially a mental touch. It was as if his fingers were on physical controls. He could virtually feel pressure, vibration, temperature, and other sensations without ever actually touching the object.

"Wait a minute. If there is a haptic connection here, then can I control it the same way I can control a drone?"

He jumped back into the feeds and his previous host. It was attacking the base of the control panel. Colby reached out to it, taking his virtual hand and grabbing the thing's real hand. Nothing happened. The green plant arm passed through his virtual hand as if it was, well, *virtual*.

"Shit, Edson, concentrate!"

He tried again, this time building up the hand, adding bones, tendons, and ligaments. The plant soldier's arm might have hesitated a moment, but it wasn't stopped, and it tore another piece of the machinery apart.

"What am I doing wrong?" he asked.

He tried several more tacks, even running through his Troubleshooting checklist, but nothing was working. The machine, whatever it was, was soon turned into scrap, and the plant soldier moved to the next one.

Colby switched to another plant soldier but didn't have any more success. He knew he was making tiny adjustments in their actions, but not enough to stop any of them from destroying the factory.

Where're the facility's security forces? Are they going to just ignore this?

The factories were the lifeblood of New Mars, and to much of the Republic. Most were automated, but still, there were Marines and local security forces on the planet for a reason. They should be reacting to the assault.

Colby paused from his efforts and widened the awareness of his host so he could simply take in the scene, hoping to see signs of the cavalry riding in to save the day. All he saw was destruction. The entire wall of the factory was gone, and a good half of the machinery destroyed. All of the plants were working with a single purpose.

Well, all except one. A single solder was whirling around aimlessly, knocking into the others. It stopped and stood still for a moment, then lashed out erratically with a ropy arm. . . at the same time that Duke jerked at his side.

What?

His fingers were not restrained, and he could feel Duke's warm body. He pushed out into her, and she jerked within her restraints. At the same time, the crazy plant soldier jerked.

"Duke, Duke, who's a good girl?"

The plant soldier stopped, then wiggled.

"Duke, are you controlling that plant? Are you?"

He pushed harder into her with his fingers, producing a yelp. Immediately, the plant solder stopped wiggling and marched to join the rest at the nearest machine.

He couldn't believe what he'd seen. His eyes told him that the soldier and Duke had somehow been attached, but his mind screamed that was ridiculous. And it was ridiculous. A dog couldn't control an enemy soldier, could she?

Unless this really *was* a dream brought about in his last seconds of life in a hypoxia-induced death, it sure looked like the two had been connected. It made a perverse degree of sense. Somehow, he was connected to the plant soldiers as they rampaged. Why not Duke? They were both inside a womb of sorts in the locker. Colby had the sneaking suspicion that the ship's tendrils had not only kept them alive, but somehow plugged them to the plant ecosystem. They'd been connected to the command and control.

And it hit him. Duke had stopped the plant soldier in its tracks. Colby had been trying to stop an arm by simply holding it back. He should have been doing as Duke did and *become* the host, for lack of a better term.

He turned back inwards to his host. Instead of trying to control its movements, he pictured himself sinking into it, being subsumed by it. Nothing happened, but he wasn't going to give up. If a dog could do it, so could a human. He closed off every possible input he could, seeing himself sink into the quicksand of the soldier. This was too reminiscent of his nightmares, so he changed that to sinking into a warm bath. He could feel the plant's very being, but he could not find a way in. He adjusted, shifted, changed the force of his projections, and suddenly, something opened up, and he started to fall in. . . and immediately clawed for freedom.

He'd felt himself being controlled, instead of him doing the controlling. The plant mind was not like anything he'd experienced nor imagined. It was so. . . alien. It wasn't what he'd imagined a science fiction hive mind to be, but it sure wasn't human, and that scared him to the quick. He'd almost been taken over by it.

Marines don't quit, however, and Colby knew he had to do something. But what? He'd pictured himself sinking into the plant. What if he reversed that image? What if the plant sunk into him? Or if he surrounded it?

He formed a new image, one of his body flowing around the plant, taking it in like an amoeba eating a bacterium. He'd already formed a type of resonance with this plant soldier, and far quicker than he'd expected, he'd drawn the plant in. Colby was still Colby, and he thought he was in control of the plant. The soldier was attacking another machine, and Colby reached out with his mind with a command to stop. The soldier hesitated, but after a moment commenced again.

Frustrated, Colby sent out a powerful order, a mental scream. The soldier stopped dead, ropy limbs still grasping the machine. Another plant pulled the machine parts from his soldier, and still, it remained motionless.

Carefully, Colby withdrew, waiting for the plant to start in on the attack again. It remained motionless. If he could, he'd have raised a fist into the air in triumph.

There had to be more than a thousand of the plant soldiers inside the ruins of the factory, and Colby sensed that there were far more destroying other factories. It was too much for him to grasp the magnitude of what he was trying to do, so he refused to think about it. Every journey began with a single step.

He shifted to another host to begin the process again.

****

"Stop that plant," Colby sent, then waited to see what would happen.

After an hour, he'd only stopped thirty plants from their rampage of destruction. It became clear that he was fighting a losing battle, and his finger in the dyke wasn't going to hold back the ocean. He had to change tactics, and this was his attempt to do more.

His implant was continually improving the interface with each interaction, and with a specific command, he was hoping he could get soldier to fight soldier. If he was successful, that would make his impact that much greater. Instead of a single plant standing still, he would take out two: one being held, and the other doing the holding.

In the back of his mind, he kept wondering about the boss plant. Topeka had taken off the thing's head, but he now believed what he'd seen with the head scuttling across the ship's bridge. Something had started the plant army on their rampage here on New Mars. Was its objective the same as back on Vasquez? Was it orchestrating this attack? And if it was out there controlling the assault, why hadn't it ordered any of the stopped soldiers back into battle? All good questions, but Colby lacked sufficient intel for more than guesswork, besides which his immediate focus was consumed by taking over the plant soldiers.

Ordering one soldier to attack another was different that simply stopping it. His target plant reached over and wrapped up the soldier next to it. That one kept reaching for the last pieces of the machine it had been dismantling, but Colby's plant was like an octopus. They both teetered for a moment before falling over. They lay intertwined on the grounds, ropy plant arms twisted in each other's grip.

"Two for one," Colby said.

Duke answered with a piteous yelp. He knew she had to be confused and scared, but there wasn't much he could do about it.

Unless I can get one of the soldiers to come back and open the locker and free us?

He'd tried several times to free a foot and start hunting for the hatch release, but he hadn't come close. He knew he was in the locker for the long haul unless he could figure out a way to be rescued.

But if I get out of here, can I still control them?

Whatever was holding them was probably what allowed him and Duke to interface with the plant soldiers. It boggled the mind that two different forms of life could connect like that, but the universe was filled with amazing things, and the proof was right there in front of him.

For the moment, he and Duke were safe, and he could control the plant soldiers, so it was probably better to stand pat and create more havoc. He checked on his quisling, which had managed to tear off one of its opponent's arms, but was now in danger of losing one of its own. He was hoping it could make short shrift of the other, but as the two combatants slowly maneuvered for the upper hand, he realized that wasn't going to happen anytime soon, if at all. He gave it another command to attack, figuring it wouldn't hurt to reinforce his last command, then withdrew, looking for his next target.

He was able to take over this one in less than a minute, and it unhesitatingly turned from a half-destroyed fabricator of some sort to fall upon the soldier next to it. It took another minute for the victim to seem to realize what was happening and turn to face its ally-turned-enemy. None of the other soldiers seemed to notice the pair and they wrapped each other up in mortal combat.

As his implant fine-tuned the process, the time to take over a soldier became less and less. By his tenth "grab," as he began to think of it, the process took about thirty seconds. The fabricator that had been this group of soldiers' target was out-of-action, but no more damage was being done.

Colby felt a thrill of victory before he widened his perceptions. This factory had to still have a couple of hundred as of yet undamaged machines, and there were hundreds of plant soldiers still bent on destroying every last one of them.

"No time to admire your handiwork, Edson. Get your ass back to work."

****

Just over thirty minutes later, Colby had set another fifty-six soldiers against their brethren, so 111 were out of the demolition sweepstakes. It was only 111 because one of the ones Colby'd attacked had managed to tear off all the arms of the one he had taken over. It limped back to join the others while its attacker tried to inchworm-hump after it. Colby paused to watch the victor for a moment, he needed the break. His head ached with the onset of a killer migraine, just like the ones he sometimes had when first learning to use his implant.

The tips of his fingers rested on what was probably Duke's haunch, and the contact was an anchor. He was sure she appreciated his touch as well. He wasn't connecting with her like he was with the plant soldiers he'd commandeered. But there was some sort of connection going on, just the tiniest bit of backsurge in the tendrils that held them both fast.

He breathed deep, and took control of the limping soldier, ready to send it to attack one of the others, but with only half of a single arm left, he realized that the thing couldn't do much damage. He was about to shift to another soldier when a blinding light filled his head, a flash of intense pain flooding him for an instant before it was gone.

What the...

The jolt had been a flash, almost too short to feel, but his nerves trembled as if remembering pain. His headache intensified, and he struggled trying to bring his hands up to his temples.

He forced himself to concentrate, trying to select another frame to figure out what had happened. It was easier to slip into his previous captive, and from it, he could see the limping soldier, or rather, what was left of it. Bits and pieces were strewn haphazardly around the floor and walls, a green mist hovering in the still air where his host had stood.

A streak of red light flashed past his/the plant soldier's field of view, and one of the soldiers tearing into another piece of machinery exploded into a thousand bits of plant. More green mist bloomed over the spot.

Colby knew that flash for laser light. Specifically, the laser from a M88 rifle, and that could mean only one thing—the Marines had finally arrived!

Several more lasers reached out, exploding the soldiers. The lasers weren't doing the damage—they were merely the spotting tool, like an old-fashioned tracer round. The M88 was a microwave rifle, sending out two megajoules joules at 20 GHz in .25-second pulses.

It was a perfect weapon for rapidly heating water—and objects which contained water tended to come apart with extreme prejudice. Plant soldiers evidently contained *a lot* of water.

An M88 could fire five hundred times on a single charge, taking only five seconds to recharge the capacitor between shots. As he expected, five seconds after the initial volley, another one reached out, exploding six more plants into mist.

"Get some!" he shouted, his voice muffled by the vines holding him.

The soldiers might have been single-minded in tearing the factory apart, but they were still soldiers, plant-things or not. Almost as one, they turned to face the threat and surged forward.

Colby shifted his perspective, and a platoon of Marines was entering the building in perfect assault formation through the destroyed back walls. His heart raced with excitement, and he longed to be out there, a lieutenant again, leading the assault. In their mech battlesuits, Marines were a menacing sight to most bad guys, but to him, they were comfort, pride, and. . . yes, love, all rolled into one.

He needed to let the Marines know what they were facing. He tried to pull them up through his implant, but it was like barreling down a highway only to hit a stone wall. Nothing went through, and he wasn't sure why. He started a troubleshooting worm to work on it, then turned his attention back to the fight.

Another volley of lasers cut down the soldiers in the front of the rush towards the Marines. The soldier next to Colby's exploded, the force knocking his viewpoint plant to its knees? Lower extremity? A wave of panic roared through him. He'd just had one host under his control killed, and it was not something he wanted to go through again. He shifted his focus away from the action, jumping to one of the soldiers outside the building.

"Damn!" was all he could say.

He'd been focusing on the factory, knowing there was much more going on, but not to what extent. Every factory or warehouse in sight was flattened or close to it. Thousands. . . *tens* of thousands of plant soldiers were pouring out of the wreckage, converging on what looked to be two rifle companies, about two hundred Marines. Three crew-served M280 particle-beam cannons were spewing nano-pulse beams of death, mowing down the plant soldiers like so much genwheat in the path of an unrelenting harvester.

The toll on the soldiers was frightening. A thousand had already died, the particulate flurry of their remains giving rise to that green mist. More frightening, however, was that the wave of vegetable bodies inched closer and closer to the Marines.

"You are too dispersed!" Colby yelled out to the commander, even knowing no one could hear him.

Almost immediately, the platoon that had been entering the building started to pull back, and for a moment, Colby watched in shock.

Can I control the Marines, too? No, that's impossible. The commander was taught the same as I was and is seeing the same thing.

Marines are taught to take the fight to the enemy, to seek them out and destroy them. But with thousands of plant soldiers eagerly advancing on the Marines, sometimes the best offense was a good defense. By creating a strong defensive perimeter, the Marines could employ interlocking and mutually supporting fields of fire, creating an impenetrable wall of energy.

In theory.

The M280s were devastating weapons, but they were big, bulky, and not very maneuverable—not so much due to the cannon itself, but from the powerpack. Particle beam weapons were energy hogs, better suited for tank bodies or Navy ships. The cooling coils alone were larger than the projector tubes. For a crew-served weapon, the Achilles heel was changing out the power cell. In normal operations, a three-cannon section would rotate the power cell switch-out so at least two cannons were up at all times. This time, the numbers of plant soldiers closing in were so huge, the firing was so intense, that the choreography was interrupted, and two of the weapons had gone offline at the same time.

With a huge gap, the Marine riflemen couldn't keep up with the mass of the charging plant soldiers, and they reached their Little Big Top, breaking into the line of Marines. Monomolecular blades took over from rifles as the fight devolved into hand-to-branch combat, but while the M88 exploded the plant soldiers, cutting them was far less effective. Even missing arms or with huge chunks taken out of the bodies, the plant soldiers kept up the attack like zombies seeking brains.

Hell, do something, Edson!

He'd been so caught up in the fight, switching from one host to the other, that he'd forgotten that he could still affect the battle. At least fifty of the plant soldiers were amongst the Marines, and several Marines were down. One lay still on the ground, left arm gone while three plant soldiers were tearing the cerroalloy ISP armor apart. The same armor that could withstand a 105mm artillery round was like papier-mâché to the plants' relentless strength.

A Marine stepped up, and with a tremendous blow from the monomolecular blade extending from the battlesuit's arm, sliced one of the soldiers attacking the downed Marine in half, separating the lower ambulatory "legs" from the rest. Even so, it still kept prying apart bits of battlesuit.

Colby swooped in, a hawk on a rabbit, flooding one of the three soldiers, and took control. His host released its hold on the broken edge of the battlesuit's chest carapace, and at Colby's direction, shifted to the other fully functional soldier, intertwining its arms in the other's, immobilizing it.

Marines closed in, firing kinetic handguns, which didn't bother Colby much, but also swinging bladed arms, which hurt like hell. What had been simply vague impressions of pain were now much more pronounced. As his implant's control of the interface had improved, the tactile transfer had grown stronger as well.

Colby stayed in place, however, absorbing the pain until he felt the soldier's remaining arms starting to lose their grip before withdrawing. He didn't want to risk being connected when the thing died.

His skin still tingled, as if he'd been cut himself. He took a couple of deep breaths, then dove back into the fray. He pulled two more soldiers off Marines before the soldiers inside the lines started exploding again.

About freaking time!

A Marine battlesuit could take a fairly good pounding from a microwave weapon, and getting "hosed down" was an accepted course of action when the enemy was intermixed with Marines. The cannons must be back online, so the Marines who'd been concentrating on keeping more plant soldiers from reaching them could focus on their buddies and clear the lines.

Colby shifted outside the Marine lines to one of the soldiers in the back of the mob. What had been thousands was far, far fewer as more and more were cut down. That green mist was now a thick green fog, which was not good for the Marines. Particle beams were amazing weapons, but they lost power through electrostatic bloom, and that effect was heightened with particulates in the air. The cannon beams cut the air with a shimmering glow, but that glowing meant energy was being diverted.

Some of the plants around him didn't have the same fervor, if he was reading plant body language correctly. A couple hundred broke off from the rear of the pack, including his host. For a moment, he thought they were quitting the field of battle, but no, there was a purpose to the movement. They had not lost their fervor--this group was maneuvering to flank the Marines. If the body of plant soldiers were being controlled by the boss plant, then the boss must have realized it was wasting bodies, and was changing tactics.

These were not mindless automatons—well, perhaps the soldiers themselves were, but not the force guiding them. That made them much more dangerous.

Colby jumped to one of the lead soldiers and commanded it to divert, hoping the others would follow. They didn't. They bypassed his captured host and kept marching. He was about to order his host to tackle one of the others, but it wouldn't do much good. The fight was well out of his hands.

Instead, he turned his host around and sent it to the back of the main body where it would hopefully become a Marine target. He pulled out of it, then tried to digest what the remaining thousands of frames showed him. If he could see a pattern in what the plants were doing, then get that to the commander, then he'd be contributing. . .

Beside him, Duke yelped piteously and struggled for a moment, before settling into a whine.

"Calm down, girl. I'm here," he said, stroking her side with the tips of his fingers, a tiny motion, but one that seemed to help her.

He wondered what had set her off before it hit him. He'd felt what it was like to be in a host when it was killed. He'd wager Duke had been out there, inside one of the soldiers when the Marines had destroyed it. For a moment, his anger rose against the Marines, the bastards, the—

What the hell, Edson? What are you thinking?

He'd never, ever, thought bad about the Marines, not even when he was being cashiered out of the service. He'd hated a few other Marines during his career, and he hated Vice-Minister Greenstein with a passion, but that wasn't the Corps. He loved the Corps, and he felt an overwhelming sense of guilt over what he'd just felt.

How could that have happened?

Something taking over a large proportion of the frames caught his attention, diverting him from his guilt. It was the Marines, launching into their attack.

"Oo-rah!" he shouted, wondering if that was still from his heart.

The Marines poured in tight company wedges designed to pierce the remaining plants with maximum firepower to the front and flanks. One company headed to cut off the plants that were trying to envelope them. Colby should have known that the commander would have been aware of the situation and had recognized the same thing he had.

"Just let him fight. You're not in command," he muttered.

With the cannons remaining back to deliver supporting fire, the Marines tore through the diminished numbers, blasting plant soldiers into bits and pieces. The green fog of death intensified and more soldiers were vaporized, but as the Marines closed in, their weapons kept spitting out death. The two companies were machines, killing machines. The plants didn't have a chance.

More and more of his frames winked out, and he began to lose his situational awareness of what was happening. There were too many gaps, but that was a good thing. It meant the Marines were winning. Within an hour, he was down to seven frames, seven left from the thousands or tens of thousands—he'd never been able to determine just how many there'd been. From what he could tell, these were from seven immobile soldiers, probably wounded too much to continue to fight.

One was at what looked to be the old defensive position. Colby took a chance and slipped around it, taking it captive. He tried to get it to move, but while he could sense it trying to respond, nothing happened. It lacked arms it could move, or legs stalks to escape. It couldn't even wriggle its body. From the larger pieces of green chunks around it, Colby thought it had to be one of those that had reached the Marine lines only to be chopped down by the blades.

At least its senses worked. Colby slipped back out, but gave its frame his primary attention. A few Marines were within its sensory range, beyond which was the thick green fog of dead plant bits. A breeze picked up, slowly blowing the fog away and revealing the Marines, like monsters emerging from the schlockiest holovid, as they returned. The sight was impressive, and Colby hoped the surveillance drones that had to be flying overhead were recording this. Images like these convinced young men and women to enlist.

But something was wrong. Some of the Marines were limping, their battlesuits giving uncharacteristic lurches. Marine battlesuits tended to either work or not. They could be blasted to smithereens by heavy kinetics, they could be fried by energy weapons that overcame their shielding, but they didn't tend to get merely damaged. Once the armor or shielding failed, it was usually a catastrophic kill.

As he watched the Marines form up, more and more were in obvious distress. Colby was baffled. He switched among his remaining seven feeds, but the one from the defensive position provided the best view, and that revealed nothing. More and more of the Marines lurched about, and several platoons moved into defensive positions, weapons outboard.

One Marine stopped dead in midstride, then another. Others froze as well. Within minutes a good third of the Marines had become unmoving statues. A battlesuit was effective because it both protected a Marine from fire while allowing the Marine to close with and destroy the enemy. Without maneuverability, it was just a pillbox waiting for the enemy to outmaneuver it. Colby wasn't surprised when first one, then in a rush, Marines were molting, getting out of their suits. Wary

Marines, now armed with the smaller man-packed weapons, took positions by their dead battlesuits, facing outboard, and probably wondering just what the hell had happened. Colby wondered that as well.

The two companies of Marines had won a decisive battle, overcoming a veritable horde of enemy plant soldiers with what might have been a single friendly casualty. Now, after the battle, the Marines had somehow been stripped of their biggest advantage.

The Marines had won the battle, but from what Colby could see, it was a Pyrrhic victory.

Interlude II: A New World, A New Infestation

The Gardener's supply-pod-turned-escape-vessel skimmed across the atmosphere of the mud-red planet, venting velocity and attempting to limit temperature extremes as it descended. The limited sensory details it could access revealed a barren world, one that would take thousands of revolutions of effort and planning to transform into a garden. Robotic vessels appeared to come and go from a single point, a slight deviation from the mud, presumably the destination for the unthinkable, space-faring Meat. As terrifying as that prospect was, it was also the only place to have the living resources needed to restore itself, or to grow the tools needed to protect itself from the Meat.

It adjusted its course and fell from the sky. There was no way to know what technological capabilities this new Meat had mastered, and the Gardener's best course was to act like an insignificant bit of space debris, some remnant that was left from a larger chunk that had all but burned up in reentry. Moments before striking down, its sensors discerned the shapes of artificial structures much like the invading Meat had built within its garden world, but also thousands of vast containers, each easily as large as its former vessel. Several of the containers were open and its sensors detected organic material, much of it similar to the material contaminating the garden it had recently purged.

It could work with that.

At the last instant, the Gardener manipulated mathematical constructs, twisting gravity and velocity. Its pod still crashed, but did not crater the ground or destroy its cargo. Moreover, it had positioned itself near one of the containers. It reviewed its stock, reviewed the plans it had made, and released a plume of tiny seeds high into the air. A portion would enter the container, take root within the material it found there. In less than a rotation of this muddy world this new seeding would yield the Gardener's first wave. The Meat would be stopped.

****

Protocols existed for every contingency, hundreds of thousands of scenarios and situations which had never occurred had nonetheless been modeled and analyzed, extrapolated and resolved. If the Gardener felt any distress, it was less about its situation than the peculiarity of finding itself utilizing such procedures.

Complexities of redundancies defined its people's life view. What point even conceptualizing a venture if one were to begin without all possibilities accounted for? Viewed in such a light, its current predicament was at worst a minor inconvenience.

The initial seeding required only a two-percent success rate. Given sufficient time, even the most arid or acidic environment would yield success. But Meat, regardless of its manifestation, was always short-lived, which in turn meant that time was a limited resource. Fortunately, there was evidence of spillage around the target cargo container to suggest they contained a variety of organic matter, and in such profusion that inspection had resulted in a sample of the cargo escaping. The Gardener's released seeds absorbed the bits of debris and pursued the genetic option that it had activated in them before their dispersal.

Seven purge agents—the same tools it had lately planted by the tens of thousands on its garden world—took form and together advanced on the nearest container, working in concert along an accessible seam. Two pressed immature forward tendrils into that seam, even as the other five dedicated their brief existence to generating and transferring the powerful acids that allowed the initial pair to create microscopic runnels adequate for their pollen, which continued the process. These five withered, but had served their purpose. Complex carbon chains were altered, co-opted, shattered. Cracks radiated from several places along the seam, and just that simply, the two surviving purge agents breached the cargo container. The entire process had taken scant minutes.

The pair hefted the now-desiccated remnants of the other five purge agents that had already gone to seed and tore them into smaller bits, stuffing the pieces through the cracks into the organic matter below, grain of some form, more than adequate for the current need. These seeds fed upon the grain, broke it down, produced a new generation of seeds that in turn consumed still more grain and germinated into more purge agents, hundreds of them. They tore the cargo container apart from the inside. Half moved toward structures that the Meat had erected for their own inscrutable but offensive purposes. The remainder split into smaller groups, each targeting other standalone containers and, further afield, whole stacks of containers, to repeat their genesis. Soon, thousands of leafy agents advanced on the structures, tearing them open. Some entered to attack their contents—absorbing any organics and destroying inorganics, according to their genetics directives—others applied their talents to breaking down the Meat's structures themselves, guided by the directives the Gardener had built into their every fiber.

From the shattered safety of its pod, half-buried in mud and dirt, the Gardener directed its agents with a light touch, *the majority of its focus devoted to ratiocination and the need to incorporate so much novel data into a plan to alert its people.*

It scarcely noted when the remnants of its vessel arrived, delivered like plucked weeds and shattered branches to the far side of the array of cargo containers. In the fullness of time it would grow a new vessel, but that was a future concern and not something it allowed to intrude on its thoughts. Eventually, a more insistent interruption broke its concentration. Several squadrons of Mechs arrived, pulling its focus to their actions as they spawned confusion. With brutal efficiency the Mechs began destroying its purge agents with energy waves. But no, not actual Mech life, these nuisances were more Meat, Meat that had developed technology to mimic the appearance and behavior of Mech. Their presence dictated a more nuanced response than it had built into the genes of its purge agents.

The Gardener had itself changed since arriving upon this world. Even as its agents had begun their work, a dedicated few had returned to it and sacrificed their newly grown bodies, supplying it with more base material. It had built up the ambulatory ganglia that supported its cranium, even as it had expanded the volume of its brain case and coaxed its cortex to expand to fill it, growing its cognitive abilities. As the tech-wearing Meat attacked, it spun off a trio of strategies, any one of which might resolve the conflict at hand.

From its pod's remaining seed bank, it jettisoned a precious few mega seeds, the advanced form of the utilitarian purge agents that could combine and grow to gargantuan proportions for those tasks that required macro rather than micro scales of action.

Next it unleashed a burst of anaerobic symbiotes. A fraction landed upon some of its purge agents and took over a portion of their surface area to generate aerodynamic pollens too small to be seen. These in turn wafted toward the Meat.

And finally, it reached into the dormant communication network that bound its purge agents, taking direct command of the different contingents of them to use them more strategically against the Meat foe.

Such an approach, hasty and multiplicitous, violated the Gardener's training and experience. When designing a world, it would expend vast time determining the one best and true way to accomplish its goal. But contingencies had forced it to invoke other methods. Any one strategy might be required, or two, perhaps all three. But when it was done, the Meat would be destroyed and there would be sufficient resources left for it to select a more purposeful course of action, alert its people to this new danger, and put end to the threat of the Meat.

Part III: Seeds of Doubt

Colby lay in the darkness, his fingertips intertwined in Duke's fur—the only sensory input he had. The last of his plant hosts had been cut off five, ten, fifteen minutes ago. With only his thoughts, it was hard to keep track. It occurred to him that the Marines might opt to destroy the broken ship he arrived in, weighing the advantage gained by eliminating an unknown threat over the loss of alien technology. That possibility slowly grew, like a loose thread unraveling on a sweater, until it came to the fore and took over most of his thoughts. He needed to communicate, to let them know he was in here. But nothing he tried had yet allowed him to contact the Marines, and the troubleshooting worm he'd initiated during the fight had revealed nothing. It should have been simple. His implant should have inserted itself effortlessly into the comms net, but when he reached for the system—and he'd used the comm system on New Mars tens of thousands of times—it was as if nothing was there.

He'd been locked out, and it didn't take much effort to guess who had done it. Vice-Minister Greenstein. The asshole, probably fearing that Colby would have started a rebellion when he was relieved of command, had blocked his implant from the tactical net.

The tiniest of vibrations reached him, pulling his attention away from all competing thoughts. Had it had been real or just his imagination? Then, a few moments later, he felt it again. What did it represent? Was the ship taking off, ready to be shot down, or were the Marines boarding it? Were more of the plant soldiers being harvested inside the ship? Colby didn't know enough to hazard a guess.

"It's OK, Duke," he whispered.

And then, like water in the desert, oh so faintly, he heard voices—*human* voices.

"In here!" he shouted, "In here!" as Duke let out a half-whine, half howl. The talking outside stopped, and he shouted out again, "I'm in here! In the wall!"

Nothing happened for a long minute. His mind swam with images of Marines firing their weapons into the ship's locker, prompting him to keep up a steady stream of pleas to help him.

Light cut the darkness of the locker. Colby squinted, eyes tearing with pain, but nonetheless tried to tilt his head up to see, but the vines crisscrossed his face, leaving only tiny gaps to see through. A Marine peered in, M86 pointed at him.

"What the fuck?" the Marine said.

"I'm Lieutenant General Colby Edson, Marines. Get me out of here!"

The Marine leaned back, passing out of Colby's view, and he said, "Sergeant, you're not going to believe this."

Colby felt a tap on the bottom of his foot, as if poked with the barrel of an M86. A man-packed version of the larger M88, it still fired the same rounds, any of which would be more than enough to end Colby's journey through life.

He caught a glimpse of a second figure. Keeping his voice calm with a huge force of will, he said, "Listen, Sergeant. I'm Lieutenant General Colby Edson, Republic Marines. I need you to get me out of here. I've got vital intel that has to be passed to higher headquarters."

"We don't got no General Edson on New Mars," the sergeant said, distrust plain in his voice.

"I'm retired now. But I'm still a Marine."

Duke chose that moment to whine, and the sergeant jumped back out of view.

"He's got a dog in there with him," someone said.

Colby didn't know if it was Duke or him that convinced the sergeant, but he said, "I'm sending a runner to get the lieutenant, sir. You hang on."

He didn't want to hang on, he wanted to be free. He was tired and hungry and had to get word to someone in charge because it was damn sure that Greenstein hadn't shared the report he'd sent before entering the wormhole. And to top it off, something about the light or maybe his interaction with the Marines was causing the vines to constrict even more. Colby recognized the early warning signs of a panic attack. He had to get out of the locker and out of the grasp of the ship.

"What's your name, Sergeant?"

"Sergeant Prius Mannigan, sir."

"Sergeant Mannigan, I've got to get out of here now. While we're waiting for your lieutenant, can you try and get me out of here?"

The sergeant hesitated, then asked, "What happens if I touch that stuff?"

"I. . . I don't know," he said, suddenly ashamed that he hadn't considered the question before asking. He didn't want to put the sergeant at risk. "Better not touch it, but if you've got a blade, maybe you can try to cut me loose?"

Asking a Marine if they had a blade was like asking them if they breathed.

"Corporal Lin, cover me," the sergeant said to someone out of Colby's sight. "I'm going to try and cut the general out."

The sergeant leaned forward, and a moment later, a searing pain shot up his leg. He screamed and Duke howled.

"Stop, stop!"

"I didn't cut you, sir. I know I didn't," the panicky-sounding sergeant shouted.

"Just don't do it again," Colby snapped, as waves of pain washed through him for a few moments before it diminished to more of an ache. "Let me think."

20/20 hindsight assured him that the vines hadn't just connected him to the plant soldiers, they'd bonded to him as well. He had to figure out a solution that didn't harm the vines. There was no way he'd survive being cut out.

"What's going on, Sergeant Mannigan?" a woman's voice reached him.

"There's some general in there, ma'am."

"And a dog," another voice added.

A new Marine took up position beside the sergeant and peered in. "Who are you, and what the hell are you doing in an enemy ship?"

"I'm Lieutenant General Colby Edson, Republic Marines. How I got here is a long story, and I'd prefer to only tell it once. Who's your commanding officer, Lieutenant?"

Only silence answered him. Colby had run out of patience. He snapped, "I'm not a fucking plant-soldier, in case you haven't noticed!"

"He looks like one, all trussed up like that," someone muttered from beyond his limited line-of-sight.

There was another long pause, then, "Captain Sotherby."

"Your commanding officer, not company commander," he said, struggling to hold back from erupting again. He might be a retired Marine Corps general, but he was trussed up like a New Year's hog on the spit, and this lieutenant had a platoon of armed Marines out there.

"Lieutenant Colonel Manuel Sifuentes, sir," she said grudgingly.

"Manny? Manny Sif?" Colby could have wept with relief. "Get word up to him. Tell him that I know what he did on Harris Reef!"

"Sir?"

"Just tell him who I am, and mention that I know about Harris Reef."

Manuel Sifuentes, of all people. "Manny Sif" had been a company commander for him, back when he was a colonel and the commanding officer of Marine Deployed Reaction Force 33. While at Harris Reef on a liberty call, the young captain. . . well, suffice it to say that events unfolded so that the captain had shown up stark naked at the liberty shuttle, begging the Navy chief for a ride back up to the ship. Colby had listened to the captain's story of woe, took pity on him, and decided that he'd been more of an innocent—well, not completely innocent—victim than a transgressor. He'd covered up for Manny Sif, ensuring nothing official was entered on his record.

The Marines outside the locker spoke in low tones while Colby lay there. At one point, someone muttered, "Just burn the suckers. They'll let go then."

"No one do anything until your CO gets here!" Colby shouted out. The Marines fell silent after that.

It took at least fifteen minutes before Colby heard activity outside. A familiar voice said, "So, just what is going on in this thing?"

Colby could see the lieutenant step back, and a moment later, an older-looking, but still recognizable, Manuel Sifuentes came into his view.

"Who are you?"

"Colby Edson, Manny." The colonel frowned and pulled back just a hair. "MADREF Thirty-Three, Harris Reef, a certain captain and a local young. . ."

"Shit! General Edson! You were shit-ca. . . you retired and went off to be a farmer somewhere. What the hell are you doing here?"

"Yes, I was shit-canned. And I was a farmer on Vasquez, and that's where the boss plant first invaded. I fought them off and took its ship, but as you can see, things kinda went to hell, and I'm stuck in here."

"These aliens attacked Vasquez? Why didn't we hear about that before they landed here?"

"I sent a report up, to Vice-Minister Greenstein."

"Nothing was promulgated. They surprised the shit out of us when they landed. What the hell are they, anyway?"

"I've got some ideas," Colby said, and I need to brief the staff. Who's the CG?"

"Brigadier General U Te, sir."

Well, it could be worse. She was a bit of a brown-noser when she was a battalion commander, but she should listen to reason.

Despite the importance of New Mars, despite the presence of a Marine Sector command, the planet only had a reinforced Marine battalion and the local militia for defense. The civilian officials on New Mars liked having the generals with them, but they feared combat troops that could theoretically take charge, though nothing like that had happened for over four hundred years. But as a result, the Marines were limited to a single combat battalion. That battalion was part of Ninth Division, but the bulk of the division was based on Mongut III, two wormhole jumps away.

"I really need to brief her and her staff, but I can't do it like this. You've got to get me out of here."

"We tried to cut him out, sir, but he screamed as soon as we cut the vines," the sergeant said.

"And the dog cried, too," another voice called out.

"Manny. . . uh, Colonel," he said, "I'm somehow connected to this thing. I feel what's happening to it."

"Are you still, you know. . . are you still, you, sir?" the lieutenant colonel asked, leaning his head into the locker and speaking too softly for his men to hear.

"Yes, I'm still me," Colby said.

I hope I'm still me.

"Sir, Master Sergeant Jelavić comes from a farming family. Maybe he can figure something out?" the lieutenant said.

"Well, hell, it can't hurt to see if he's got any ideas. Good thinking, Lieutenant. Someone get him over here.

"How the hell did they shut down our battlesuits, General?' he asked Colby, turning back to him. "We're down to 17 percent effective. Do you know how they managed that?"

Colby didn't know, but the image of the green mist of atomized plant bodies came unbidden to his mind. Something told him the mist was part of that.

Before he could articulate even that vague thought, Sifuentes held up a hand to silence him with the familiar look of someone listening to an implant.

"Major Lyme, did you get that?" he yelled out to someone out of sight, probably his XO or operations officer. "OK, get the company commanders ready. We need to move. All of you inside this ship, get to your companies now!"

"Manny! What's going on?"

"Sorry, General, you're going to have to stay put for now. I'll send someone back for you when I can."

"Why? What's happening?"

"One of your plants broke into the food containers and is growing out-of-control. We've got to stop it before it gets God knows how big!"

****

Colby was going batshit crazy. He had light now, at least, but he still couldn't move. Wiggling his fingers and toes just didn't count. Duke clearly felt the same way; since the Marines had left she hadn't stopped whining and nothing he could say calmed her. Her discomfort only fueled his own frustration. Manny Sif could have left at least one Marine with him, maybe that farmer master sergeant who could figure out how to free him.

Then he felt a little guilty for feeling put out. Colby had seen the giant plant warriors back on Vasquez. They'd been like some vegetable version of the daikaiju from the Hollybolly remakes of ancient B-movies. And like those movie monsters, these plants had been powerful enough to tear apart a massive launch cannon and they looked pretty unstoppable. With a full Marine division and a couple of cruisers, they'd make short work of the plants, but he wasn't sure how a reinforced battalion, especially one down to 17 percent battlesuits, would fare. He wished he could be out there with them. It hurt to know Marines were marching to danger while he lay there like a piece of cargo. He had to get out of the ship to help in any way he could.

"Hell, Duke. I guess it's up to us, huh girl?"

He'd already tried to push his consciousness to whatever was out there growing, hoping that he could somehow affect it. But there was nothing. When he reached out as he had with the plant soldier he couldn't find anything to connect to. It was as if he was lost in a sea of black cotton that held him tight inside his green prison. Everything beyond the ship's hull was an empty void. At least inside, he had some input. If he looked down, he could see the lump of vines that was Duke, and straight ahead he could see a narrow sector of the ship's bridge. It wasn't much, but it was so much better than the blackness he'd endured before. Without that little bit of light he would be crazy, and probably wondering if Manny and the other Marines had just been a fevered dream.

Inside the ship? I can't sense anything outside, but I can see inside, and what is this thing but just another plant?

He felt a slight jolt of excitement. He'd felt pain when the vines holding him had been cut, which meant they were connected. All he had to do was figure out a way to open than connection, and then maybe he could get the vines to release him.

"But how the hell do I do that?" he said aloud, reverting to his habit of talking things through. "OK, think of it like an enemy comms network, shielded from eavesdropping. How do we break into that? Standard operating procedure would be to use either subterfuge, worm my way in, or a resort to a brute force attack."

Colby had enough respect for the boffins he'd met over the course of his military career to know he didn't have the brain power to hack into a system even if he had a controllable interface. But he did have his implant, and that gave him some pretty impressive power options. It took him a good ten minutes to go through the mental gymnastics required to set up what he wanted. He ran a quick self-check, and it looked like it would work. Maybe.

He hesitated a second before starting it. There was no way to know how the ship would react. It could recognize the attack for what it was and take action to eliminate the source. Colby didn't think getting strangled by vines would be a particularly comfortable way to go. But that was a chance he had to take. Visualizing a big red button, he mentally pressed it.

He didn't feel any different, yet he knew the implant was sending thousands of thrusts at the ship, trying to find a crack in the alien operating system and forcing it wider. Colby tried to focus, ordering the vines to release them, pushing against nothing in hopes that his implant could open, identify, and exploit even the tiniest of portals. It was difficult, though, with Duke whining, but there was nothing he could do about that. The poor dog had reached her limit.

Twice, the vines jerked, giving his heart a jolt as he pictured squeezing the life out of them, but his attempts to control them got nowhere. He was beginning to feel the futility of it all when suddenly, as if picked up by a tsunami, he was carried. . . somewhere? He was inside the ship. Not like his body was inside the locker, but more intimately within the core of it.

Stop! he ordered his implant.

Odd sensations streamed into him, some hybrid of the connection provided by the vines and the efforts of his implant. He reached out tentatively, trying to figure out just what/where he was, trying and rejecting analogies and metaphors until he found one that fit. As best as he could comprehend it he was almost an extension of the ship—or it was an extension of him. He couldn't tell. He focused on the vines, and ordered them to release him. Nothing happened. He could see them, he could almost feel them as they held Duke and him fast, but they wouldn't respond to his commands. Unlike the soldiers, it was as if they couldn't understand what he was ordering them to do.

"Hell, I'm being undone by the stupid ones," he said.

He cast around the ship, hoping there were any mobile plants left. He'd seen plenty of them back on Vasquez, taking readings and scuttling about on plant tasks that looked to have more to do with fieldwork than invasion. It was then he realized that, other than the boss plant, he hadn't seen any mobile plants since he'd been aboard.

"They've got to be somewhere."

Colby started projecting himself through the ship, taking a virtual tour. . . except, it wasn't virtual. Part of him was actually traveling around the broken ship, noting the damage done by the cargo drone and poking into every compartment.

Meanwhile, the rest of him was stuck inside the locker. It felt different than when he was controlling the soldier plants.

He didn't find any of the little, diagnostic plants hiding out, nor anything he could use to free himself. He found one compartment that reeked of potential, if that made sense. Literally, it was as if something pinged his brain about unnamed possibilities when he focused his awareness on that tiny section. But there was nothing there over which he could take control.

When the first search turned up empty, he did it again. Still nada. The only thing that tickled his senses was the small compartment that felt like potential. And then it clicked.

"Seeds!" he said. "They've got to be seeds! What else defines potential for a plant? If I can—" But the ramifications and his own reservations halted his words.

Somewhere outside the ship, Marines were in battle with giant plants. Those plant warriors, not the smaller soldiers, were the problem, not the solution. More of them would only add more to the mess.

Or would they? I could control the other soldiers. What if I can sprout new ones and then use them to fight?

He didn't consider how long it would take to grow new fighters to soldier-size. On Vasquez, it had taken over a day, but if he understood what Manny Sif had said, the daikaiju were growing at an exponential rate. Maybe he could get these to grow that fast, too. A little of Señor Fukimaru's Wonder Grow went a long way back on his farm to increase yield, and there had to be an equivalent here on the ship that could do the same thing.

You might have been a Marine general, but you've been a farmer for the last two years, for goodness' sake. Just figure it out, Edson!

Before he consciously decided to actually germinate the seeds, his mind was questing inside the compartment, and almost immediately, he recognized what had to be a nutrient feed system. He hesitated for only a moment before he tried to trip it. He might not have been able to control the vines holding him, but to his welcome surprise, the nutrient broth started to flow into the mass of seeds.

Almost immediately, the seeds, well, *stirred*, as if waking up. He nervously monitored them, hoping he hadn't a mistake. He might be compounding his initial sin of letting the plants onto New Mars.

Within a minute, the seeds began to sprout, tiny green tendrils reaching out. Colby tried to reach them, but other than an itch in his mind that he couldn't scratch, he didn't feel a connection.

Maybe they don't have a developed enough whatever-they-had-for-a-brain yet.

There had to be thousands of the seeds. As the green tendrils grew larger, longer, the new sprouts used them to start pulling themselves out of their separate bins and onto the deck. Within five minutes, five-centimeter-tall "starts," to use farming terminology, were crawling out of the compartment and invading the rest of the ship.

Colby couldn't see any of them yet. His very limited field of vision was a little above waist height and only with a few degrees of arc. He wasn't sure, for that matter, just how he was "seeing" any of this. He knew it was through the ship itself somehow, but he didn't have a clue how that worked. But he could see it, and that was all that mattered for now.

More of the starts poured out of the compartment. To Colby's surprise, two of the immature plants started to bond to each other. For a moment it seemed they were fighting, like fetal sharks inside their mother's womb, but then they *merged*, forming a single, larger plant. The newly formed double plant then sought two more merged plants, and within a minute, had combined into a single, still larger plant.

The top of something green passed into Colby's vision for a second and then was gone. A moment later, another appeared as the plants—he couldn't call them starts any longer—continued their combinatorial dance.

Two leafy arms reached up into the locker, gained purchase and pulled the body of a plant up to join him.

"Stop, stop!" he yelled, focusing his effort.

The plant barely hesitated. It pulled itself further into the locker, climbing the wall somehow, not touching him yet. Another followed it, then a third. Duke started snarling, but the plant paid no attention to the dog. Colby attempted to struggle, remembering how his neighbors, the Gustavsons, had been killed by the plant soldiers, how they had attacked him on the farm and in Blair de Staffney Station. He didn't want to die trussed up like this. Striving to remain calm, he sent out waves of orders for the plants to leave the locker. He could feel them, better than when they were sprouts and starts, but he still couldn't control them.

The first plant reached out to touch one of the vines holding his leg. That vine went limp, almost swooned. It released Colby and started to merge with the larger plant. Other plants reached in, tendrils questing one by one for the vines that imprisoned him, and those vines released him as well. When one of the plants encircled his leg with a supple branch of an arm, Colby tried to jerk back, afraid that somehow, he'd be absorbed, too, but as if tasting him and finding him unworthy, the arm jerked back.

The locker filled with writhing plants, their number decreasing as they grew from absorbing vine after vine. Duke started barking and wriggling beside him as each gripping vine let go in turn. Colby felt a final vine across his chest fall away. He sat up, pushing at the plants in his excitement to be free. With no more vines, they slid out of the locker, presumably to seek more fodder for mergers.

Duke didn't care why they were gone—she bolted from the locker with a yelp and out into the mass of smaller plants on the deck of the ship. She started jumping and spinning, crashing into them as she exulted in being free. The plants she knocked over ignored her antics and simply picked themselves back up.

They looked identical to the ones that had invaded Vasquez, but they acted in a different manner.

Colby had been filling in a picture of the alien species, and he was pretty sure that the boss plant controlled the others. If so, then was it possible that they had to be programmed or ordered to attack humans? Which meant that these plants, of which the boss had no knowledge, hadn't received such orders yet. Did that mean he had an opportunity to program them? The larger they got, the more Colby began experiencing whispers of plant-thought, as if their brains were only now beginning to reach some critical mass needed to be controlled.

But that still left the question of the plant boss. Colby had no doubt that cabbage-head was alive and out there, controlling whatever giant plant warriors were now attacking the Marines. Would the boss show up here and take over these plants? Colby vowed not to let that happen. Now he just had to figure out how to back up promises with deeds.

Before he could do that, though, he had to get out of the ship. More than a dozen of the plants had grown to his chest-level in height. A few seemed to be merging with the ship itself. He'd been able to control the plant soldiers when they were attacking the factory outside while he was trapped in the ship, then by the symmetric property of equality, he should be able to control those on the ship from outside of it.

This wasn't algebra, he knew, but he really *had* to get off the ship. Claustrophobia had him on the edge of a panic attack that he couldn't currently afford.

"Duke! Let's go, girl," he shouted.

She barked what he assumed to be her assent. He started pushing his way through the unresisting plants towards the ship's hatch, she darted under them, weaving her way between their stalks.

The aft end of the ship had been heavily damaged by the cargo drone's arms, and the ship had created temporary patches to stop the flow of air even after Colby had climbed into the locker. He hadn't seen them before, more worried about breathing than in admiring a feat of biological engineering. As he watched, the obvious patches were fading. All around him plants were reaching up and being absorbed into the bulkhead, like so much vegetable wall putty.

"Shit!" he said, wondering what was happening to the hatch itself. It had been a tight fit before just to get through it into the ship—he hoped it was still there. He couldn't see it through the mob of plants pressing themselves against that part of the wall. He couldn't even see Duke any more, and only knew her location when he she gave another yelp. Plants flew left and right and as Colby ducked down, he could see his dog shoving plants out of her way as she pushed her way to the open hatch. His heart dropped as he saw it already closing.

"Wait, Duke!" he shouted, scrabbling forward on his hands and knees, but Duke, seeing sunshine, was not waiting for anything.

She darted ahead and through the opening. Her passage through spurred the sphincter-like hatch to begin closing faster. With a burst of speed, Colby darted forward, following Duke's example and sending plants flying. He could see the dog on the outside as she stopped and looked back at him, barking furiously.

"I'm coming, girl!" he shouted, crawling as fast as he could, but in the best Hollybolly tradition, the opening kept shrinking, and in this case the hero didn't make it. By the time he reached it, the opening wouldn't have even accommodated a child. He stuck his hand through the hole, desperate to force it back open, but he couldn't even slow it down. Duke licked his hand before he had to jerk it back for fear of being trapped—or worse, losing his arm.

"Son-of-a-bitch!" he yelled in frustration, kicking out and scattering more of the smaller plants.

Even among the plants from which he had torn limbs, they all ignored him. But that didn't mean they wouldn't notice him if he started taking them all on. He leaned back against the bulkhead, letting his emotions drain away until his mind felt numb.

Only, it wasn't really numb. There was an incessant buzzing that he'd at first thought an actual sound before realizing his ears weren't hearing any of it. He opened his mind, staring at one of the merged plants, this one about a meter-and-a-half tall. He imagined himself enveloping it, as he had with the plant soldiers in the factory, and he told it to stop.

It did.

Evidently, the plants had to grow large enough, or merge with enough others before their neural network could pick up commands.

"Open the hatch!" he ordered it.

Just as with the plant soldiers, he doubted they understood his words per se, responding instead to the underlying intention. Whatever the mechanism, the plant moved to the correct spot along the bulkhead and pressed up against it.

And, of course, given his luck, nothing happened. The hatch did not reappear, and the bulkhead remained as featureless as before. Colby left the plant mindlessly striving to open a hole in the hull of the ship and shifted his attention deeper into the ship itself. He was just as attuned to the vessel as the individual plants, but he couldn't control it. He could sense the capability just out of reach, but even with his interface, he lacked some critical piece that would allow him that connection.

He could feel the ship growing all around him, changing in response to the plants he'd unleashed from seeds. More and more plants melded into the walls of the ship, emerging and continuing to grow on the outside, branches extending across the ground in all directions even as it enveloped the ship itself in ropy vines reminiscent of the ones that had held him prisoner. Following some blueprint he couldn't fathom the ship began to transform. Finally only a few plants remained inside the ship's compartment and these spaced themselves at even intervals from one another and began to sprout heavy branches, filling up more and more of the available space.

The process wasn't entirely comfortable. Colby felt as if he had gas, his stomach spasming as he explored the ship through his connection. It seemed as if the ship was no longer the central entity, as if the plants kept merging into a larger and larger form, one that had opted to incorporate the ship into itself. Somewhere in the process it had stopped being a ship that he was using to grow plants in.

If it isn't the ship, but another plant, can I control that?

He reached out, the connection familiar and different but tenuous, like trying to understand Italian when all you spoke was Spanish. Before he could try to exert control, the ship lurched, throwing Colby backwards across the deck.

Those branches were legs! This thing has become one of the giant plant monsters!

Colby reached out to the plant itself, ignoring the capsule that was the ship, and he let his awareness flow into it. There was no disorientation as there had initially been with the plant soldiers. This was even more familiar than slipping into an old pair of shoes that knew his feet from long use. He'd done this a thousand times before, in a Republic Marine Corps battlesuit. It didn't matter if a giant plant was really the same, or if his implant was translating the process into something his mind could comprehend. Those kinds of questions could wait until later. What mattered now was that he felt more in control than he'd been since leaving Vasquez. A few tentative impulses flickered over him, expressing a vague concern, or possibly opposition from the plant warrior around him, but it took no effort for Colby to squash them.

With a simple mental flick, he was aware of what was outside of him. He was aware of a small golden dog biting a tiny corner of his leg. He was aware of combat in the distance, of Marines, almost all on foot, being attacked by thousands of suicidal plant soldiers. He was aware of three more giants much larger than the pair that had torn apart the launch cannon back on Vasquez. These plant warriors ignored the puny attempts by humans to stop them as they destroyed what he recognized as the governmental administration complex.

"Sorry Duke," he said as he stepped forward, careful not to accidentally fling the tiny dog aside. "Looks like I'm getting into the shit after all."

****

Like a Norse Jötunn emerging from the earth, Colby stood up, towering over the shattered factories and cargo containers. It should have felt odd, but it didn't. Perspective aside, the metaphor held. This was no different than donning a battlesuit. Muscle and nervous memory took over, and he strode forward. He didn't have to "think" each tree-like leg in turn, no more so than he would to take a normal stroll—he wanted to move forward, and the legs took over.

Despite his ability to control the giant plant, he had not been absorbed into it. He may have expanded his sense of self, but the core of who he was resided in the human body that slumped on the deck of what had been the alien ship. That body rolled at each lurching step. Much more of that and he'd awaken to a mass of bruises when all was done. He sent out a tentative command, and this time, the bulkheads of the ship obeyed, sending out several tendrils that delicately wrapped around his body, like the harness inside a battlesuit. With his physical body secure, he turned his attention back to the outside world. The process had taken only seconds.

There were small eddies of green mist dotting the ground, like puddles after a rain. They stirred as he stepped into them, rising in swirls around his legs, attaching thousands of tiny potential-plants to him. He could feel the life force they contained, life force that translated into brute power. Colby knew without knowing how that it was power he could tap.

His perception of distance skewed as he settled into his new height. Up ahead he could see the tops of three giant plants—*daikaiju*, he thought, recalling the term once more. They rampaged in what he knew to be Christiaan Huygens City, the capital of the planet. He didn't have to see them, though, to know where to go. He could *feel* them, their presence shined like a beacon in his mind, the distance to them defined in terms of the number of strides he'd need to reach them. It didn't have to make sense, it just was.

Reflexes honed by endless hours in a battlesuit had him reaching through his implant to call up a targeting routine with the intention of painting the three giants and assigning a series of missiles to each once he locked on. His implant pinged back empty, unable to mesh with the software or access the requested armament because of course he wasn't actually in his familiar battlesuit. The analogy only went so far. Colby would have to carry the battle to his foe the old fashioned way. Still, missiles would have been nice.

He crushed immobile battlesuits as he strode along. He wasn't trying to stomp on them, but there wasn't much open space to place his huge feet, not if he wanted to take the most direct route and reach the fight ahead. He could sense firing, he could sense the battle, but couldn't hear the sounds of the conflict. He briefly wondered if the plants even had hearing in the way that humans did. It didn't matter. Whatever sensory capability came with his daikaiju was more than adequate to understand what was going on.

With his mind wandering as to whether he could hear or not, he almost crushed a pocket of a dozen Marines who were being attacked by smaller plant soldiers. The Marines turned to face him, firing their puny weapons which were about as annoying as gnats to him—less annoying, in fact. Colby paused for a moment, taking the time to sweep a huge hand through the attacking plant soldiers, knocking them down like ten-pins. He grasped a handful as he resumed walking and tried to push them into his thigh, to absorb them. It didn't work, so he let the mangled bodies fall to the ground as they released more spores.

The fighting ahead was getting heavier, and Colby tried to break into a run. The result was almost comical. He stumbled, almost fell, as he became aware that he possessed a multitude of arms because he windmilled them wildly to keep his balance. Whatever else the daikaiju were, they were not built to be runners. He went back to walking, marginally increased his speed, and had to be satisfied with that.

His sense of time had turned fuzzy as well. In something more than five minutes but less than ten, he entered the city. Marines in battlesuits were attacking the three daikaiju with heavy weapons, but their massive bodies seemed to simply absorb what was fired at them. Which isn't to say they didn't notice. One of the three picked up a huge chunk of what had been part of the planetary administrative building and flung it at the Marines. Several battle-suited Marines were knocked out of the fight.

As he approached, some of the remaining Marines fired at him. Their missiles and heavy rounds were beyond gnat-annoying, but not by much. Colby would rather they not fire at him, but he could bear it. Nukes might be another matter. He knew the militia had them, but as long as the city still functioned, and as long as there were humans still alive in it, he doubted the clearance to deploy them would be given. Which was just as well—he didn't want to test his new body against that kind of destructive power.

Not my new body, he told himself. *I'm still me. This is just a huge, organic battlesuit.*

He wasn't quite sure what he was going to do as he strode down Morrison Way and approached the administration building. There were three giant plant warriors there working their way through the huge building. It wasn't until he entered the square, where the Victory Fountain lay in rubble, water shooting into the air, that he realized he was *looking down* at the other three. He didn't tower over them, but he was taller. Looking down at the branches that served as arms, he realized that he out-massed them, too. Together, they were three to his one, so combined, they out-massed him, but he was larger—and hopefully more powerful—than any single one of them.

A missile streaked out and hit Colby low in his torso.

Hell, guys! Stop it! he thought, turning around to face them.

He didn't have any vocal chords, nor any way to make a sound, however. He swung his many arms as if waving off a troop carrier landing, but far from communicating his desires it just triggered two more missiles. There wasn't much he could do about them, and it was only an annoyance—even if they did hurt—so he swung back to the other three diakaiju.

As if sensing him, two of them parted a few steps, giving him room to join in the mayhem. He took advantage of that, getting closer before he sent out a focused metal command for the one on his left to stop.

It didn't.

He tried again, but the giant plant didn't even hesitate. Colby didn't think he'd even penetrated the giant—it was as if there was something blocking him, like a shield. It was as if they were on different frequencies—or something more powerful was in control.

Where is the boss plant? Colby asked himself, turning around to scan the city. Was it aware that he'd taken control of some of its plant soldiers earlier, and had it found a way to block him?

He didn't expect to actually see it, Life had never come at him so easily. Besides, the damn thing could be anywhere. But on the off chance that it was there and within range of being crushed by a well-placed massive foot he'd had to look.

There was nothing left for him to do. With a mental sigh, he reached from behind the nearest giant and wrapped it up with his arms. When he had it thoroughly entwined in his grip, Colby lifted it off its feet. The giant squirmed in his grasp. It was ungodly strong, but Colby was stronger, and without its feet to brace it, it had no leverage. It grasped at him, pulling, desperate to grapple. Colby lost a few minor arms in the attempt. He braced himself, expecting to go into shock as he felt limbs being torn from his body, but his connection ignored that—too human—reaction. After all, it wasn't like he didn't have plenty of limbs to spare, so the loss of a few was really inconsequential.

The realization was both disconcerting and liberating. He shifted the daikaiju in his grip, and began swinging it like a baseball bat, beating it against the side of the half-demolished building. Bits of marble, granite, and plasticrete broke off—along with larger bits of green plant matter. Chunks of plant flew in all directions as Colby swung again and again, effectively smashing the plant to bits. Still, the arms grabbed at him, even when half of the plant was spread all over the building and into the square. He kept swinging and only stopped when his opponent finally went limp.

He dropped the broken remnants and turned to face the other two, who had paused in their own rampage. They didn't have eyes, but there was no doubt that they were "looking at him."

Getting orders from above, huh?

As one, they moved forward to engage him, and Colby stepped back into the square. He might be bigger than either of them, but two-to-one were not great odds. He needed room to maneuver. If they managed to close with him together he wouldn't stand a chance.

As he backed away one thing immediately registered. They bumped each other in their single-minded determination to rend him into his own green mist. They shared an objective but were not working as a team, and that sparked the beginnings of a plan. Two could defeat one as a team in almost every situation but only when working in tandem. A savvy fighter could turn their inability to work as a team into an advantage.

Colby was a savvy fighter, courtesy of the Marine Corps Martial Arts Program. All those hours of pain, all those hours where Master Sergeant Burke Dorcas tortured him within a centimeter of his life, came flooding back to him. All those bouts fighting two other Marines at the same time—which almost always ended up with him getting the shit kicked out of him—had imbedded muscle memory that took over, even after all these years, even applied to a giant plant body that he happened to be wearing.

He backed up, leading them out of the ruined building, and just as they reached what had once been the Grand Rotunda, he feinted to the right. Both of his opponents wheeled to cut him off, which was just what Colby wanted. He pivoted on one leg, delivering what had to be the most powerful spinning back kick in the history of the human race. It connected low on the closer giant, sending it backward into the second, tangling them both up for long enough for him to step in and deliver a stomp with all of the kilotons of force he could generate. A chunk of the nearer daikaiju turned into mush. Colby tried to take advantage of the situation to deliver another stomp, but this time, as his foot hit, the other plant warrior managed to snake an arm around its companion and snag Colby's foot as he tried to withdraw. He jerked back and almost toppled, hopping away. He couldn't afford a fall here; it would be a mortal error. It was only because the other two were tangled up together that he was able to retreat back into the square and stabilize himself.

By that time, the other two had untangled themselves and squared off against him again. The first one leaked greenish fluid from two pulverized areas on its trunk. It was still in the fight however, showing no signs of distress as it advanced on Colby into the square.

There was a small explosion against one of the giant's crushed areas, as a Marine tried to take advantage of the situation. The wounded plant didn't flinch, and the Marine fire died off.

Colby had to keep maneuvering, he had to position the other two so they'd continue to get in each other's way. Most of all, he couldn't risk getting tangled up with both of them a second time. If he was caught, he was a dead man (plant).

He dredged up every single trick he remembered from his MCMAP training—and then added in some from pure street brawling for good measure. At one point, he ripped a cerrosteel support beam out of a ruined building and started swinging it around like a madman, raining blows on the other two, sending plant bits flying. It was gratifying but not all that effective, and it cost him an arm when he got too cocky and one of his opponents latched on and yanked back.

He darted in with kicks and blows, trying to hit and retreat before they could react. More often than not, his greatest opportunities came when the other two got in each other's way. The first one, the one he'd stomped, was slowly being broken, blow by blow. One leg, leaking a green ichor, buckled. Colby feinted, and the other tripped over its comrade in its eagerness to get at him. Colby had been waiting for this moment, and he grabbed the fifteen-meter-tall statue of Admiral of the Navy Fergusson Bianci, which had graced the square for centuries. He ripped it off its granite foundation, confident the admiral would approve of his plan. Spinning it around as if it were made of paper-mâché, he lunged forward and drove it into the base of what Colby thought of the giant's neck, pushing the admiral's upraised arm through the plant with enough momentum to both knock his foe over and drive the statue's arm into the ground.

It spasmed, reaching for the statue with a trio of limbs, but its power was gone. It wasn't dead, but it was out of the fight, for the time being at least.

The second giant closed with him before Colby could recover, but the time for running was over. Colby was hurt, missing minor arms and a chunk of one massive thigh, but so was the remaining giant. Now was the time to take on his opponent and let mass carry the day.

Mass nearly wasn't enough. Evidently, giant plant warriors had their own hand-to-hand combat techniques, and when they weren't getting into each other's way, these could be very effective indeed. They grappled like titans and crashed to the ground with a force that threatened to topple the surrounding buildings. Colby got on top of the other giant, which should have been a huge advantage but he somehow found himself slowly being crushed as a dozen arms wrapped around his torso and all but two of his own arms and grinding them to splinters. His connection flickered and he knew he didn't have long. With his remaining arms he grasped the other giant's nominal head and started pounding it into the stone slabs that made up the square. This was going to be a race to see who could remain conscious the longest. Colby sensed he had only seconds left when the other plant stopped applying pressure, its body limp. He'd won, but barely.

Never, ever underestimate your opponent, Edson!

He'd managed to take out the first daikaiju by using his brains and training, but assuming that might made right, he allowed the fight to be controlled by his opponent—that mistake almost cost him his life.

Colby got to his knees and slowly stood up. The plant beneath him was dead, green mist already forming. Behind him, the other giant was still alive weakly pulling at Admiral Bianci. There was no way he was going to give it a chance to recover. Crossing over to the impaled giant, Colby pushed one of his smaller hands into the creature's wound and imagined reaching through his fingers into fallen plant, questing for control. He'd been blocked before, but whether from the physical contact or its weakened state he felt a flicker of contact. Even as he tried to exploit it he could feel new walls being erected, batting aside his commands for the daikaiju to quit, give up, surrender.

Let's see how far we can push the whole battlesuit analogy.

He cleared his mind, imagined the heads up display of his battlesuit and pictured the emergency molt button. As he pressed it, he willed the logical sequence of events into his opponent. A sequence that, even if that damn boss plant cabbage head was calling the shots, it would never see coming.

With a spasmodic jerk the plant warrior went completely rigid. An instant later wisps of green mist drifted free from all over its body.

"Elvis has left the building," Colby said to himself. He was three-for-three and the enemy had been defeated. He let out a huge mental sigh. . . as a missile slammed into his gut.

Oh, come on, guys!

He already ached from his to-the-death wrestling match, and this missile hurt. He didn't know how many more he could absorb, but he certainly couldn't attack the Marines to get them to quit.

"C'mon, Edson, figure out how to show these people you're on their side before they bring out the big guns and you're taken down by friendly fire."

He was overthinking it, thinking, in fact, like a general. That was the problem; the Marines firing on him weren't generals. He had to give them something they'd understand, right down to the greenest private.

Only one thing fit the bill. Colby drew himself to his best drill field position of attention, held it for a count of five before he very deliberately moved into a position of parade rest, then froze. A few rounds hit him, then they petered out.

He waited like that, five, ten, who knows how many minutes. Finally, there was motion at the far end of the square. Thirty Marines appeared behind a mobile artillery piece, the 155 mm gun aimed right at him. He recognized one of the Marines, to his relief.

Slowly, so as not to startle the Marines into firing, he came back to a position of attention and using only a single arm rendered the best salute he could given he was working with a massive tree branch.

He couldn't hear anything, but he could sense Lieutenant Colonel Manuel Sifuentes ask, "General Edson?"

With as much grace as he could manage, Colby cut away the salute and nodded his giant, leafy head.

****

Colby took a sip of the coffee, savoring it. Duke lay on her back at his feet, sound asleep. He still hadn't processed what had happened—he was aware of everything, but he wasn't quite sure how to analyze things, and he couldn't bring himself to discuss things with Manny Sif. While only a lieutenant colonel, Manny was the de facto head of the government on New Mars, the second most important planet in human space.

The administrative building had been destroyed, and all the civilian staff as well as General U Te, had been killed in the attack. After Manny had sent a full report through the wormhole, the response from Earth had been brief and clear. He'd been ordered to implement martial law, with himself in charge, until someone could come to relieve him.

Colby had sent off his report as well, but he was glad that this time there was corroboration. A certain vice-minister couldn't accuse him of inventing an emergency as a way to worm himself back onto active duty.

The surviving Marines were congratulating themselves on their victory. At Colby's suggestion (retired, he couldn't give orders, only suggest, but taking out the trio of daikaiju had earned him their respect), they had burned the three giant and smaller soldier bodies. The regular soldiers had surprisingly collapsed when the giants had been defeated, and Manny Sif thought they were related.

Colby wasn't so sure. Maybe because he'd spent so much time connected to the plants, he was attuned to them. He could swear he'd felt another presence out there, operating beneath the level of his own connection. He was sure it was the boss plant. If he was right, then a far more likely explanation was that after losing the three giants, the plant boss had cut its losses and bugged out, all the better to prepare for another effort.

There certainly was enough raw material for another plant army. There hadn't been any way to collect up all the spores that had been released when the plants died. Manny Sif was sure they'd achieved victory, and Colby didn't think the brass back on Earth understood the gravity of the situation. From their perspective, a single battalion had defeated these aliens, so how could they be a threat to all of humanity?

A follow-up message from Earth included orders to seal off the wormhole to Vasquez, but that had to be put on hold, at least temporarily until a rescue party could go back and rescue Topeka and Riordan and anyone else who might have survived.

Colby saw no point in sealing off the wormhole after the rescue party returned. It would be like closing the barn door after the horses escaped. The plant boss was somewhere on New Mars, and it would be plotting—and maybe communicating with wherever its kind called home.

In a way, he felt sorry for it. He didn't want to admit it, but he'd been one of them, in a way. Maybe it was Stockholm Syndrome, or maybe he just had some deeper insight that had seeped into him, but all the death and destruction hadn't had a malevolent feel to it, any more than when he had dusted his crops on Vasquez for weeds. Was all the death and destruction just a terrible mistake? If they could just communicate, might it be possible to make peace with the plants?

Oh, come on, Edson. Next you'll be singing Kumbaya.

This wasn't over, not by a long shot, and the risk was still unimaginable.

At his feet, Duke whined, deep within a dog dream, one that Colby could guess.

"Yes, you know girl, don't you? We've got to find that boss plant."

END OF BOOK TWO

Book 3
BITTER HARVEST

Part I: Weeds Amidst the Rubble

Duke whined as Colby stood at the apron, watching the shuttle come in for a landing. The dog had been glued to him since the end of the battle.

"It's OK, girl," he said. "They're the good guys."

Lieutenant Colonel Manuel Sifuentes, Colby's former protégé and the senior active duty Marine left on New Mars, had been trying to organize what remained of the planet's only major city in the aftermath of the battle with the plant soldiers, and the last thing he needed was to worry about the contact team from Earth. Without a real job, Colby had volunteered to meet them. As a retired lieutenant general, he'd had plenty of practice dealing with bureaucrats while still on active duty, and if this could free up Sifuentes, then Colby was happy to help.

No, not "happy." "Willing" would be a better description.

He patted his front pocket where he'd put the list. Government bureaucrats could be—and usually were—a pain in the ass, but they could also get things done. He and Sifuentes had come up with a prioritized list to fix the mess that New Mars had become. The list was not all-inclusive, just what they needed to address the immediate concerns. He had no idea who was on the shuttle, but he was going to give whoever it was the list and get them going on it. Like most bureaucrats, they'd have their own ideas and priorities, no doubt conceived without a proper understanding of the situation here on the ground; Colby's task was to delay or possibly derail their objectives and get the things on his list done right away, even if he had to beg or browbeat them into it.

The shuttle slowly landed, kicking up dust that still had a tinge of green. During the heat of the battle with the plant army, a green mist, created from the bodies of dead plants, had risen, coating everything. Now, a day later, most of it had disappeared. If it were not for the utter destruction of the city, he could have thought that all of the fighting had been a dream. Almost all traces of the plant soldiers themselves were gone.

The shuttle door opened, and the steps unfolded. First to debark were two Capital Guards who rushed down, then took up positions at the bottom of the steps, facing inboard.

Colby kept his face neutral. Like all Marines, he had a very low opinion of the SUTAs (Sticks-Up-The-Ass). They were wannabees, peacocks in fancy uniforms who strutted and pranced, chests puffed out as they reveled in their self-importance. Marines tended to ignore them, but their presence always meant that someone high on the food chain was around.

Someone aboard the shuttle was powerful enough to rate their own praetorian guard, and that changed the equation a bit. He wasn't going to be able to browbeat them into getting his list filled. Colby had lots of experience dealing with the type, and usually the best course of action was to convince the bigwig that whatever Colby wanted had been what they wanted in the first place.

He plastered a smile on his face and thought about skimming the list of likely high-ranking politicians who might be arriving, but his implant had been offline since the battle with the plant daikaiju. His patience, like his smile, was manufactured, but sufficient as he waited to see who had decided to make a personal appearance on the scene. Whoever it was, Colby would just have to deal with them.

An underling, bright and eager, popped her head out of the shuttles hatch, spotted Colby, and ducked back inside. His smile faded just a bit, and he had to force it back to full wattage.

Many of the high and mighty were sticklers for protocol. The fact that there were two capital guards standing at attention at the bottom of the steps meant that whoever was in the shuttle was high-ranking, and that they expected to be met by the appropriate party, not a scruffy-looking farmer and his dog. If he was still on active duty and in full uniform, with an honor guard behind him, that would have satisfied any visiting dignitary, but not as he was now.

He expected an underling to come out first to see who he was and if he was befitting of receiving the head of this group. This nonsense was just wasting time while his list burned a hole in his pocket. He was tempted to march up to the shuttle and announce himself. Even retired, a lieutenant general still carried some weight, and maybe throwing his around wouldn't be such a bad thing.

He'd just taken a step forward when two more guards appeared, stopping at the top of the steps, then turned inboard.

Colby raised his eyebrows in surprise. Maybe this was going to work out after all. Blinded by his own prejudices, he might have judged too soon. Not everyone who was serving at the top levels was an asshole, and if they were willing to come out to meet someone who looked as common as he did now. . .

Colby's optimistic spin reverted to his original judgement of "asshole" as a familiar face appeared at the shuttle's hatch.

Vice-Minister Asahi Greenstein took a moment to look over the wrecked landscape, before settling his gaze on Colby, a half-smile on his face.

This was the corrupt piece of crap who'd ruined Colby's career. All the rage and hatred that Colby thought he'd worked through during his time spent farming on Vasquez surged in him, as fresh as if everything had happened just yesterday.

He would have expected literally anyone else, from the lowest government flack to the commander in chief, anyone besides the vice-minister. The man rarely left the confines of the capital complex on Earth. He was not a "field guy."

But, in a way, this made sense. Colby had sent a report to the vice-minister from Vasquez, so Greenstein would have been among the first to know that humanity had been invaded by an alien species. He'd have had a jump on his rivals, and in the never-ending game of state, that could have huge benefits down the road. That big an opportunity for self-advancement could have been enough to get Greenstein out from behind his desk and into a war zone.

Colby hated the man, but he could still use him. The vice-minister certainly had the heft to get everything on his list filled and then some.

His face ached with the smile he'd plastered on as he watched the man walk down the steps, trailed by the top two guards. As soon as he stepped foot on the ground, the bottom two SUTAs performed an immaculate facing movement in unison, stepping off to precede Greenstein as the five walked up to him.

"Vice-Minister Greenstein, it is good to see you here," Colby said, hand outstretched.

The vice-minister looked at Colby's hand as if it were a rotten piece of meat, then said, "Mister Edson, I am surprised to see you here. Most criminals flee the site of their crimes."

"Excuse me?" Colby asked as his smile slid from his face, replaced by an expression of confusion, his hand still outstretched.

"I might be surprised, but I am grateful. It saves me the trouble of searching for you." He turned to one of the four expressionless SUTAs and said, "Guard Captain Heuhn, arrest this man."

****

Colby ran his tongue over his lip. It was puffy, and he could taste the coppery tang of his blood. The guards had been both brutal and efficient, overwhelming him before he'd had a chance to adequately defend himself. Four-against-one odds had certainly worked against him as well.

He'd gotten in a few shots, and he was pretty sure Duke had bitten one of them, but he'd borne the brunt of the fight, and now, hands cuffed behind him, his body was protesting. At least Duke had gotten away. He hoped she was OK, but if he found out they'd hurt her, there would be hell to pay.

Not that you can do much about it, Edson, locked in this room. They hold all the cards.

He still didn't know why he'd been arrested. Greenstein had beamed while his guards took Colby down, a look of eager anticipation in his eyes. The vice-minister had enjoyed it, like some well rehearsed fantasy, Colby realized.

Two of the guards handcuffed and laid Colby on the deck while the other pair went to find a "jail cell," as the vice-minister told them. Three civilians came out of the shuttle and stood glancing down at Colby, staring at him as if he was a rabid dog. He didn't give them the pleasure of reacting in the least.

Unless there were more civilians in the shuttle, this was a very small contact team to start the recovery ops. Something wasn't adding up, and not just the fact that he'd been arrested. He just couldn't figure out what was going on.

After a long half-hour, the two guards came back with a report of a suitable room. Greenstein waved them off and returned to the shuttle, followed by his three minions.

"You gonna walk?" the guard captain had asked, at least giving him the choice.

What had the vice-minister called him? Heuhn? Maybe he wasn't a total peacock after all.

They led him several blocks through the ruined city to the remains of a small, one-story building. The front was smashed, but the back was still intact. They took him to a good-sized room and sat him down in a chair, hands behind his back.

The four left him in the room, but Colby wasn't naive enough to think he was really alone. He tested his cuffs, more because it was expected of him than in hopes he could break free, then settled in to wait.

He drifted off to sleep, so he wasn't sure how much time had elapsed when a guard opened the door and the vice-minister entered.

The guard exited the room and closed the door behind Greenstein, leaving Colby alone with him. The vice-minister pulled up a chair in front of Colby, turned it around, then sat on it, legs straddling the back and arms crossed over the top.

"You really screwed up, Mister Edson."

Colby didn't say a word. The vice-minister was trying to get a rise out of him, calling him "mister" instead of "general."

Normally, Colby would have reacted and corrected him, but there was nothing to be gained by it given the situation. Colby recognized it for what it was: nothing but pettiness on the vice-minister's part.

"Did you really think you could conspire against humanity?" the vice-minister asked. "And you being an ex-Marine at that. I'm shocked."

Greenstein was playing a game, and Colby remained silent, waiting to see where the man was going.

"I've been trying to figure out what you hoped to gain by starting a war with an alien species. At first, I thought it might simply be anger at how your life has turned out. But then, traitor though you are, you've always had ulterior motives. So, I wondered. Maybe an investigation into your financial holdings would reveal something?"

Really? I don't have enough to my name to cover the cost of next year's seeds.

"We finally make first contact, and you instigate a war. Panic ensues, and certain stocks skyrocket. Am I warm?"

Colby said nothing.

"Oh, I've got my investigators working on it. They are very good, Mr. Edson, and they will find what whatever I tell them to."

Shit. Yeah, I'm sure they will.

"You know, there's a record of my report to you from Vasquez," Colby said, unable to keep quiet any longer.

"Oh, you mean this one?" The vice-minister pulled out his compad and looked at it. "It says here that you are demanding two-million credits for some 'vital' information."

"That's not what I wrote and you know it."

"But that's what's written here, Mr. Edson."

And it probably was, Colby knew. It would be nothing for his team to change the message.

"You're not the only one to see the real one I sent."

"Oh, you mean dear Erin? Yes, she saw it, but she's had a medical emergency. Stroke, you know. She's in the hospital now, and it's touch-and-go, poor thing."

You son-of-a-bitch. If my implant was online I'd be beaming this entire conversation far and wide.

And with that thought, all the pieces clicked into place. Why the vice-minister was on the shuttle, why he'd come before anyone else. Why his implant was offline, for that matter. He hadn't believed Colby's message, and because of that, New Mars had been devastated. His negligence had led to the loss of thousands of lives. Greestein was covering his ass!

"Lieutenant Colonel Sifuentes sent a report out, too. And you can't do anything about that."

"And why would I?" the vice-minister said, his tone oozing corruption. "The colonel and his Marines fought bravely after you smuggled the plant army to New Mars, wrecking your carefully laid plans to take over the planet and all its vital manufacturing."

"So, what is it, Greenstein? I'm manipulating stocks or conquering planets? You're just throwing shit up against the wall to see what sticks."

The vice-minister's eyes narrowed a fraction, and Colby knew he'd drawn blood. Greenstein had come to cover his tracks, but it was a weak strategy and lacked any supporting tactics. The man was trying to wing it, and he didn't have a firm plan yet that would pass the sniff test.

"I'm not the one in the shit, Edson," he said with cold certainty. "You can be assured of that."

Colby recognized the tone, the confidence of the criminally clueless. Given an opening, he'd be able to use that to bring the asshole down. Not for the first time he wondered how Greenstein had risen so high.

The vice-minister prattled on, "You had a good thing going, you know? A fourth star, a cushy life after retirement. But no. You had to go sticking your nose into where it didn't belong. You had to go all white knight, ready for the joust. But you forgot this very vital fact. Sometimes, knights tilt at windmills, things beyond their control.

Colby stopped short of rolling his eyes at the mangled metaphor. As if Greenstein had ever read *Don Quixote*. Likely he'd seen some watered down Hollbolly vid that missed the whole point.

"Whatever happens to you, remember, it was your choice."

Finally, the vice-minister must have tired of hearing his own voice. He stood up, and without saying another word, let himself out. A few minutes later, one of the guards came back with a bottle of water. He had a black eye, courtesy of Colby and their little fight.

"Captain Heuhn says you deserve humane treatment, even if you are a traitor. I'm supposed to stay here while you drink, so no funny stuff, OK?"

"Scout's honor," Colby said, mentally shaking his head at the young guard's naiveté.

A real soldier would not trust an enemy.

The irony was, Colby wouldn't try anything. *His* word was good. Maybe the guard wasn't so naïve after all.

The guard unlocked the cuffs, let Colby work some blood back into his hands, then handed him the water. He stood on the balls of his feet, ready to react, but at least he hadn't drawn his weapon.

Colby drained the bottle, then held it at his waist and asked, "May I?"

The guard nodded, and Colby filled it while the guard watched. He didn't care about that. He was a field Marine, and when nature called, there was no such thing as polite modesty.

He shook his hands out one more time, then put them back behind the chair. The guard reattached the cuffs, picked up the full bottle, and left. As Colby settled in, trying to get comfortable, he realized that there was some give in the cuffs.

He pulled at them, and his right hand started to slide. His hopes jumped. The young kid had made a cardinal sin—he hadn't checked to make sure the cuffs were secure.

Colby pulled, almost tearing the skin off his wrist and hand, but after five minutes of tugging, his hand popped free. He stood up, cuffs dangling from his left hand. Ignoring the pain in his right, he swung the cuffs around a few times. They didn't have much weight, but they'd make a passable weapon.

Creeping, he approached the door. He couldn't hear anything on the other side. He leaned forward, pressing his ear against it to hear better, and the door moved. He jumped back, stunned. It had opened a crack. They hadn't even locked it.

He put his hands against the door, ready to give it a shove and jump whoever was out there when sanity caught up with him.

Capital guards were not Marines, but they weren't totally unprofessional in what they did. Even a young guard would not make the mistake with the cuffs, and they would not have left the door unlocked.

He tip-toed back to the chair and took a seat.

The vice-minister had the upper hand, but no matter what the bastard did, Colby could—and would—fight. And no matter how well-crafted the story the vice-minister concocted, some people would believe Colby. All it took was for the vice-minister and his minions to slip up once, and their carefully crafted story would start to unravel.

A traitor who was killed trying to escape, however, could not proclaim his innocence.

Colby sat back and waited for the next move.

****

The door crashed open, jerking Colby awake. He jumped up, holding his left hand back and ready to use his cuffs as a weapon. Two Marines rushed in, then hesitated when they saw the wild-eyed man standing in front of them.

"Not a grateful way to greet your rescuers, General," Lieutenant Colonel Sifuentes said as he entered the room. "Are you going to take us all on with those cuffs?"

"Manny Sif, I'd never would have guessed that I'd ever say this, but you are a sight for sore eyes," Colby said as he lowered his arm. "I take it you are the cavalry, but how did you get Greestein to agree?"

"He didn't. The Commandant insisted that you be released, the First Minister objected, and those two are fighting about it now. I told Greenstein that in the meantime, I was taking you into custody until they could get it straightened out back on Earth."

"And he agreed?"

"I've got over 300 Marines. He's got four SUTAs."

Colby nodded his understanding. Might makes right—and this time, in his favor.

Still, he was in debt to the colonel. Sure, he held the practical power right now, but when everything was sorted out, if Greenstein somehow swayed the first minister and triumphed in the end, Manny Sif's career was over.

Colby felt the lump growing in this throat. This is what he'd missed most after being cashiered from the Corps: the loyalty and bond all Marines had for each other.

Lieutenant Colonel Sifuentes made a show of looking around the room, then said, "Unless you are really attached to these accommodations, General, I'd suggest we diddiho out of here before a firm decision on your status comes down from on high."

He left unsaid the fact that he'd have a much harder time breaking him out if the director general came down on the side of the first minister. It would be better for both of them if Colby was out of Greenstein's reach before and if that was the decision.

And that decision wouldn't necessarily be based on the facts of the matter. Neither the commandant nor the first minister knew the truth. The first minister was backing his Number 2, and the commandant was taking issue with any former general, even a shit-canned general, being held by one of the ministries, even if that was the First Ministry and the minister technically outranked him.

Colby held out his left arm, from which the cuffs still dangled. One of the two enlisted Marines stepped forward, took out his multitool, and a moment later, the cuffs dropped to the deck. Colby rubbed his wrist, and then followed the two Marines out of the door where ten more Marines waited, not exactly guarding two SUTAs, but making no effort to hide that they were waiting for anything.

The guard with the black eye stood casually, thumb stroking the butt of his sidearm as he watched Colby emerge. Colby could see the animosity the young man held for him, and he probably wished he'd just shot Colby earlier, then dragged him out to stage an escape.

You can't hesitate, son, not if you want things to go your way.

Colby gave the young SUTA a huge smile, then nodded his head. The guard's eyes tightened, and for a moment, Colby wondered if he'd be foolish enough to draw his weapon.

Leave him alone, Edson. He undoubtedly believes I'm a traitor, fed by Greenstein's bullshit.

He shifted his gaze and walked alongside the colonel, flanked by the Marine squad, and left the ruined building. He felt a wave of relief as he passed through the shattered door that almost made his knees buckle. Inside his makeshift cell, he'd kept his spirits up by vowing to fight, but as the sunlight hit his face, he realized how deep into the shit he'd been. Without Manny Sif's intervention, he may have not even lived to see another day.

"Are you ready for an update, sir?" the colonel asked as they made their way through the ruined square where the giant daikaiju, including the one Colby had controlled, had fought to the death just two days before.

Colby immediately said yes, slipping back into general-mode before remembering he was no longer on active duty and really had no "need to know," as the military termed it. Still, if the colonel was willing to brief him, he would sure as shit listen. Manny Sif was a heck of a Marine, but he was still just a lieutenant colonel, and this was some pretty heady stuff going on. If Colby could give him any advice based on his years of service, then he owed it to the younger Marine.

"I sent off a cargo pod with what I could scrape up of the different plant soldiers to Lanie Wasserman right after the battle. Lanie is a research fellow at GSI. We were classmates at Command and Staff."

"A civilian?" Colby asked, surprised.

"I had to do something quickly. The plant material was disintegrating as we collected it. We froze some and vac-packed the rest.

"GSI is contracted to the Second Ministry, and Lanie's got clearance. But I routed it through an Academy classmate who's in MCRDD, and he sent it on, cc'ing the chief of staff."

Colby nodded. Yes, that would work. With Manny Sif's chain of command wiped out by the plant soldiers, he couldn't send it up the chain, and the Marine Corps Research and Development Division would be a logical alternate destination. Keeping Lieutenant General Godfrey, the current chief of staff, in the loop covered Manny's ass while getting the samples into someone's hands. They wouldn't stay within the military's control forever, but with Greenstein and his shenanigans, Colby was glad the samples were in military hands for now and not in the civilian side of the ministry.

"Get this, sir. We've already got the initial results. Whatever those plants were, they did not have terrestrial DNA. They are alien."

Which was no surprise to Colby. He'd fought the damned things, he'd *been* one of the damned things. He knew whatever primordial ooze had spawned them had not originated on Earth.

"Interesting, but why do I get the idea that this isn't the main thing you want to tell me?"

"Because it isn't, sir," the colonel said, looking around at the Marines accompanying them. "We do have a DNA match. Well, not a complete match, but type-match, is what the message said. The DNA is from the Alpha-Nine class of lifeforms.

From the way Manny Siff had said "Alpha-Nine," it was clear the colonel expected him to recognize the designation. If his implant hadn't been offline, Colby would have run a simple search. Instead he had to dredge his memory. He had a vague recollection from some report that had crossed his desk decades earlier.

Alien life had been found throughout human space, something like 43 different types. Most were various types of microorganisms, but a good 15 or so were multicellular. Colby was a Marine, though, and not a xenobiologist, and while he remembered enough to recognize what the colonel was talking about, the specifics were lost to him.

"I'm sorry, Manny, but I'm not up on alien life. What is significant about the Alpha-Nine class?"

"That's what was originally on your planet. I mean your new planet. Vasquez!"

His hair stood on end for a moment, and he wasn't sure why. He'd known that there had been alien life on Vasquez before it had been terraformed, and it still existed in parts of the planet where humans had not yet tilled the soil for terrestrial crops.

Were the plant soldiers native to Vasquez? he wondered. *No, Vasquez had been cultivated for nigh on 40 years. We would have seen giant broccoli soldiers before now.*

"Anywhere else?" he asked. "Aren't there some classes that are found on multiple worlds?"

"That's the thing, sir," the colonel said, lowering his voice even more. "It's the same class as on fourteen known planets."

"And let me guess, all in the Eidleman Quadrant?"

"Yes, sir. All in the Eidleman Quadrant."

Vasquez was on the outskirts of human space, pushing outward in the Orion Arm. Most of the human diaspora was inwards, toward the galactic center where more densely packed solar systems offered a greater chance of finding Goldilocks planets to settle or terraform. But that didn't mean space beyond Vasquez was empty. With over a billion stars in the Orion Arm, there were still hundreds of millions of stars out beyond his adopted home, hundreds of millions of stars that could harbor an untold multitude of lifeforms.

Something tickled the back of his mind, almost like the touch of his implant when he was taking control of the plant soldiers. A need to expand, to find a new. . . garden? What if the boss plant wasn't an invader, but a defender? Hell, what if its troops weren't actually soldiers? He'd spent most of his life in the military, so it only made sense that he'd interpret the situation from that perspective. But he'd been a farmer these last years, and from that point of view the boss plant wasn't an adversary, it was just. . . a gardener! Panic started to bubble up, and he physically shook his head to clear it, pushing uncomfortable thoughts deep to where they couldn't surface.

". . . Sixth Ministry has already gotten wind of it and are demanding access," Manny was going on.

Colby focused on the here and now.

"Sixth Ministry? They're the science arm of the government, so that makes sense," he said, acting like he'd heard everything the colonel had just said.

And they don't have the power to do much else, he thought, still concerned about his own future.

The huge organism that was the government would be shifting to take over the situation. An alien invasion had been the fodder of the media since the 20th Century, and every agency had to have contingency plans ready for this. It wasn't up to Colby to play hero anymore, so his thoughts went to self-preservation. And as he'd learned when he fought corruption before, that might be difficult to attain. With the military under the control of the First Ministry, there wasn't much even the commandant could do if the first minister wanted his scalp.

****

Lieutenant Colonel Sifuentes handed Colby a readout. He gave it a quick read, then crumbled it up and tossed it to a trash can, bouncing it off the rim and to the floor of the Marine's CP.

"He won't quit, will he?" Colby said in disgust.

It had been a copy of yet another message to the first minister, demanding that Colby, Manny, and all the Marines on New Mars be arrested for traitorous actions against the Republic. Clearly, Greenstein was in panic mode.

Was he even aware of how ridiculous he sounded? Did he seriously expect that anyone would authorize the arrest of 300-plus Marines? And not just any Marines, but the very same Marines whom he'd already lauded for turning back the plant-soldiers attack. But the man was a politician, first and foremost. He didn't have to make sense. The rest of the Marines were just bargaining chips in a larger game. Greenstein wanted his ass, and now probably Manny Sif's as well. He likely thought that if he could yell loud enough and long enough, it was possible that the commandant would concede, just to shut him up, and in the process give up the two of them.

"You know, you didn't have to make a target of yourself. You didn't have to take action on my part, Manny."

The younger Marine looked up at Colby, and his eyes hardened for a moment. "With all due respect, General, I am rather insulted that you would even voice something like that. You're a Marine, an honorable man despite what happened, and Greenstein is scum. There was no other choice, sir."

Dutifully chastised, Colby nodded. He'd been wrong. Manny had acted on his honor.

Still, he was very grateful for it.

"OK, then," he said, anxious to change the subject, "where do we stand with the power grid? Is there anything I can do to help there?

"Not unless you have a G-39 in your backpack, General. Until we get the Corps of Engineers in here, I'm afraid that power is going to be—" he started before he went glassy-eyed in the manner of a person getting messages over his implant.

Colby automatically queried his before remembering he was cut offline.

The colonel listened for a full minute before he snapped back and shouted out, "Sergeant N'belle, get the major over here ASAP and put the battalion on Deployment Alert Bravo."

He got to his feet, and Colby asked, "Can you tell me what's happening?"

"Oh, of course, sorry, sir. That was the commandant herself. It seems as if she and the Chief of Naval Operations took notice of our reports, and they're not waiting for the first minister or the director to get off their collective asses.

"The RS *Pattani*, a corvette, and a packet destroyer have just entered New Mars orbit. Our orders are to lead a mission back to Vasquez, retrieve any survivors, and assess the situation. If there are still enemy there, we're to engage them. But our prime mission is to keep any more of them from getting to New Mars. Up to and including, if necessary, destroying the wormhole from the Vasquez side."

Colby felt the familiar surge that accompanied the call to battle, and jumped to his feet, anxious to return to action. It took a conscious effort to calm back down. This wasn't his fight anymore.

"And Greenstein?" he asked. "Are they coming to arrest him?"

"Greenstein? No, unfortunately. The commandant said to treat him with kid gloves for now. Politics, you know."

And the commandant still doesn't know which way the wind is blowing, he thought bitterly.

Which wasn't fair. General Piper Nilson bled Marine Corps green. She was from the Basic Officers Class just after Colby's, and she'd been nothing but professional since then. If she ordered Greenstein to be treated with kid gloves, then she had a good reason for that. Which didn't mean the asshole wouldn't eventually get his just desserts somewhere down the line.

"What Marines are on the ships?" Colby asked. "Are you still in command?"

The *Pattani*, as a frigate, had a minimal crew and normally no Marines on board, but between the three ships, they could carry up to a battalion-minus of Marines or a mix of special operation-types. That would probably mean a full bird colonel in charge.

"Sir?" Manny asked, looking perplexed.

"Are there other Marines in the task force? And are you still in command?"

"You didn't. . . wait one, sir." He went glassy-eyes again, and Colby could see his throat moving as he sub-vocalized.

He turned back to Colby a long minute later and said, "Sir, G-8 is. . . well, hacking the block on your implant. The commandant is confident that they'll get it back online with all its previous functions reactivated. That's probably going to take a few hours, but the paper pushers will need that long to go through all the protocols anyway."

"Protocols? Why?"

"With all due respect, General, I should think that would be obvious. Your commission is being reactivated. You're in command."

Interlude I: Adjusting for the Impossible

By the time the destruction ceased, the Gardener had completed the regrowth of a minimal body sufficient to its need. The new form secured its enhanced cranium in a snug space beneath the rubble of what had once been one of the structures so prized by this brand of Meat. There was adequate airflow to bring it information, enough moisture to suit its current requirements. From its dwindling supply of resources it had generated and repurposed data collectors into sentries and scattered them around its location. It was safe, for the moment, or at least as safe as any Gardener enduring such circumstances might manage.

Reality, such as it was, could no longer be trusted. Although it had never itself indulged, the Gardner possessed knowledge of a variety of potent alkaloids capable of altering one's brain chemistry. Profound and disturbing hallucinations might be achieved, or, with the right combinations, schisms and even complete breaks from reality were possible.

It found the concept offensive. Trained in design and empiricism, it struggled even to entertain the thought experiment that reality could be subjective. It was nonsense. One could not design a garden, let alone the landscape of an entire world, without an unwavering appreciation for and understanding of objective reality. One gardened by obtaining a mastery of the interplay of complex but predictable patterns. A garden did not spontaneously reject its nature. Grassland did not transform overnight into forest, mosses did not become ferns, conifers did not choose to change themselves into liverworts. Reality operated by rules, laws that could be deduced and observed. It was vast but fixed.

Except no one had bothered to inform the Meat, not here on this world of mud and Mech, nor back on the planet that it had intended as its latest garden. The purge agents it had unleashed on this world should have overcome local resistance. This was an established fact. Yet, somehow, they had been destroyed down to the last leaf.

No matter. The mega seeds it had planted had been hard-coded at a genetic level to possess sufficient response patterns to defeat any assortment of Mech or Meat in the known galaxy. For them to do otherwise was as inconceivable as rain falling upward to fill the sky with clouds. But again, reality, as it appeared to be defined in this place, among these Meat, had proved otherwise.

No Gardener felt threatened by any configuration of Mech. At worst, they were an inconvenience and short-sighted, hasty. No Gardener feared Meat, even more ephemeral and chaotic. Nuisances, nothing more. And while this Gardener had been surprised by the antithesis of Meat wielding Mech—Meat that had learned to overcome its native gravity well and venture into space, infesting other worlds, other systems, with filth and sprawl and thanatopic entropy— still it had expected to overcome the creatures readily enough.

The Gardener had not imagined that the same Meat that had obtained a modicum of mastery over Mech would somehow merge with its own much more sophisticated vegetable systems. But this Meat had. This Meat had commandeered its vessel. This Meat had compromised its purge agents. This Meat had even launched its own mega seed and, not content with that gross deed, had used its own paltry consciousness to override the mega-seed's behavioral programming and subvert the mighty structure to its own heinous purposes.

Reality should not allow even the possibility of such a synthesis of Meat and Mech and Veg. Had not, in all the time since the primal flash. Until now.

If reality, as it understood it, no longer held sway, if order had surrendered to chaos in less time than the simplest of seeds might germinate, the empiricism demanded that this Gardner must embrace chaos.

But only in a very orderly manner, flush with internal consistencies born out by direct observation, repetition, and revision.

Several rotations of this muddy and underdeveloped world occurred while it grappled with these fundamental changes. During that time the lifeless pieces of its purge agents had broken down beyond the cellular level. This had been part of their reality, to return to the soil, to be carried away upon the air, to circulate in the water upon whatever planet they were unleashed. The trio of shattered hulks constructed on the templates of its mega seeds had similarly begun to decompose. Even the usurped creation of this Meat had begun to give way to the natural process. Entropy will out.

In this new unreality, pursuing its own version of synthesis was not the answer, would not defeat the blend of processes this Meat had employed. No, the Gardener resolved to maintain its integrity of vision. It would not taint itself. But chaos did require sacrifice. Purity would be lost. It could not stand apart from what this Meat had done, not if it had any hope of restoring reality and then warning its fellow Gardeners. It would have to blend as well, remain itself, separate but no longer apart. Only through thorough empiricism would it find the means to defeat such repugnant chaos. Only by learning from this Meat could it achieve a state where all such knowledge might be stricken from the galaxy.

It had expanded its ratiocination to its theoretical limits and examined the situation from every angle, every perspective, evaluating each and every known and unknown, selecting from the resulting options and scenarios until it had found one that offered the most promising outcome. And then it had begun allowing its massive brain to decay. Soon after, the rest of its body began to follow suit. Little time remained to this form.

The particulate remnants of all its creations, even the recent data-gathering sentries, hung in the air. It required little effort to produce a pollen that altered these bits into the iota of a vast network. As the pollen spread, the network expanded throughout the air in all directions. And as the Gardner itself came apart, it distributed its intellect and sense of self to this network. The near infinite scintilla of itself, endless, nearly invisible specks of green, smaller than the smallest of spores, in time landed upon and adhered to every surface of Meat and Mech, and continued to spread further, carried by its unwitting hosts.

In this form, conscious but bodiless, the Gardner would wait, would observe, and when it had gathered the critical data that would yield its success, it would strike.

And the Meat—despite its mastery of Mech or its recent impertinent synthesis with Veg—being clueless Meat, would succumb, likely without any awareness of how much trouble it had caused or how it had summoned its own eradication.

Part II: Thorns, Weeds, and Roses

"Did you think you could hide from me, Edson?" The sneer in Greenstein's voice grated on Colby's nerves.

Colby turned away from Wendi Utica, Manny Sif's logistics officer, and said, "Excuse me, Captain."

The task force had received a warning order to be ready to deploy back to Vasquez, and even with only a single, understrengthed battalion, there were a million moving parts that had to be coordinated.

Kid gloves, Edson, kid gloves, he repeated the mantra in an attempt to be civil to the vice-minister. He looked up at Greenstein, a half-smile on his face.

It didn't work.

"Captain, where is your commanding officer?" the vice-minister demanded from Utica.

"Colonel Sifuentes? I think he's in the armory, sir," she answered automatically before her face fell, and she looked at Colby, asking, "I mean, if that's OK for me to say that."

"Why do you want to know, Vice-Minister?" Colby asked, almost choking on his words.

Greenstein stared at Colby, then turned his body so that there was no doubt that he was snubbing him, and said, "If your commander isn't here, then I order you to arrest this man."

"Sir?" Captain Utica asked, clearly confused.

"Did I stutter? I told you to arrest this man. He was in my custody until some. . . *people in military uniforms*. . . released him. Those people will be found and prosecuted, but as I know your name, Captain. . ." he said, turning to look at her name tape.

Captain Utica kept turning away from him, keeping her name tape from his sight, and he almost chased around until with a shout of victory, said, "Utica!

"As I know your name, Captain *Utica*, it won't be hard for me to find you if you do not obey my orders. So, get your Marines and arrest this man now!"

She looked up at Colby, clearly out of her depth, then said, "I. . . I can't, sir."

"What do you mean, you can't? Can't or won't? I'm warning you, your career is about to come to a very unpleasant end."

"She can't, Vice-Minister. You have no authority to give her any such orders."

Greenstein had been deliberately ignoring Colby, but at this, he turned towards him, his face turning red as he almost choked before managing to get out, "What the hell do you mean, Edson? I have the authority, and you damn well know it."

"In that, you are sadly mistaken," Colby said, a smile forming despite his half-ass attempt to control it. "You do *not* have the authority."

Greenstein stared at him, mouth gaping open. He turned to look at the two of his capital guards as if for support. The SUTAs glanced about at the eight other Marines in the room, Marines who were taking an intense interest in what was going on. Greenstein's guards evidently decided that discretion was the better part of valor because they failed to look the vice-minister in the eyes. They might be jerks, but that didn't mean they were stupid.

Even without their moral support, the vice-minister did not back down. Instead, he ramped up the rhetoric, pitching his voice as if surrounded by media recording him for the evening news, and addressed everyone around him.

"I am First Ministry Vice-Minister Asahi Greenstein. I have declared Colby Edson in violation of Civil Code 1402.3b. As such, it is within my authority to request assistance from any Republic constabulary or federal troops to carry out arrests and detainment," he said before breaking down into normal speech, "That means you Marines. You have to arrest Edson."

Captain Utica had regained her composure. She stepped around Edson and said, "If the general were a civilian, you could charge him with whatever that code is. But since he is a Marine, all charges have to be referred through the Commandant of the Marine Corps via SJA-1."

"Edson? A general? He used to be a general, Captain, but he got cashiered," Greenstein said, the gloat in his voice almost enough to make Colby step up and punch him. "Now he's nothing but a farmer at the ass-end of the galaxy."

Four of the Marines stepped forward at his words, and the two SUTAs instinctively took a step closer together. Colby held out his hand, palm outward, to stop the Marines.

Before he could have the satisfaction of giving the vice-minister the news, Captain Utica said, "He may be a farmer, sir, but he's also an active duty lieutenant general of Marines."

Once again, Greenstein looked poleaxed. This time, Colby didn't hold back the grin.

"That's correct, Vice-Minister Greenstein. As of. . ." he said before checking the time, ". . . eight hours and thirty-two minutes ago, I've been recalled to active duty. Signed, sealed, and delivered."

"But. . . but you were cashiered. You were kicked out for cause."

"You're never completely out, vice-minister. You're simply transferred to the inactive list, there to be recalled at the whim of the director."

"She signed off on this?" he said, a note of panic in his voice.

Colby could practically see the wheels turning in Greenstein's mind. If the director had signed off on Colby's reactivation, then that could portend a new political wind, and ever the politician, he was acutely aware of how things could change.

"As I said, signed, sealed, and delivered."

The vice-minister stood there silently for along moment, and Colby could almost hear the gears spinning furiously in the man's head.

"I'm going to want this confirmed, Edson—"

"General Edson."

The vice-minster almost snarled, but said, "General Edson. I want to speak with the commandant. I assume you realize that as a vice-minister, I have the authority to dema. . . to request that?"

"Of course, sir." He turned to the captain and said, "Please relay the vice-minister."

"I'd be happy to, sir," she said with sarcastic enthusiasm.

As a civilian, even a high-ranking civilian in the First Ministry, Greenstein did not have a military implant. His commercial implant could connect him throughout human space, but only through the commercial relays. The main relay on New Mars had been turned into so much rubble by the alien daikaiju, so to call back to Earth, he either had to use his ship's comms and then request a patch to the military side of the ministry, or he could be patched right to HQMC via Captain Utica's.

"Sir, code two-three-bravo-niner-six-foxtrot-zero-four-four," the captain said.

"Thank you, Captain," Greenstein said as he flipped down his earset.

He turned away as he started sub-vocalizing, not that Colby could have picked up what he was saying even if he tried. The reason he'd had the captain relay Greentein's call was that his implant was still offline. Now, if he'd had it, as a Level 6 implant, he *could* listen in.

Captain Utica caught his eye and raised her eyebrows. She could listen in without too much trouble. Colby shook his head, suddenly feeling guilty for his own thoughts along those lines.

The vice-minister was getting angry, pacing back and forth, punching the air with his right hand in a fist. That made Colby happy. The guy should be rotting away in a federal cell, preferably on some planet with heavy gravity and noxious air, but for now, no matter how petty it might be, Colby was enjoying this.

Until the vice-minister suddenly stood up straight, his right hand raised to his ear. He nodded, then said aloud, "So, I am the senior First Ministry rep?" He nodded a few times, then said, "Thank you, General McTimmons. I'll pass on to the first minister how cooperative you've been."

Colby's stomach gave a lurch. General McTimmons was the Assistant Commandant of the Marine Corps, who, along with the two force commanders, was on an equal level as a vice-minister. And if Greenstein was happy with whatever the ACMC had just said, Colby was pretty sure he was going to hate it.

"Thank you, Captain," Greenstein said in a saccharine voice. "You've been a great help."

He turned to Colby but made a show of stowing his earset, keeping him waiting.

"Well, General, it seems that you have been reactivated after all. Congratulations are in order, I guess. We'll worry about the charges after this operation back to Vasquez is over."

Colby waited for the other shoe to drop as the vice-minister looked at him with triumph gleaming in his eyes.

"Is that all?" Colby finally said, losing the battle of wills.

"Oh, no, now that you mention it. It seems that I've been made the senior First Ministry rep for the mission—you know, to make sure this thing is actually done correctly. And as you are part of the First Ministry, and, of course, as I out-rank you, I am in command."

Colby stared at the vice-minister in shock.

He's in command? Of a military operation?

"I'm going back to my ship, General. I'll expect a full brief in. . . oh, let's give you time to get this done. . . in two hours?"

With that, he wheeled around, snapped his fingers at the two Capital Guards—who seemed more than eager to leave—and marched back out of the room. As soon as the hatch closed behind him, Marines broke out into questions.

Colby started to activate his implant before he remembered he was still cut off.

"Quiet!" he shouted before turning to the captain and saying, "Get to the ACMC's office and find out just what is going on."

Colby had felt like taking a victory lap only ten minutes ago, but victory had been snatched right out from under him. If Dickhead was right, this mission had just turned to shit.

****

"General, the vice-minister wants to inspect all the Marines," Major Nkundlande-Siphers passed. "What do I tell him?"

"Excuse me, Captain," Colby said, holding up a hand. "I need to handle something."

Greenstein was being a pain in the ass, but it hadn't been as bad as he'd feared. First, he was not in command of the task force, as much as he wanted to believe it. Task Force Roundup was a military operation, pure and simple, and Colby was in command. Still, the first call he'd received once his implant had been reactivated—the Marines hadn't been able to hack it yet, but as part of the compromise with the civilian side of the First Ministry, the block had simply been turned off—had been from the commandant himself. He told Colby to humor Greenstein for the moment. Colby had objected, wanting to arrest the man, but what had been simply a request from the commandant immediately became an order that brooked no argument, and Colby immediately shut up about it.

The vice-minister had cancelled the brief he'd told Colby to give him (which was just one less possible confrontation as Colby had planned on sending a junior officer to do that). He'd stayed in his ship, emerging once the Navy arrived and again just now. He'd spent five minutes making sure the Navy knew he was in charge, and now, eight hours later, he'd come out again with his latest demand.

Colby knew the man was just trying to let everyone know he was in charge. It was petty, but Colby could play the game, too.

With his implant back to its full capability, he didn't have to subvocalize. Years of experience enabled him to "think" his messages, and the implant sent them.

"Take a squad from Alpha, have them lay out their full gear in component mode, weapons disassembled. Give him a checklist, then we'll see how long he lasts."

"Oh, sir, with all due respect, you are a cruel man," the major said.

"How do you think I got three stars, my young major. Edson out."

Marines absolutely hated a component inspection, referred to as "junk on the bunk." It was onerous to set up and easy to fail. With so many parts, it was almost impossible to have them all in perfect condition. What the junior Marines didn't necessarily realize is that the SNCOs or officers conducting the inspection hated them even more, if that was possible.

"I'm sorry about that," Colby told the Marines and sailors in the small, almost-intact room he'd commandeered as his CP. "Captain, you were saying?"

Captain Alicia Whitehorse was the composite fleet commander as well as commanding officer of the *RS Pattani*, a Naha-class frigate and the designated flagship of the task force.

Colby had not been familiar with her, which was not surprising. She'd just made captain, and he'd been out of circulation for awhile. A quick scan showed that she was an up-and-comer, one of the Navy's brightest stars. Highly experienced and decorated, Colby was glad that it had been the *Pattani* that was close enough to answer the call.

It wasn't that the other two captains and ships were lightweights. Commander Deshal Brockmorton of the corvette *RS Portnoy Bay*, and Commander Nick Pierce of the packet destroyer *RS Gazelle* had excellent records as well—no one got command of a Navy ship without being one of the best—but Whitehorse and the *Pattani* were one-percenters.

With the ongoing crisis with the Borealis Pact, Colby was surprised that the Navy had even sprung the three ships. It was necessary, as the plants represented a clear and present threat to humanity, but the plants were an unknown to the command while they understood the very real danger of the Borealis Pact.

"Yes, General," the captain said. "There was some talk about waiting for the *Surrey County* to arrive so you could have assault craft for your Marines, but based on your initial report, the sector commander thought time was of the essence."

The *RS Surrey County* was a Ground Assault Carrier, designed to forcefully insert Marines on an enemy-held planet or moon. Vasquez might still be technically enemy-held, but Colby didn't think that the *Surrey County's* capabilities would be needed to land his Marines.

The sector commander had been right, time was critical. Topeka and Riordan were still there, and Riordan needed medical care. Chances were that more survivors were on the planet as well who'd managed to hide or run, and while Marines could stand up to the plant soldiers, he knew civilians couldn't face them head on and survive.

"The *Pattani* has more than enough spaces for your Marines, and with our ship's shuttles and my gig, we can land you in two waves. With your warning order, we've tentatively chosen two locations, here and here," she said, waving her wand. Vasquez appeared over the table, then the image zoomed in to DeStaffney Station, where Colby, Topeka, and Duke had battled the plant soldiers and found the enemy ship, then it rotated to Tennison, the second collection point for the planet's agricultural products.

"Once you debark, we will take the guard position at the wormhole while the *Portnoy Bay* and *Gazelle* remain on call for any support you need."

The image of Vasquez disappeared, to be replaced by images of both of the smaller ships, along with their armaments. As always, Colby was somewhat in awe of the power even a smaller capital ship had. A corvette was a pirate and smuggler hunter, and the packet destroyer was a ship killer, but either one of them had more firepower than a regiment of Marines. He was confident that if his Marines needed fire support, either ship would be more than capable to supply it.

Neither ship could touch the firepower of a frigate, however.

"Explain to me one more time why the *Pattani* is going to remain by the wormhole and not in orbit."

Colby had received the ship disposition already, and even as the task force commander, there wasn't much he could do to change it, but he wasn't quite sure of the whys and wherefores as of yet.

"If we have to destroy the wormhole, sir, then the *Pattani* is the only ship of the three of us capable of doing that."

Destroy the wormhole? Then Vaquez would be isolated. Why? he started to wonder before it hit him. *Of course. We killed the plant boss here on New Mars, but if a new one can. . . sprout?. . . then we cannot risk it getting through here, and then to other systems.*

"And why only the *Pattani*?"

"Neither of the other two ships have a Pluvian Doomfist. The *Pattani* does. Imploding a wormhole is, well, it's a balancing act between brute power and a delicate touch. The ship has to be in the exact center of the wormhole, and you know how they keep shifting with gravitational fluxes. Then, the PD has to be set for a close-sphere field induction. And trust me, General, if the induction fails to spark full pluviation, imploding the wormhole will be the least of your problems. We're talking a wave of quantum instability spreading out from both ends.

Colby couldn't understand half of what the captain was saying, but he nodded sagely.

"And that will destroy the wormhole?"

"If we keep the induction field at max output for between 20 and 30 seconds, yes, sir, it should."

"That can't be good for the ship and crew."

The captain laughed, then said, "No, sir. It won't. We'll get the crew off on the life-capsules, but the ship itself will be lost."

Colby knew how captains felt about their ships, and he was surprised that she was so matter-of-fact about the potential for her ship to be destroyed. He decided right then and there that not only did Captain Whitehorse have a sterling record, but he rather liked her. She was the kind of warrior he understood. She was his kind of people. The kind of officer who would unflinchingly sacrifice her own career much as he had done. He hadn't met many in his long career, and stumbling over one in the current situation struck him as an omen of sorts.

Well, Edson, that means you need to make damn sure she doesn't end up sacrificing herself to close that wormhole. What a waste that would be.

"And the *Surrey County*? Does this have the Puluvian. . . Ploovi. . . uh. . . the same capability?"

"No, sir. None of the amphibs have the PD. Frigates and battleships, and only the newer ones at that."

It was just as well, Colby thought. Ever since humans left their caves to fight one another, those in charge always wanted more firepower, it didn't matter if it was bigger clubs or bigger spaceships, that need had never changed. He didn't have to like it, but Colby knew that when the time came, he would make full use of whatever they had.

"Well, let's hope it never comes to that," Colby said. "So, what are we looking at for leaving orbit?"

"We're ready when you are, sir."

"Colonel Sifuentes?"

"Without the armor, we're light. Top Wunton's already aboard the *Pattani* doing a quick embark brief, but we'd be ready to load out in 30 minutes."

The armor was a sore spot. It had proven extremely effective against the plant soldiers, but somehow, they'd almost all been disabled, gummed up, and CWO4 Mikhailov, the battalion armorer, had said that some components couldn't be repaired. With 331 Marines, the task force had exactly five working sets of battle armor.

"We always say that it's the Marine who're the dangerous weapons, not what we arm them with, so this might be the time to prove it."

Colby watched his officers. Manny's attempt to suppress a grin was less successful than Whitehorse's effort not to roll her eyes. "Let's start the embark. I want every ass-slap onboard in ninety minutes. Can we do that?"

Even with a diminished battalion of only 331 Marines, that was asking a lot, but as a commander, he knew when to push.

Manny Sif looked to Captain Walsh, his S4, who gave the slightest of nods in return.

"Yes, sir, we can."

"Then let's do it. Captain Whitehorse, Colonel Sifuentes, I would like to see you and your principle staff on board as soon as we depart the system."

Colby didn't need his implant to know they were both relaying instructions down the lines of their respective chains of command.

"Are we all good?"

"Yes, sir," came the chorus of the gathered staff.

Colby stood up, signaling the end to the meeting, and the Marines rushed out, leaving the space to Colby and the sailors. Colby shook the hands with each of the Navy officers and the command master chief before they left.

Better get yourself ready, too, Edson.

He hadn't even been issued a weapon yet. Time to find Mikhailov and rectify that situation.

He'd taken only two steps when he felt the telltale ping and his implant took an incoming call from Major Nkundlande-Siphers.

Hell, what does Dickhead want now? he wondered before accepting the call.

"You were right, sir," the XO said. "Greenstein only made it through half of Corporal Mont Arif's inspection before he gave up. Told me to finish it."

That's not even as long as I figured.

"Doesn't surprise me. We're embarking now, though, and you've got the vice-minister watch. Go tell him to get to the shuttlepad."

"He thinks he's taking his little Markus X, sir."

"Last I heard, a Markus X's a luxury corporate ship, not a military man-of-war. If he wants to come, he'll join us on the *Pattani*."

"Uh. . . sir. No disrespect intended, but I don't think he's going to listen to me. He still thinks he's in command here."

Damn, Edson. You can't delegate every interaction with that bastard.

"You're right, Major. Let me handle di. . . with the vice-minister. You've got more on your plate that you need to deal with now."

Generals normally didn't worry themselves with the details of getting individuals aboard ships, but this was a unique situation. Besides, the more he thought about it, the more he knew he was going to enjoy telling the vice-minister that he couldn't take his fancy ride to Vasquez.

****

"Any signs of life?" Colby asked. "Human life?"

The last two hours on and then in orbit around New Mars had been hectic, a case of controlled chaos as the Marines embarked aboard the *Pattani*. He'd had one last meeting with the Navy and Marine Corps staffs, but once they left orbit and headed to the Vasquez wormhole, the Navy took over, leaving Colby alone with his thoughts.

Those thoughts veered into territory he'd just as soon avoid, but once started, they wouldn't let go. He'd left Topeka and Riordan on the planet when he'd commandeered the alien ship to get back to New Mars, and he couldn't help but feel that he'd abandoned them. The planet hadn't been secured from the alien threat, and for all he knew, the plants could have sprouted up armies of the daikaiju since he left.

"Not much, sir," the sailor on the bioscans said. "I count just four-hundred and thirty-three humans."

Four-hundred thirty-three?" Colby asked.

"That's all. Sorry, sir."

Vasquez had been a highly automated colony, and prior to the invasion, there had only been just over 2000 inhabitants on the entire planet. Sixteen hundred people killed was horrid enough, but over four hundred survivors was more than he could have hoped for.

"And at DeStaffney Station?" he asked.

"I've got forty-one, sir."

That doesn't mean Topeka made it, but if there were that many people there, he'd bet she was already in charge of them. He felt a load lift off his shoulders.

"Sir, do we proceed?" Manny Sif asked.

"Nothing else out of the ordinary?" Colby asked the rest of the Navy CCC crew.

The holovids showed Navy captains battling aliens from ships' bridges, looking out through vast windows into space. There was nothing like that in actuality aboard a Navy ship. The *Pattani* was controlled from the CCC, the Combat Command Center, located deep in the center of the ship and heavily shielded from enemy attack.

All 15 of the scantechs shook their heads. Colby realized that none of the ships extensive scanners was set up to identify specific plant life, but several systems would notice 30-meter tall plants roaming the landscape, and with 433 humans still alive, the planet had to be relatively secure.

"Captain Whitehorse, are we ready?"

Her eyes lost focus for a moment in the manner of someone on her implant, then she was back, giving Colby a thumbs up and saying, "Shuttles and the gig are up and ready."

"Very well. In that case, Colonel Sifuentes, let's launch."

He gave a quick order to his implant, and a moment later, a dedicated circuit was created, linking him directly to Captain Whitehorse.

"I'd like you to keep this circuit open," he passed. "Just in case."

If she was surprised at his voice suddenly sounding in her implant, she didn't give any hint of that. She nodded once, then passed, "Will do, sir."

"Well, you keep the Navy ready up here in case we need a ride off Vasquez."

"Aye-aye, sir," she passed as he turned to make his way to the hangar deck. "Go with God, sir."

Colby stopped and slowly turned around, a smile on his face, before uttering the standard response, "Don't need God for this. I've got my Marines."

****

Duke gave a yelp of joy as the captain's gig hatch started to open and Vasquez air flooded inside. She broke past the Marines and bolted over the half-opened hatch to the sunshine, jumping around like a puppy.

I know what you mean, old girl, he thought as he started to push forward.

"Sir, you need to wait until we clear the area," Sergeant Dela Cruz told him, his voice grave with the heavy responsibility of making sure nothing happened to him.

Colby wanted to order him to stand down—Manny Sif, who'd landed in the first wave up at Tennison, had already reported no sign of vegetable combatants, only some very relieved civilians, happy to see the Marines. It had been bad enough acceding to the lieutenant colonel's insistence that he wait until the second wave, but to have a Marine squad, led by someone who looked like he should still be in secondary school, was very frustrating. He wasn't an invalid, and he could still fight the fight, if it came to that.

And, surprisingly, he was excited to get home. Yes, "home." He'd only been on the planet three years since his exile, but he'd gotten used to the pristine air and pace of life. He could see Duke cavorting around, stopping to roll in the dirt, and he wanted to get out of the gig and feel Vasquez's sun on his face again.

He couldn't do that to the sergeant and his squad, however. The young Marine was taking his mission seriously, and even a general had to bow to how the Marines conducted things.

He waited as the hatch fully opened and Sergeant Dela Cruz gave his orders to his squad. The Marines rushed out, weapons at the ready while Colby cooled his jets, still watching the deliriously happy Duke cavort before she suddenly looked up and bolted out of his view. He was just about to ask the sergeant what was going on when the Marine returned to the open hatch and said he could come out.

With a little more emotion than he'd have thought, he stepped out of the hatch and onto Vasquez soil, the good loamy aroma reminding him of just what made the planet such a perfect place to grow crops. A better place couldn't have been created by all the agritechs in humankind. He almost knelt to touch the soil, to test if it was about ready for pyro berries.

Come on, Colby. You're not a farmer anymore. You're a Marine again, and you don't need to be checking out soil conditions.

He raised his gaze from the soil and toward the station, where Duke was attacking one of about 40 civilians who were being held back by a fire team of Marines.

What the. . . he started to wonder before it came into focus. Duke was lunging at a familiar person's face, to be sure, but to lick, not rend.

Colby strode across the field, two fire teams of Marines forming a wedge around him. Hopeful faces watched him approach, only a few he recognized. Lassie Heldreman ran a farm with her son Jack about 20 klicks farther from the station than his, and he'd helped them erect a new silo. He scanned the others, but he didn't see Jack, which might account for the look of sorrow on her face. There was Father Demopoulos, the defrocked Orthodox priest with whom Colby had bartered snap beans for a decent wine. David and Jia Li Manus, with little

Foster grasping his mother's hand, stood smiling hopefully at him. He saw Lazer Montgomery, one of the planet's four equipment techs, someone who'd probably visited most of the people on the planet at one time or another.

He didn't recognize most of the others, which gave him pause. There hadn't been many people on the planet to begin with, and he'd must have been living like a hermit not to know them.

But there was one other familiar face, and Duke was right there, her tail whipping back and forth.

"Took you long enough, Edson," Topeka Watanabe said, her hand patting Duke's head.

****

"Well, he's full of himself," Topeka remarked.

"I call him Dickhead," Colby said, as the vice-minister walked away after making sure he told the gathered civilians that not only was he in charge, but he'd ordered this mission to rescue them and they owed their very lives to him.

"Dickhead? Why General, I'm shocked and befluttered that you would stoop to such gutter language, and around my delicate sensitivities at that," she said in a highly affected voice.

"You don't know him like I do," he said, unable to keep the bitterness out of his voice.

That took the smile off her face, and she said, "I think there's more to the story here than meets the eyes, and you've got a history with him."

"You could say that," Colby said, leaving it at that.

He was not going to get into how it had been Greenstein who'd railroaded and got him kicked out of the Corps and exiled to Vasquez in the first place. That was too close to the bone, something that was personal. Somehow, some way, he was going to make sure that the vice-minister paid for his sins—not for screwing him over, but for the corruption that Colby uncovered that had led to Greenstein taking him out first.

"Well, if I wasn't such a lady, I'd say that if that motherfucker messed with you, then I'll be glad to kick his fucking balls so far up his ass he'll need a mining permit to find them."

Colby looked at Topeka first in shock, then in relief as he laughed out loud. At first glance, she looked innocent, a petite young woman with the face of an angel. By now Colby knew she was a kick-ass terror who would make a sailor blush with her language.

Whether she meant to or not, she reminded Colby to get to the task at hand, not worry about some pissant vice-minister whose days were numbered—hopefully, that is. Even that bastard couldn't pull enough strings to cover his ass over ignoring the plant invasion after being warned about it.

Then again, he got away with stealing from the Corps.

He shook off that line of thought and said, "OK, you were telling me about the new growth."

"Yes, sir," Fiorio Slavas, a hop-bean farmer from the Thames Creek area, said. "The first plant-things, they stripped my fields bare, you know. Like what you said happened to you down here station-way. We barely got out ourselves, with those things chasing us until we got on the outcropping."

Colby had never met Fiorio until 30 minutes ago, and he'd never known that north of DeStaffney Station, the terrain was dotted with close to 50 rock outcroppings that sprung out of the otherwise flat ground like kopjes.

"Me and Leda," he said, nodding to a florid-but-smiling-faced woman who was looking on with interest, "we stayed up there for two days. We could see the smoke and all from station-way, but we didn't know what was happening. Finally, we came down, 'cause we were mighty hungry, you know like.

"We went back to the farm to see what we could scrounge up, and our fields, they were covered."

"Tell him how fast, Fiorio," Leda said.

"I'm getting to that. Like Leda says, these weren't no sprouts or nothing. They was like two meters high."

"Three," Leda said.

"Three meters high," he corrected himself. "Only they weren't nothing from Earth, that I can tell you. I didn't want to touch them, so we left to come to the station here."

"And what did we see?" Leda prompted him.

He looked a little puzzled, then said, "The station all destroyed like this?"

Leda rolled her eyes, then stepped in front of her husband, saying, "What he means is that while we were walking here, there were kilometers of the alien plant forms. They'd taken over the entire terrain. What had been a nice big pine forest was gone, an alien horticulture in its place, but one far more developed than our own terraforming could do in thirty years."

Colby mentally counted out the days since the attack. It had been less than a week, either five or six days. His trip to New Mars and back had screwed up his calendar somewhat.

He looked to Topeka who nodded and said, "It's like that all around here. Big swathes of land have been repopulated with non-native plants."

Well, all of our crops and plants are non-native. We introduced them here, he thought, but kept that to himself.

"Hold on a second," he said, raising his hand, palm out.

"Manny, I'm getting reports that new vegetation is taking over large areas here, supplanting Earth-vegetation. Is it the same thing up there around Tennison?" he asked over his link.

"Wait one and I'll find out," the lieutenant colonel passed back.

"And none of the new plants attacked you?" Colby asked Leda, ignoring her husband.

Several voices broke out, too many to hear what was being said, and Colby had to hold up a hand again to shut them all up.

"Leda, if you please."

"None of them pursued us, if that's what you mean, and some of them, you could touch without anything happening. But others, some of the smaller ones, the ones with the shiny trefoil leaves, they're like guards. Touch them and you'll regret it."

"They burn!" David Manus said, holding up an arm with a wicked-looking red blotch that ran from his wrist to his elbow. "I barely got away with my life."

"All hands, avoid contact with any shiny plants with trefoil leaves," he passed to the Marines while he listened.

The entire force had been ordered not to come into contact with any non-Earth vegetation, but this little tidbit deserved greater dissemination.

"Did they chase you?" Colby asked David. "After you got burned."

"We were coming in to the station with Kob 'Mbelle," he said quietly. "I got burned, he started swinging a scythe he'd managed to make. We ran," he said, pointing at Jia Li and Foster. "Kob stayed to fight, and they swarmed him."

"There was nothing we could do," he said, his eyes pleading for Colby to agree, to release the burden he'd been carrying.

Maybe David could have pulled Kob away, maybe he couldn't. That was not for Colby to say, but he did understand the guilt. Every commander who'd sent men and women to die in battle had felt the same thing.

"You had to take care of Foster," he said.

He didn't expect David to accept that, and from his expression, he hadn't. He'd have to deal with that demon himself.

"So, if you attack them, they will attack back. But they won't hunt out people and chase them down?"

"Not that we know," Topeka said.

"I'd like to see some of these," Colby said as Sergeant Dela Cruz came alert. "Can you show me?"

"There's some not too far," one of the women he didn't know said. "I can show you."

"Sir—" the sergeant started before Colby cut him off.

"Don't worry Sergeant. You're coming with me. And we're just going to see them, not touch them."

"General, what's going to happen to us?" someone else asked as he started off to see these guard plants.

212

I guess I never told them that. Of course they want to know.

"For now, we need you all to hold tight. We'll bring down some more supplies, but the first thing we need to do is to make sure the planet is secure. Once we've done that, the republic will send in a liner. All of you who want to leave will be taken to New Mars for transit onward."

"But you said New Mars was hit, too," someone shouted out.

"Only Hellasland was hit, so the rest of the planet is functioning. Besides, our wormhole only leads there, so that's the only way out from here.

"I should also say that there will probably be a significant monetary incentive to stay here on Vasquez. That's far above my pay-grade, so I don't know the details. but the Republic wants the crops we've grown here."

"I hope they like alien crops," someone muttered as Colby turned to go see the guard plants.

They'd only gone a hundred meters when Major Nkundlande-Siphers came running up to them.

"What, Sergeant, did you rat me out?" Colby asked.

He knew the Marines thought he had to have protection, but this was getting ridiculous. He came to a stop and waited for the major, ready to cut the man off.

"General, I didn't want to pass this over the net. But you know that plant-boss thing?"

"Yeah," he answered, a sudden hollowness forming in the pit of his stomach.

"From how you described it, I think it's back. First platoon saw it, or another one just like it, running away from the captain's gig and into the trees. A couple of the Marines fired on it, but they think it got away."

"How did they miss?" Colby asked, his voice a little too strident.

"They were at the station, sir. There wasn't an obvious reason to put a guard on the gig."

Which was true, Colby knew. But that left an opening, that left hope.

"So, the gig is 500 meters from the station?"

With the station landing pad torn up and covered with debris, the shuttles and gig had landed in an open field outside of the rubble.

"Yes, sir, about that."

"So, they might have been too far to see clearly?"

"Two meters tall, broccoli-looking thing that moved along a bunch of roots?"

Whatever hope he'd been grasping at was gone. He looked to Topeka who had a resigned look in her face.

"The Gardener's back," he said.

Interlude II: Passage and Illumination

Boarding the Meat vessels had been simplicity itself. Its consciousness was borne upon uncounted numbers of specks carried aboard each of three craft in the days before departure. Greater numbers of specks were left behind on the planet itself, but the Gardener simply withdrew its awareness from them, passing those portions along to bits upon the vessels. Initially, once it understood that the trio of arriving vessels would soon depart, the Gardener had considered maintaining its consciousness upon all three. It abandoned that strategy when it became clear that the Meat that had interfered with its garden on the earlier world would be leaving as well and traveling aboard a specific craft. That Meat had stolen its vessel, co-opted its purge agents, imposed its will upon a mega seed. None of its fleshy associates had given any indication of such capabilities. Obviously then, the greatest opportunity to nullify this species involved marshaling its powers in proximity to the only Meat that had demonstrated any intelligence beyond the simple destruction that defined all of them.

Much as it had withdrawn its awareness from the specks scattered outside of the three vessels, the Gardener abandoned its presence on the other craft and consolidated its intellect and cognition aboard the vessel that would transport the Meat it now considered its only real opposition. Once that had been accomplished, it applied itself to a better understanding of the Meat, the better to eradicate the pest from its garden and, potentially, the rest of space.

Gardeners did not measure time in the frenetic way of Meat. Time was subjective, different for different things. The life cycle of growth, the seasons of a world, the movements of planets, the generations of limbs and roots within every different plant and tree and shrub. None of these were the same, not like the units of seconds and minutes that so entranced these Meat, defining their lives at every step. The Gardener balanced both forms of perception. The rotations of this world, prior to the vessel's departure, contained both a billion Meat busy moments but also, for it, only a single contemplative point, even given its consciousness distributed across so many specks throughout the Meat vessel. Each speck observed, recorded, sorted the data presented through its limited sensorium. Each passed every datum forward to be collated and compared and considered by the gestalt of all. The data flow might be vast, but it hadn't yet yielded true knowledge. Nor had the Gardener expected it to; little learning occurred at the level of the microscopic specks.

Exceptions existed. It only required the loss of several tens of thousands of specks to the vessel's crude atmospheric filtration systems before the Gardener's consciousness learned of the brutal assault on so many of its components and steered its elements away from the numerous passive intake valves found in every space aboard.

In counterpoint, it also identified numerous, out of the way nooks where it could gather and reproduce its constituent numbers to more than make up for the losses from the vessel's systems. Moreover, as small, clumpy layers of green accrued on the underside of consoles, along containers in seemingly locked storage areas, and throughout the exterior lengths of conduits hidden from regular view, the Gardener generated nodes of concentration and processed the massive influx of information. It came to understand, to its astonishment, the nature of this variety of Meat.

They engaged in meaningful, complex behaviors that resembled true language. Many forms of Meat in the Gardener's experience made use of audible signals for basic communication, but these had been limited to Call systems, finite subsets of content limited to informing others of danger, the presence of food, or sexual availability. But this form of Meat actually spoke to one another. The language was crude, to be sure, but also open-ended.

Once the Gardener had realized they had language, it discovered something equally astonishing. They had not inherited the Mech at their disposal, they had created it themselves. However unthinkable, the parsing of their newly acquired language as well as the trickle of details from its countless observers left no doubt. This Meat had developed and designed the means to remove itself from its planet of origin and was well on its way to infesting large swaths of the galaxy. Moreover, they had discovered a technology that its own people had missed. Gardeners understood how to fold space, from the edge of one solar system to the edge of the next, eliminating the need to traverse the empty space between. This Meat lacked that ability but instead had harnessed portals that traversed space of orders of magnitude greater. But typical of Meat, they did not truly understand what they did, could not control it, and used it only opportunistically.

Thus had they left the worlds of their infection far behind when they discovered its garden and bespoiled it for their own purposes. That passage had presumably skipped over vast regions of space, systems where other Gardners toiled for their art or nurtured the seeds of society's successive generations, each side utterly unaware of the other. Cluelessly, the Meat had reached beyond the safe range of worlds unknown by Gardeners and intruded where they did not belong.

All this it had learned and one thing more. The specific Meat of its attention on this vessel, and the other two craft besides, were returning, back through the far-from-understood portal. All unknowingly, they would be taking it back, back to a region of space it understood, back where it had resources scattered in caches across the planet from its seeding two hundred cycles before. Regardless of its own fate, in less than a rotation upon that world, it could encode everything it had learned into messenger probes to be sent on to its people. This rabid and uncontrolled Meat required action, preparations for defense, contemplations for its eradication, likely even a long-range plan to identify, locate, and purge the hundreds of worlds it had already infected. It was. . . ambitious, the kind of plan that would require incalculable spans of time. But then, what was time to a Gardener?

Part III: Pyrrhic Melons

"We need to track it down, Captain. Period."

"Yes, sir. We'll do our best."

"No, you won't, Captain," he snapped. "Your best isn't good enough. You'll get it done. Am I understood?"

"Yes, sir. We'll do it."

Colby looked at the crude sketch of the area drawn by one of the survivors. The Gardener had been spotted running into the small pine forest on the far side of the captain's gig, the same one where it had landed its spacecraft during the initial invasion.

It's not staying there—it's only passing through the Earth trees. It wants its own kind, he realized, *"because it's not behaving tactically. It's not some kind of vegetable soldier, it's a Gardener!*

"Captain, change of plans."

"Sir?" Captain Wallace Singh asked, clearly confused.

Be clear, Edson. That's on you.

"Your mission is still to kill the boss plant, but it's not in the pines."

"Where is it, sir?"

"Leda, come look at this," he said, calling the woman over. "This area right here is the pines over there," he said, pointing. "And over here, this is how you came to the station, right?"

"Uh, yes, I think so," she said, her eyebrows scrunched up as she tried to make sense of the sketch.

It's not that hard. This is just a map. Look at it, he thought, before he realized he was being too demanding. *Calm down Edson and give her a break. She's never seen a printed map, much less one hand-drawn from memory before.*

"Look, your home is up here. You walked down this road, so you must have passed the area on the other side of the pines, right."

She pulled it closer, and after a moment, Colby could see the understanding flood her face.

"Yes. Yes, we came that way."

"OK, you told me that most of the area had been taken over by the alien plants, right? So, are there alien plants on the other side of the pines?"

She studied the map as if she could see the answer in the drawing, before she said, "Yes. They were the alien plants. I'm sure of it."

He thanked her, then turned back to the patiently waiting company commander, saying, "OK, Captain, I don't think the plant boss is in the pines. I'm betting it'll be over here. I want you to go around the pines at the double time, then look for signs of its passage."

He considered having the captain try and surround it, but the area was just too big. No, his best bet would be to run the thing down, like Early Man running down a gazelle.

"And I'm coming with you," he blurted out before thinking.

"Sir?" the captain asked.

Two minutes before, he'd told the captain that he'd be staying at what was left of the station to coordinate the two landing areas, and now he'd changed that, too. The man had to be wondering if Colby had lost his mind, but his training kept any such thoughts off his face.

"I'm coming with you. I've had more experience with this thing than anyone else."

Beside him, Sergeant Dela Cruz stepped up, a protest forming on his lips, but Colby stopped the Marine short with, "And you're coming, too."

"And don't forget me," Topeka said quietly—but leaving no doubt that she was not asking permission.

"Fine," he said, not wanting to argue.

Within two minutes, Captain Singh was moving his company—minus a squad that was left with the civilians—out. Colby and Topeka were in the rear of the formation, surrounded by not only Sergeant Dela Cruz's team, but two squads from Singh's company. They'd only gone about 20 meters when Duke broke free of the man Colby had asked to hold her and streaked through the Marines to him.

He just accepted her presence, reaching down to pat her head just before the company broke into the double time. Topeka grimaced, but she kept up.

Colby had led the way five days prior when he and Topeka had run to the Gardener's ship, and he'd been the one pushing the pace. That was then, and this was now. Surrounded by fit, young Marines, Colby was feeling his age in comparison as they jogged to go around the pine forest. He kept his face steady, smiling and nodding at the Marines who kept looking at him, but inside, his gut was in spasms, and his lungs cried out for air. He was glad when they got off of the natural ground and onto the hard road that led north out of the station. He was still sucking wind, but at least the footing was easier.

Beside him, Topeka was in worse shape, but she struggled ahead. At least Duke wasn't having any problem, darting back and forth between the Marines and Colby.

Within a klick, they rounded the pines and started the gentle downslope into the bottomlands. Going downhill was easier on the lungs, but it changed his stride. Beside him, Topeka was struggling, and he thought she was going to stop until a Marine stepped up, told her to grab the back of his assault pack, and dragged her along.

She looked mortified as Colby caught her eye, but he knew that telling her to go back would be useless. She was seeing this through.

They'd only gone another 800 meters or so when the Marines in front of them slowed to a walk. Like an accordion, the formation collapsed on itself, and Colby stumbled, running up the back of the Marine in front of him.

"You OK, sir?" the Marine asked, turning around.

"Fine, son. No problem," he said, keeping his voice calm despite his burning lungs and trembling legs.

All senior Marines, officer or enlisted, thought that they were the same private or lieutenant who'd first joined the Corps.

It was hard to accept that bodies aged, let alone admit it. Several of the younger Marines were breathing hard, but Colby was not going to show he was suffering even if it killed him.

He was tempted to query Captain Singh about what was going on—more than tempted. But he held back, slowly trying to recover his breath. And then, they rounded the last bend in the road, the entire bottomlands stretched out before them. In the far distance, he could see the tops of the Hastert Hills through the light haze.

Just 200 meters ahead of them, the agricultural richness of the bottomlands began, and the lead platoon was deploying from a column to a line, getting ready to enter the nearest field.

"This was Megan Tines's farm," Topeka said quietly between deep breaths as they looked out over the bottomland.

Colby had never met the famous Megan Tines, one of the first farmers to receive a charter on the planet, and one of the most successful. She'd grown the delicate vacuberries, a good money crop that Colby wouldn't have attempted on his farm until he had far more experience.

What had been acres of the low vacuberry vines had now been replaced with large, round, vaguely melon-looking things—two-meter-tall melons. They were a bluish-green, evenly spaced, each one about four meters from the next. Between them were smaller plants. The transformation had taken only days.

Something about the larger plants bothered him, like an itch he couldn't scratch, but for the life of him, he couldn't put his finger on the reason.

"Has anyone reported seeing those, yet?" he asked Topeka.

"Nothing like that."

"Take a full bio scan of the field 70 meters to my zero-two-zero," Colby passed to the watch officer on the *Pattani*. "Let me know what they show."

"Roger that, sir."

Colby didn't know what had sparked that thought, but sometimes, a commander had to go with his gut. If nothing else, this would be just more data for the science-types back on Earth to pore over.

Without an immediate threat to the wormhole, Captain Whitehouse had switched rolls with the *Pattani* in geosynchronous orbit over DeStaffney Station, and the other two ships doing a detailed ground scan of the planet.

Ahead of him, the first platoon was about to enter the field. Colby watched nervously, taking a couple of steps forward. Sergeant Dela Cruz and Private Queen, a huge, 130kg Marine, matched him, step-by-step.

OK, OK, Sergeant. Don't get excited. I'll be a good boy and stay back.

He could monitor the company net, though. With a brief mental command, he was listening in to the Marines.

"We've got movement," a Marine—Colby's implant identified him as Lance Corporal Morganstein—said.

Colby ordered a direct feed from the Marine, and he could see what looked to be several meter-high plants moving forward. They weren't the trefoil type, but there was a sense of purpose to their movement.

Stupid feed. Why isn't it clearer? he fumed, trying to determine what was about to happen.

Only the feed was normal, he realized. It just didn't compare to the immersion he'd experienced back on New Mars, when he was "seeing" through the plant soldiers.

The *cracka-cracka* of a burst of automatic fire reached him, and Colby pulled back from Morganstein's feed. More Marines started firing. Colby resisted the urge to run forward and take over, but he'd learned long ago that would be an invitation to disaster. Generals could set the stage for their Marines, but when it got down to brass tacks, it was up to those same Marines to fight the fight. Trying to get involved would only confuse matters, and that would get Marines killed.

He flipped from the orbital feed to the captain's and then to his own eyeballs, settling on the latter. The Marines, some 15 meters deep into the plants, were being attacked by the smaller, one-meter-tall plants. The big melons remained motionless. Hundreds, if not thousands, of the smaller plants were swarming the Marines, who were retreating in good order, firing into the mass. There were too many for the slug-throwers to cut down, so the Marines had switched to their M88s. A fine green mist rose up between the rows of melons. Waves of plants were exploding into bursts of green goo as the water in their bodies was excited to a boil by the beam weapons.

Not all, though. Colby saw one Marine, then another, then three more fall beneath the onslaught. If the plant soldiers had been able to tear a Marine in a battlesuit apart, Colby knew these Marines stood no chance.

"Sir, we have to retreat," Sergeant Dela Cruz said, pulling on his arm.

Colby whipped the arm free. He wasn't going anywhere while the Marines were in contact.

If the Marines had retreated pell mell, then more would have fallen, but their disciplined retreat, with each Marine's fire supporting the other, kept most of them alive as they emerged from the field. Orders were flying over the net, but Colby kept quiet, letting the NCOs fight the battle. And he was proud of what he saw. He knew how terrifying the plant soldiers could be, things out of nightmares, but the Marines never faltered.

The plants did, however, much to Colby's surprise. They stopped at the edge of the field, green arms waving, but not moving forward even as more fell to the Marine fire.

"Cease fire, cease fire!" Marines shouted, passing on the order as they stopped 20 meters away and faced the plants. Colby could see NCOs checking their Marines.

"General Edson, what are your orders? Do you still want us to advance?" Captain Singh asked him over the person-to-person net.

Colby stayed silent for a moment, trying to get his thoughts in line. Something told him that the Gardener was out there among the melons and small soldiers. If nothing else, the fact that the small soldiers had stopped at the edge of the field was indicative that they were being controlled.

"No, stand ready for the moment," he ordered the company commander.

He switched the link and called Captain Whitehorse. "Captain, can you drop the hammer on the alien lifeforms at these coordinates?" he asked blinking in and uploading them. "I'd like it with one fell swoop."

"Let me check, sir. Wait one."

"What are they doing?" Topeka asked.

Colby shook his head, reaching one hand down mindlessly to pat Duke's head.

"General, the disposition of the alien plants is haphazard, so our GIP Cannons would require multiple salvos. Additionally, you and your Marines are too close. You'd have to retreat back a minimum of 500 meters."

Crap.

If the Gardener was in there, he wanted it trapped. If the *Pattani* had to fire in salvos, that would give the boss plant warning, and it could slip away during the bombardment.

Wait, can't they adjust their beam cannons?

"What about your. . ." Colby started before he had to query his implant to see what the *Pattani* carried. ". . . your BTY-1210. Can't you start that in a circle, then focus it in on itself?"

"With Betty? That's affirmative."

"Great! And is that danger close? I mean, do we have to move back first?"

"No, sir. It's focused finer than a gnat's ass. You won't be touched."

"OK, then I want you to encompass the entire growth here. Burn the native. . . I mean the Earth crops as well, but I want this entire field eradicated. Nothing escapes, understand?"

"Got it, sir. I'm passing this to Guns now."

"Guns" was Lieutenant Commander Tannibeth Rystal, the ship's weapons officer.

"I want that in 60 seconds Captain."

"Uh. . . no can do, sir."

"What? Why not?"

"We've got the ship-to-ship lens on Betty now. We need to change that out."

Colby wanted to lash out. In typical Navy fashion, the *Pattani* had its most powerful weapon in ship-to-ship mode, leaving the rest for ground support. The Gardener hadn't shown signs of naval warfare, and as it turned out, the ground-and-pound guns were not suitable for this mission.

"How much time do you need," he asked, fighting to keep his voice calm.

"Twenty minutes, maybe less."

"Make it fifteen."

He cut the connection, scanning the field with his naked eyes. Fifteen minutes seemed like forever, and he had visions of the Gardener slipping away before the *Pattani* could fire.

"Captain Singh, stand by. We're going to ash the plants in fifteen. As soon the *Pattani* stops firing, I want your company in there. If there's a speck of green left, burn it."

"Roger that. No problem."

Colby told Topeka what was going to happen, then checked in with Manny Sif. Manny reported huge swathes of alien life, but none of the melon pods. Three Marines had been burned by plants, but none of the plant soldiers had actively attacked them.

It was only here, between the hop-bean farms and DeStaffney Station that the plants went into attack mode. That had to signify something—just what, he didn't know.

"Give me a countdown," he told Captain Whitehorse needlessly.

"Roger that," she said, probably wishing he'd stay out of her knickers.

OK, that's the last time I ask.

Nine minutes later, he asked how much longer it would be.

"Look at that," Topeka said before the captain could answer.

In unison, like a sped-up version of sunflowers following the track of the sun, the melons moved to "aim," for lack of a better word, at the eastern sky.

"Captain Singh, get ready!"

But the captain had already acted. The Marines aimed their weapons, ready to take on whatever came their way.

"Captain Whitehorse, we need your Betty now!" he passed to the *Pattani's* commanding officer.

Several things happened at once. The small soldier plants, the ones that had attacked the Marines, seemed to collapse. The nearest line of melon pods twisted to orient on the Marines, and the rest shot up into the air, like watermelon seeds squeezed between two fingers.

"Fire!" he shouted at the Marines, taking over the company net.

The first salvo let loose just as the nearest line of melons. . . spurted. . . a greenish-yellow mist.

"Nose filters!" rang out over the net from a dozen voices as the mist flowed toward the Marines, engulfing them in seconds. Nose filters or not, the Marines started to stumble and fall as Colby shouted out for the platoon around him to fall back.

It was useless. The mist rolled over them, and Marines began to tumble. Topeka, too. Colby held his breath for as long as he could, running to get out of the mist, Duke on his heels. Finally, he had to breathe, and he knew he'd be taken down, too. He gulped in the air. . . and nothing happened. There was a minty taste to his mouth, but he was fully functional. As was Duke, who sat and looked up at him, head cocked to one side.

All around them humans were on the ground. Only the two of them were upright. There had to be a reason for that, but he didn't have time to figure it out. Most of the melons had taken off.

"Captain Whitehorse, we've had a launching. Burn everything leaving the planet."

"We see it, General. There are over a thousand of them all broadcasting signals similar to the telemetry recorded from the alien ship you commandeered."

"Just burn them, Captain," he roared aloud.

"We can't, General. We just got the ground lens on. Betty is no longer configured for ship-to-ship. We're engaging with all other weapons systems and missiles now, and I've called back the *Portnoy Bay* and the *Gazelle*."

"Get them all. Not one escapes."

"Sir, there are thousands, and they're tiny. I. . . I'm not sure we can. Sorry to cut you off, sir. I've got a fight on my hands."

The captain cut the connection. She knew her duty. They couldn't allow any of the melon pods to escape.

She'd have made a helluva Marine.

He looked around. Marines were on the ground around him. His heart rose to his throat as he dropped to his knees next to a Marine, a lance corporal with "Kukuro" on his name tag. The Marine's eyes were open, and Colby could see the fear in his eyes.

He's alive, at least.

"Lance Corporal Kukuro, can you hear me?" he asked.

The Marine didn't respond, but there was something in his eyes that lent belief that he was conscious.

"If you can hear me, roll your eyes."

Was there the tiniest bit of movement there? That might be wishful thinking, but something told Colby that the Marine was alive. He looked around. All of the Marines he could see had open eyes.

There was nothing he could do for the hundred-plus humans at the moment, so he marched down to Mz. Tine's farm. The front row of pods, the ones that had spit the green mist at him, had collapsed upon themselves and hung limply among the small dead soldiers. Colby gingerly stepped between two of the pods, stamping on the plant soldiers. Beyond that front rank, the pods had all gone, leaving a base of leaves that were wilting as he watched.

"General Edson," Captain Whitehorse passed on the net.

"What is it? Have you stopped them?"

"Negative, sir. We've downed a couple hundred, but there're too many. And there's no doubt about it. They're heading for the wormhole."

Shit, shit shit!

"See what you can do, Captain. Get as many of them as you can."

"You know I can't do that, sir. You know I have my orders."

"But. . . but, that means. . ."

"That's why we get paid the big credits, sir. We'll do our duty. Commander Brockmorton will take over and pursue all the surviving pods."

There was nothing else he could say. Their orders were clear.

"It's been an honor, Captain, a true honor."

"Likewise, sir, likewise. Well, if you'll excuse me, I've got quite a bit on my plate at the moment.

The connection was cut as Captain Alicia Whitehorse maneuvered the *Pattani* to enter, but not pass, the wormhole.

"Commander Brockmorton--" Colby started to pass.

"I've got it, sir. We're chasing the pods, but their awfully small and agile."

"No matter where they go, you're not to give up, understand?"

"Roger that, sir."

Colby felt defeated, and he shook his head. Duke whined beside him.

"Why us, girl? Why are we still standing?"

Because we've got some of the plant in us now. We're connected. We've both been touched by the damned things.

For a moment he wondered if he was being controlled somehow, and that scared him. But he felt like Colby. He thought he was still himself, still Colby.

As his gazed wandered, he realized that there was one pod still upright.

Malfunction? he idly wondered.

He wandered over to it, hoping to gain an insight that would help the two remaining ships destroy them. As he approached, the pod split open from top to bottom. Colby stepped back, and pulled his sidearm out of his holster, suddenly feeling vulnerable.

Like a baby passing the birthcanal, the Gardener emerged, looking much like it had in the moment before Topeka had cut off its head. Duke erupted into a flurry of barks and lunged at it before Colby could grab her.

Instead of attacking, the Gardener knelt, one of its leafy hands outstretched to the dog. Duke stopped, whined, then leaned forward, her nose almost touching the thing. Suddenly she wagged her tail and licked the arm.

Colby was flabbergasted. What had just happened?

His implant activated as if receiving a call, but it wasn't from Captain Whitehorse or one of the other two ships. He wasn't sure what it was for a moment as the transmission swept back and forth as if trying to find the right frequency. He almost understood something a few times, but then it was gone, leaving a trace of familiarity.

Realization hit him. It was the Gardener.

"What do you want?" he sent to it.

Maybe it took both of them sending, because almost immediately, the Gardener's thoughts filled his senses.

«*Extraordinary Meat. Meat with language. Meat with the trappings of Mech. Meat in space, on other worlds, on this world. My world. Short-lived, arrogant meat. This world was barren thousands of cycles past. Barren until I arrived. I seeded its oceans with plankton to change the atmosphere. I introduced fungi to change the surface of the land. I set these in motion to to do my work and went away. I returned two hundred cycles past, and as I intended this world was ripe for planting, for the garden I had planned. It was majestic, exquisite, but still so young. I fine-tuned the design, adjusted the ecosystems I'd spawned, and went away again. And then you, arrogant foolish Meat arrived. You ignored what your own senses told you, and sought to undo all my efforts.»*

Colby had already suspected this, he realized. He just hadn't wanted to admit it, that it might be humans who had been the aggressors here.

«Meat destroys. It always has. Your own history acknowledges this, though you choose not to apply this truth to your own species. You despoil everything you touch. You will go. You will take these others with you and leave my world so that I may restore this garden.»

"But it doesn't have to be this way. We didn't know you were here. Hell, we didn't know you existed. There has to be another way here, one that does not result in death and destruction."

The Gardener seemed to dismiss the concept, but there was something, a hint, a germ, that Colby picked up. The possibility intrigued the boss plant. He tried to formulate another tack when a voice shouting "Edson! My God, where are you?" reached him.

What the hell is he doing here?

"I see you, Edson, I see you!" Vice-Minister Greenstein shouted out even louder as he daintily picked his way through prone Marines, arms held high as if to avoid contact with them.

He pushed into the field and approached Colby.

If you want to knock out my Marines, why not knock out him, too? he thought at the Gardner.

There was no answer. He received the slightest whiff of curiosity instead.

"My God, Edson, what happened here? Are they dead? And is that the head plant there?"

"They're unconscious—"

"Sir, I'm Vice-Minister Asahi Salinas Greenstein. I'm here as the representative of the Republic. Of all humanity. I am authorized to speak to you in the name of the chairman."

Bullshit. You don't have authorization for anything.

"And let me tell you, my friend," he said, pushing past Colby as Duke gave a low growl. "We have huge potential here. Huge."

Colby wanted to tell Greenstein that the Gardener couldn't understand Standard, but he realized that the bossplant was, not listening per se, but paying attention. Suddenly, he knew that he was playing the part of translator. He heard the vice-minister's words, and the Gardener was picking them through his thoughts.

"I've seen what you've done here, and I'm impressed. Truly impressed. We can take those capabilities and totally revamp the agricultural business. Hell, a backwater dump like Vasquez could supply all the crops needed by humanity, all of them, just using your agritech. We'll be rich, and I mean filthy rich."

Colby was shocked. This was beyond the pale, even from a snake like Greenstein. He wanted to take the man by the throat and shake him like a terrier on a rat, and only the Gardener's presence held his hand.

"How does that sound to you? I mean, you don't need Republic credits, of course, but I can give you whatever you want. Raw materials? Fertilizer? Weapons? You name it, you've got it. My family, we're big in the weapons business, so, I've got the inside track for that.

Colby felt a mental shudder emanate from the Gardener when Greenstein said "weapons." Colby was just disgusted. The man was trying to work a deal here, of all things.

"What about the Marines?" he asked. "Some of them died here."

The vice-minister seemed to remember that Colby was still standing there. He frowned, then waved a hand, saying, "That's why they get hazardous duty pay, Edson. And we can't let past. . . past *disagreements* get in the way of future cooperation."

He turned back to the Gardener and said, "Speaking of weapons, my family's are top-of-the-line, but your soldiers, they are pretty incredible. We can take that tech and make new weapons, with the best of both civilizations. No one would be able to stop us, and they'll all pay top credit to keep up with the rest who'll buy from us.

"And if someone balks, well, we'll have the weapons, so we can pretty much force them to comply, if you know what I mean."

The Gardener had been standing motionless, but after the last comment, something changed. The plant shuddered, then from out of the mic on Colby's collar, spoke.

«This is what Meat does. What it seeks. Destruction for its own sake. And being impressive Meat you aspire to ever more impressive forms of death. This one revels in it, crafts personal goals predicated on it. Short-lived Meat, why do you not savor life rather than pursue death? I have no weapons, but I can momentarily repurpose other tools to address your desires.»

A blast of mint-green mist blew out from the Gardener and enveloped Greenstein. Unlike the Marines and Topeka when their mist had hit them, Greenstein immediately started to convulse. He grabbed for his throat as a pea soup of froth came gushing from his mouth. His terror-filled eyes looked at Colby, and he managed to spit out "Edson!" before he fell to his back and lay still.

"That's General Edson to you, Dickhead."

The Gardener stayed still and silent as if waiting for Colby's reaction. He wasn't so sure his connection with the plant species would help him if the boss plant decided to take him out the same way.

"Beginning final approach into in the wormhole, General," Captain Whitehorse sent. "Will initiate pluviation."

"Understood, Captain," Colby said, a lump forming in his throat.

"I'm sending the crew off now. Take care of them, OK, sir?"

"Will do, Captain," he said, then following that a few seconds later with, "You know, you don't have to stay. You can't do anything to help the pluviation team."

"You're wrong there, General. This is my ship and my crew. I can't leave anyone to do this on their own. I'm sure you understand."

"Yes, I do. I wish there was something I could say."

"Just take care of them, Marines and sailors alike. You're going to be cut off from human space. I've got it easy. My job will be done in a few minutes. You've got the tougher task in front of you."

Colby thought of what could have happened. With his commitment to the Corps, and then his banishment, he'd never married. But Alicia Whitehorse, he could see himself with a woman like her, someone he'd admired.

"Go with God," the captain said, just as she'd done two days before.

"I don't need God. I've got the Republic Navy, Captain."

There was a moment of silence over the live connection, then a quiet "Thank you, sir," before it cut off. The net was still live, so the *Pattani* was still up there, but he knew he'd never hear from her again.

He turned back to the Gardener, angry at the wasted lives. He was pretty sure the thing knew what had just transpired, and it probably knew that Colby was angry. Anger would get them nowhere, though, especially if they were trapped on Vasquez. There might be upwards of 700 humans on the planet and one Gardener, but it had proven just how quickly it could raise a division of fighters.

"This doesn't have to end like this," he said. "Turn your pods away from the wormhole and we'll still have all the same options left to us. No one else has to die. Just turn them around."

«*They have no will that might be subverted or persuaded. No sensibility that might be reasoned with. I crafted their purpose and navigation into their very seeds. I can no more change their destiny than you can will your arm to bud new hands all along its length.*»

"So, what are you going to do now?" he asked, more to give the *Pattani* time to complete its mission rather than to hear the answer.

His implant blipped once to inform him the ship had entered the wormhole. Not much longer now.

«I will restore my garden, undo the scars you have wrought and recreate beauty and poetry. And you, the weeds in my garden, will be gone from here. Impressive Meat, flee back through your spacial anomaly. My pods will follow. You have demonstrated that your kind is too dangerous to leave its worlds. My pods will alert others of my kind, summon them with the means to contain you and end your threat.» It paused and Colby felt its attention on Duke for just a moment before it resumed. *«You understand there are higher orders. You are Meat that suborns lesser Meat, just as I command all the vegetation of this world. You do this for your own purposes and often to the benefit of that lesser Meat that serves you. You restrict it, instruct it, educate it, to the degree that any of these things are possible for lesser Meat. Such is your future. You will be restricted to your worlds. Space will be denied you, as will the means of transit. You will not be harmed, but you will be contained.»*

And that is so much bullshit, Colby thought as he waited for the inevitable. And finally, it happened. The *Pattani* went off the net. Colby sent a simple query through his implant to. . . nothing. His implant still worked, and it still had terabytes of data, but there was no connection back to humanity. They were truly cut off.

"And now you've lost. That was the *Pattani* with a handful of brave men and women, destroying the wormhole. You don't know anything about my people, where they are. We're safe from your. . . *weeding*. Meanwhile, we've got two more ships chasing down whatever of your pods are still out there. They will follow your pods to the ends of the galaxy, if they have to.

«Resourceful Meat, you continue to surprise. I had not imagined your capacity for death included self-destruction if it achieved your ends. But you have failed. My pods don't transition to your area of space. I don't need to create a beacon there for my people to find you. It is enough to inform

them of your existence, your capabilities. Many of the pods that launched seek their way home, and you have only two vessels to pursue. It is a long journey, and you are short-lived. The galaxy is vast, but we are patient. Only one needs to get through. Once they are alerted, informed of your existence and the threat you pose, my people will repurpose themselves to find you.»

While the Gardener pontificated, the Marines around them began to stir. Whatever had knocked them out was short-lived. Colby sensed that the Gardener was about to lash out, probably with its more lethal mist.

"You've lost. It's over. They're going to burn you where you stand, and destroy every atom. There will be no coming back this time."

«I am but a leaf on a tree in a single forest. My own existence is insignificant. The designs I imposed upon this world have already been set back in motion. Strike me down again, perhaps for a final time. It is your way. But it changes nothing. Not upon this world, nor elsewhere.»

"Colby!" a welcomed voice cried out from the edge of the field. He didn't turn around, but he could hear feet pounding. A moment later, Topeka was at his side, staring at the Gardener, the same one she'd beheaded a week before. Marines flowed to either side of him, weapons aimed and waiting for the order to open fire.

He didn't have to. Duke barked twice, and as if that was a signal, the Gardener collapsed, its body decomposing into mulch as they watched.

It was over. . . right?

The melon pods were ships, no doubt about that, and he knew they were being sent out as some sort of spacefaring vegetable message beacons, letting the other gardeners know there was Meat out in the galaxy, Meat that fought back. If the *Portnoy Bay* and the *Gazelle* could catch and destroy every one of them, well, all for the good. That would just delay the inevitable confrontation that would eventually happen. But humankind was aware of the gardeners now, and they wouldn't be caught by surprise.

"What now, Colby?" Topeka asked.

There were about 700 people on the planet between civilians, sailors, and Marines. That wasn't much, but it was enough to be a viable population. The planet was fertile, if they could control the gardener's plantings and make sure their own crops thrived.

"Now, we live," he said.

"Really? That's all you have to say?"

He shrugged.

"I guess you're back to being a farmer. And here I was, just getting used to calling you General."

Colby thought about that a moment. He had his Marines, and soon enough he'd also have the surviving sailors from the *Pattani*, but Vasquez had little need for either.

"You're right," he told her. "Looks like I'll have my hands full teaching a lot of people how to be farmers."

She nodded and said, "I guess I'm going to have to learn to be one too. Not much of a demand for shipping now, is there? Don't suppose you want to teach me?" she asked, looking away from him as she petted Duke on the head.

The dog wagged her tail in pleasure.

He slowly reached out and took her hand.

"Yeah, I'm a farmer again, but at least I've got my commission back.

Thank you for reading the *Seeds of War Trilogy*. We hope you enjoyed it, and we welcome your reviews of our novellas on Amazon or any other website.

SEEDS OF WAR
Invasion
Scorched Earth
Bitter Harvest

Other Books by Lawrence M. Schoen

If you would like updates on Lawrence's new books releases, news, or special offers, please consider signing up for his mailing list. Your email will not be sold, rented, or in any other way disseminated. If you are interested, please sign up at the link below:

http://bit.ly/LMSnews

Barsk

Barsk: The Elephants' Graveyard
The Moons of Barsk

The Amazing Conroy
Buffalito Buffet
Calendrical Regression
Barry's Deal
Buffalito Destiny
Trial of the Century
Buffalito Contingency

Selected Short Stories
A Fool's Death

Bidding the Walrus
Pidgin
Mars Needs Baby Seals
The Game of Leaf and Smile
The Moment
Thinking
The Wrestler and the Spear Fisher

Books Edited/Published by Lawrence M. Schoen

Alembical
Alembical 2
Alembical 3
Alembical 4
Cats in Space - Elektra Hammond (ed)
Cucurbital 2
Cucurbital 3
Eyes Like Sky and Coal and Moonlight - Cat Rambo
Rejiggering The Thingamajig And Other Stories - Eric James Stone
The Wizard of Macatawa and Other Stories - Tom Doyle

Klingon Language Works
The Klingon Hamlet
Much Ado About Nothing: The Restored Klingon Text
Gilgamesh: A Klingon Translation
Sunzi's Art of War: A Klingon Translation
Tao Te Ching: A Klingon Translation
A Pictorial Guide to the Suffixes of **tlhIngan Hol**
How to Speak Klingon: Essential Phrases for the Intergalactic Traveler

Author Website
http://www.lawrencemschoen.com/

Other Books by Jonathan Brazee

If you would like updates on Jonathan's new books releases, news, or special offers, please consider signing up for his mailing list. Your email will not be sold, rented, or in any other way disseminated. If you are interested, please sign up at the link below:

http://eepurl.com/bnFSHH

The United Federation Marine Corps
Recruit
Sergeant
Lieutenant
Captain
Major
Lieutenant Colonel
Colonel
Commandant

Coda

Rebel (Set in the UFMC universe)

Behind Enemy Lines (A UFMC Prequel)

An Accidental War (A Ryck Lysander short story published in BOB's Bar: Tales of the Multiverse)

The United Federation Marine Corps' Lysander Twins
Legacy Marines
Esther's Story: Recon Marine
Noah's Story: Marine Tanker
Esther's Story: Special Duty
Blood United

Women of the United Federation Marine Corps
Gladiator
Sniper
Corpsman

High Value Target (A Gracie Medicine Crow Short Story)
BOLO Mission (A Gracie Medicine Crow Short Story)

Weaponized Math (A Gracie Medicine Crow Novelette and 2017 Nebula Award Finalist)

The United Federation Marine Corps' Grub Wars
Alliance
The Price of Honor
Division of Power

Ghost Marines
Integration (2018 Dragon Award Finalist)
Unification
Fusion (Coming Soon)

The Navy of Humankind: Wasp Squadron
Fire Ant
Crystals

The Pumpkin Ace (A Floribeth Short Story published in BOB's Bar 2)

The Return of the Marines Trilogy
The Few
The Proud
The Marines

The Al Anbar Chronicles: First Marine Expeditionary Force--Iraq
Prisoner of Fallujah
Combat Corpsman
Sniper

Werewolf of Marines
Werewolf of Marines: Semper Lycanus
Werewolf of Marines: Patria Lycanus
Werewolf of Marines: Pax Lycanus

To The Shores of Tripoli

Wererat

Darwin's Quest: The Search for the Ultimate Survivor

Venus: A Paleolithic Short Story

Secession

Duty

Semper Fidelis

Checkmate (Published in The Expanding Universe 4)

Non-Fiction

Exercise for a Longer Life

The Effects of Environmental Activism on the Yellowfin Tuna Industry

Author Website

http://www.jonathanbrazee.com

Twitter
@jonathanbrazee

Made in the USA
Middletown, DE
17 August 2022

71561803R00139